WHITE GLOVES &
ROB ROYS

ILONA JOY SAARI

211th Street Books

*For all the white-gloved ladies who dined at Schrafft's.
And to my mom who first took me there and sipped
her perfect Rob Roy as I devoured the cheesebread.*

PROLOGUE

ASHLEY — 2000

While sitting in the back of the church listening to another heartfelt eulogy by Taffy, a distant great grandniece of the deceased, my husband Marty by my side, it struck me as odd, and a bit scary, that so many years after the advent of the women's movement, an abundance of Taffys, Lindsays, Chelseas and Tiffanys were storming the board rooms on their way to becoming the nation's CEOs. Don't get me wrong, I really like many of the names ending with an "ee" sound as long as the last letter isn't an "i" with a little heart over it. I should know, my name is Ashley. Yet, not that long ago when women were forbidden to dine alone in restaurants, take out a loan, or smoke in public there was a certain dignity to a woman's name. Solid, practical and somehow comforting. Names like Mildred, Martha, Agnes, Bertha, and Harriet. Even when they reached for the fanciful or poetic, their names had the aroma of a bouquet... Rose, Daisy, Fern, Iris. Or were names rooted or dug out of the earth...Ruby, Opal, Crystal. I want to tell you a story about four of those women. A story I've been sitting on for more than forty years.

As I mentioned, my name is Ashley. My family name is Wilkes. I know, I know, but my mother had a fixation with *Gone with the Wind* and hated the name Scarlett, and Melanie was just too "Melanie" for her. I'm a writer and thought about changing my name when I got my first byline. I obsessed over what the world would think of a writer having the name of another writer's fictional character even though I wasn't the same gender. But, ultimately, I just couldn't break my mother's heart. So Ashley Wilkes I remained.

The deceased, who was laid out in a closed coffin covered with white roses at the front of the church was Violet Rose Wilding ("Vi"), the youngest of the four women who, at a few breaths over one hundred and seven, was the last to die, releasing me from the promise I had made as a novice reporter for the *NY Daily News* more than three decades ago.

The Deputy Mayor of New York soon replaced the distant, great-grandniece in the eulogy line-up and as he droned on about Vi's considerable contributions to the city over the past century, my thoughts drifted to a group of middle-aged women shivering from the cold, their clothes covered in blood and dirt, digging a big hole in a wooded area at dawn. *I* shivered. Marty took my hand thinking I needed comfort. Little did he know that my mind had left the building. How do I tell him, a former New York City detective, now its police commissioner, the dark secret I've been keeping from him all these years?

 # CHAPTER 1

ASHLEY — 1968

It was a cold, blustery, torrential downpour Monday in October and I was a half-hour late for work. As I ran into the lobby of the Daily News building and streaked to the elevator, I left a stream of water behind me. I'm five feet five and weigh a hundred and seven pounds and I lost the battle with my umbrella when a hurricane-caliber gust of wind blew it inside-out the minute I stepped out of the subway station. I was drenched, thanks to the fact that my then trendy London Fog trench coat that cost me a week's salary wasn't really all that water repellent. When I reached my floor, I immediately threw my wet coat and even wetter, totally useless umbrella in the coat room, then headed for my desk in the crowded newsroom. The sound of typewriters clicking away filled the room. By the time I reached my desk, my dripping hair had soaked the top of my silk shirt. On the plus side, not a single person paid the slightest attention to me.

I'm a reporter. Or at least that's what I call myself. I'm a Long Island girl and after graduating a year early from Skidmore, I set out to seek my fame and fortune as a journalist, but it seemed very few newspapers wanted a female reporter. But I persevered, landing a job at the Gazette in the naval coastal town of New London, Connecticut. I wrote about church bake sales and reviewed the local high school theater productions. I covered funerals, high school football games, restaurant openings and traffic court…I even wrote an obituary or two. But after eighteen months of paying dues, I yearned to go back to New York and work at one of the big city papers. For six months I hounded every managing editor in the city and finally got an interview with Spencer Dwyre of the *New York Daily News.* He scanned my meager resume and read some of my articles, then hired me on the spot. I was moving to Manhattan! I was going to be a real reporter at a major newspaper! Or so I thought. For the first weeks, I got coffee, ran errands and was given trial assignments where everything I wrote was red-lined to death… but I was learning.

As my style developed, Dwyre began assigning me to the "style" section where I covered fancy weddings, fashion shows, charity balls and other muckety, muck events. You know…"Women's" stories. If there was a murder in someone's drawing room by Colonel Mustard with a candlestick, I wasn't the one sent to cover it. Murder was basically a "man" story. I got to write about candlesticks and drawing rooms, but never about murder. Other male reporter dominions were the White House, City Hall, and war. There were exceptions, of course, (Gloria Emerson who recently started covering "the troubles" in Ireland for the New York Times came to mind), but so far, I wasn't exceptional enough to be an exception.

I went into the ladies room and pulled out a bunch of paper towels from the dispenser and tried drying my hair. My Mom always told me I had a pretty face with a turned-up nose and auburn-colored eyes that eerily match my long mane of auburn curls, but right now in the mirror, I looked like a drowned alley cat. I had spent the night rolling my curls over large, cardboard Minute Maid frozen juice cans (empty and washed, of course) to straighten it. I had even ironed my hair a bit this morning before coming to work. So much for straight hair Tuesday. When it dried, it would be a mass of frizz that would precede me by a foot.

Back at my desk, I pulled open a drawer and found my reporter's notebook. I began going over the notes I took at yesterday's art gallery opening when Dwyre walked over to my desk. At forty-four, he looked like a successful Wall Street banker, not the rumpled "Spencer Tracy, Central Casting" version of a big city newspaper editor. No crumpled suits or bad haircut for him. Average height, with sandy brown wiry hair, graying at the temples, he had a lean frame, wore starched, custom-made white shirts by Dougie Hayward in London and navy blue suspenders. His never-rolled-up sleeves were monogrammed French-cuffed with 18K gold ball cuff links from Tiffany. His ties were always "club." His immaculate suits were Brooks Brothers' soft wool, navy or navy pinstriped in the winter and pressed tan cotton canvas in the summer.

"Give me the gallery story in the next half hour, I need you to go to Schrafft's," he said with no indication that he noticed my frizzy wet hair and water-stained blouse.

"Sure. Schrafft's!?"

"Andy Warhol is shooting a sixty-second commercial to reframe the chain's image for the youth market. It's airing in November. I want you to interview the staff and find out what they think."

"Which Schrafft's? They're all over the city."

"Doesn't matter."

"Okay."

He turned around abruptly and went back to his glassed-in office as I rolled some typing paper backed with a few carbon setups into my Selectric typewriter.

After handing in my gallery piece, I decided to check out the Schrafft's on Fifth and 46th, as it was the only one I had ever been in. I chose to go after the lunch rush, but before the dinner rush so that the staff would have a moment to answer my questions. What I was going to ask beyond "so, what do you think of the Warhol commercial," I hadn't quite figured out.

It had stopped raining and because my London Fog was hanging near a radiator, it was fairly dry when I slipped my arms into the sleeves. I looked at my forlorn umbrella, picked it up and shoved it in a trash bin outside the coat room, then left the newsroom not knowing at the time that this Schrafft's assignment would completely change my life.

The restaurant was decorated in what was called "modern British Colonial" with marble, dark woods and white tablecloths. I had been in this Schrafft's once when my mom had taken me shopping for school clothes at Best & Co. and we wanted to go somewhere for dinner before taking the train back to Douglaston. Though the times "they were a-changin'," many restaurants in the early 1960's still didn't approve of or allow women to grace their presence without a male escort. And, except for singles bars, noses were bent out of shape if a woman alone or with another woman sat at a bar or even a table and ordered a drink. It was immediately assumed, no matter how well-dressed they were, that they were "working girls." Definitely a "no-no" in New York's finer restaurants. However, women could go alone or with a female friend to Schrafft's and have a drink and something to eat without fear of being hit on, harassed or hustled out the door. It was safe, spotless, staffed mostly with women, comfortable, and served comfort food at affordable prices.

It was spring when my mom and I had dinner there shortly after I moved to Manhattan two and a half years ago. Once settled at our table, I noticed that there were a few old women (well, a decade or two older than my mother, which made them "old") sitting alone at tables eating creamed chicken on biscuits (the day's special) and sipping a cocktail. They wore a variety of hats. Some wore skirts and sweater sets accessorized with a strand of graduated pearls. Others chose tweed suits and sensible shoes. All had a pair of white gloves folded on top of their tables next to their purses. I had to smile. These women were from another time. My writer's mind raced. Who were they? What were their stories? Did any of them survive the Titanic, dance in a marathon till their toes bled, or make bathtub gin? Little did I know then that some of them actually had lives far surpassing my imagination.

Now on assignment, I looked around the familiar restaurant. A few late lunch diners lingered as the staff set up the tables for the cocktail/dinner crowd. I spotted an older woman with faded red hair and beautiful porcelain skin that probably had never seen the sun. My brilliant reporter's instincts deduced she was a waitress as she was dressed in the requisite black uniform and white apron, sporting the required hair net to keep it from falling into the food, and was cleaning a nearby table. I hoped, because she was older, that she'd been working at Schrafft's for a while and could tell me a bit of the restaurant chain's history.

I walked over to her. "Hi, my name is Ashley Wilkes," I said introducing myself. "I'm a reporter with the *Daily News*. If you have a moment, I'd love to ask you and some of the other workers a few questions about the restaurant and the television commercial Andy Warhol is making for Schrafft's."

"Good Lord, why would anyone hire Andy Warhol to do a Schrafft's commercial? What's he going to do, immortalize the cheese bread?"

We laughed as I extended my hand. "Maybe."

"Mary Jane McCarthy." Her grip was firm as she shook my hand. "OK, hon, no skin off my nose," she shrugged. "Give me a sec, I'm almost finished for the day."

She joined me at a table in the back along with one of the cooks and another waitress and, as we talked, I learned that

Mary Jane was Irish and barely sixteen when she was hired by Schrafft's the first week she arrived in America. She had long since lost her Irish brogue, but her green eyes twinkled and she was full of energy, though I guessed her age to be somewhere in her fifties. She told me how Schrafft's had been a godsend to her and to many other Irish girls arriving in America, including the other waitress and the cook who shook their heads in agreement. Mary Jane, almost as if she owned the place, proudly told me that Schrafft's was one of the only major food chains, or other companies for that matter, that for decades had hired women as servers, managers and supervisors. Most of the cooks and waitresses were women, but so were some of the corporate execs. In the throes of the current Women's Movement, this was a revelation. I wondered if Betty Friedan knew this? I didn't know if I'd use this information for the Warhol story, but I'd file it away for future reference. When I asked them about the Warhol commercial, they were less enthusiastic. They all feared that Schrafft's was no longer what the public wanted. Tastes were changing and changing its image on television without updating everything that was "Schrafft's" wasn't going to make a difference.

Mary Jane laughed. "Like me, this restaurant is a dinosaur, and associating it with Andy Warhol just ain't gonna cut it and bring in the hip crowd."

As we talked and I scribbled in my reporter's notebook (thank heaven I took a course in Gregg shorthand), a petite woman in her early seventies dressed in a tan Chanel suit trimmed with black braiding walked right past the hostess, who nodded, and headed directly to a table for two near the back of the restaurant. She smiled at Mary Jane as she sat down. Like the women I saw a couple of years earlier when my mom and I ate here, she had on a little, old-fashioned hat perched on her head and was wearing white gloves. She peeled them off after a waitress handed her a menu.

I couldn't stop myself from staring and barely thanked the other waitress and cook when they left to go back to work. Mary Jane looked at me curiously.

"Do you know Vi?" she asked.

I shook my head, no, then told her how I had noticed these older women before and wondered why they came to Schrafft's to eat dinner alone. I asked if she knew her.

She nodded yes. They met shortly after Mary Jane had arrived in America in 1937 and started working at the restaurant. Every Monday for months, Violet Wilding came in for dinner and sat in MJ's station. Finally, MJ (the nickname her fellow Schrafftees gave her) let her curiosity get the best of her. She introduced herself, they started talking, and continued to do so every Monday evening when Vi came for the night special of pan brown lamb hash with wax beans. She always had two cocktails. Perfect Rob Roys. I smiled. A perfect Rob Roy was my mom's preferred drink. I had never heard of it until we had dinner in this very restaurant and she ordered one. I remembered asking her what it was and, mom being mom, she gave me a little of the drink's history. It seems that the Rob Roy was invented by the Waldorf Astoria back in the 1800's in honor of a Broadway musical with the same name. Sort of a Manhattan, but with bourbon. What made a Rob Roy "perfect," however, was a slight change in the original recipe. Perfect Rob Roys are made with both sweet and dry vermouth—regular Rob Roys are made with sweet vermouth only. I've yet to try either one.

My attention returned to MJ who was giving me a little background on Vi…never married…successful banking career. She then alluded to a much bigger story, but politely refused to say anything more.

MJ looked at her watched. "I'm sorry, but I've got to go home and change," she said as she stood. "Seeing Jerry Orbach tonight in *Promises, Promises*. A customer got me house seats."

"Wow. Lucky you. I've been trying to gets tickets forever," I said with a tinge of envy. "But, I'm intrigued with Violet's story. I'd love to hear more sometime."

"Why don't you come by the restaurant around 10:00 Wednesday night? I'll be getting off the dinner shift."

I promised her I would as we said good night and I headed back to my apartment to write up my Schrafft's story.

As I left the restaurant, my mind was racing. I didn't understand why, but I had to know everything about Violet Wilding. Why has she been having dinner alone for all these decades? Was she widowed? Divorced? Never married? Didn't she have friends? Does she have children?

The night air was crisp and clear after the morning downpour. I could even see a star in the sky, something quite rare in Manhattan as the reflection of the lights of the skyline usually blocked them out. I decided to walk home to my little studio apartment on First and 55th while I invented all sorts of scenarios for Violet. So lost in thought, I started talking to myself… out loud. Passersby on the street looked at me like I was one of the street crazies. Maybe I was. I was at a loss to figure out why this woman with white gloves, drinking Rob Roys, intrigued me so much. I wasn't sure what a "career in banking" meant, but this was a woman who worked at a bank when very few women worked anywhere in any business. What did she need to sacrifice to be a career woman back then? My mind continued to race ahead of me and without realizing it, I was so absorbed I walked right past my apartment building.

"Miss Wilkes! Miss Wilkes!"

Someone was calling me back to planet earth. I turned around and saw Patrick, my doorman, waving at me.

"Are you OK?" he asked as I retraced my steps.

"I'm fine, Patrick. Just a little embarrassed. I was just so lost in thought I didn't realize where I was."

He opened the big glass door leading into my building lobby.

"Thank you," I said as my fingers formed their usual search party to find my keys hiding somewhere in my oversized shoulder bag. I walked to the mailroom behind a white, opaque glass partition wall framed in black wood that gave off a Japanese vibe, though my lobby hardly felt Japanese-y with its fifties, armless olive green sofas and mid-century, geometric patterned area rug on an off-white tile floor.

Armed with the day's mail, the glow of the lamp on my desk welcomed me home as I entered my compact apartment. The walls were painted refrigerator white. I wasn't fond of the trendy Navajo white everyone was using. It always looked a little dirty to me. My collection of large, light wood framed botanicals popped off the stark white walls and gave my one room a cheerful, garden flair. My sofa/daybed had white sheets and a pretty floral quilt with big pink cabbage roses I'd found on sale at Bloomie's. I poured a glass of cheap, chilled Italian white wine from the fridge and sat down at my desk to type up my Warhol/Schrafft's story.

Dwyre had given me a research packet and I condensed the information into my article. I told the story of Frank Shattuck, a candy salesman who went to work for William Schrafft, a chocolate manufacturer in Boston to sell Schrafft candy outside New England and, in 1898, opened the first Schrafft's, a small retail store to sell the candy on Broadway in Manhattan. After a few years, Shattuck's sister, Jane, who had been running the store, started serving homemade ice cream and eventually, lunches. The store turned into a popular restaurant and Frank opened more Schrafft stores. It soon became known not just for candy and ice cream, but for its cheese bread and wholesome entrees such as creamed chicken on toast and lobster Newburg.

I reviewed my notes and found MJ's quote that many of the waitresses, like herself, were just "off the boat" from Ireland and that most of the cooks were women. But Schrafft's, as MJ had mentioned earlier, was also one of the first restaurants that hired women in managerial, supervising and executive positions. Since the women's movement was underway, I thought this was a nice little bonus to the story and decided to use it. Though I did laugh when I wrote how the waitresses had to line up every morning for a cleanliness and neatness inspection. More Henry James than Germaine Greer. During the Depression, however, women were not allowed to work in restaurants after 10:00 PM, so male waiters were hired for the late dinner shift. At one point, even Kirk Douglas did a stint as a Schrafft's waiter, though that was a few years later, but a nice celebrity name drop for the article.

Recently, Schrafft's merged its fifty-five restaurant chain with outlets in eight Eastern states from Massachusetts to Florida, with St. Louis-based Pet, Inc. Schrafft's boss, Frank G. Shattuck II, came up with the plan to sell Schrafft's to a younger, hipper, career-oriented clientele by remodeling the restaurants to emphasize the cocktail bar as well as the soda fountain. Hiring Andy Warhol to sell this new image was also part of that plan, so I was surprised to learn that Andy's idea was to do a hip commercial on the chain's ice cream sundae. He called it the "Underground Sundae." How was a commercial on ice cream going to change Schrafft's image? Before going to bed I decided I really needed to see the commercial before it aired so that I could complete my article.

The next day, I used the paper's contacts in the advertising department to get an early peek. A representative from Schrafft's met me at the ad agency producing the commercial. We were shown into a cave-like room where the editor rolled tape. As the commercial began, a slightly out of focus, shiny red dot appeared on the screen which transformed into a maraschino cherry that reminded me of some of Warhol's silk-screen paintings. The cherry was plopped on top of a chocolate sundae which morphed into all sorts of psychedelic colors as the vivid background colors changed. The sundae vibrated to coughs on the soundtrack. "Andy Warhol for a Schrafft's?" asked a female voice off-camera.

"A little change is good for everybody," an announcer replied. Across the screen Andy's credit appeared.

The sixty second commercial was fun and vibrant and oh, so very Warhol. And, as the Schrafft's rep claimed, they didn't just acquire a commercial, but a piece of art. Again, I wondered why Schrafft's wanted to highlight its ice cream if it wanted a hipper, career-oriented crowd. Why not the bar, especially since singles bars were so successful for all of us trying to establish ourselves in the city and looking to make new friends. I wasn't sure a commercial about ice cream would make anyone my age want to go to Schrafft's, but I did think it was pretty.

It was late when I returned to the newsroom, but I wanted to finish a first draft of my article. When I finally made it home, I popped a frozen dinner in the oven and turned on the TV. Just another exciting, glamorous night in the city that never sleeps.

Back at my desk bright and early Wednesday morning, I polished my Schrafft's article, turned it into to Dwyre, then tried to work on a piece I was writing about the push by Wall Street firms to hire and train more women to be stockbrokers now that a total of one woman was a member of the New York Stock Exchange after Muriel Siebert bought her "seat" last year.

In the early 60's, while I was still in college, I landed a summer job at the Royal Globe Insurance Company just blocks from the Exchange. I filed and copied documents on an old mimeograph machine (memories of that smelly liquid chemical just wafted through my mind), working in a cavernous room with seemingly endless rows of open file bins alongside a bevy of middle-aged female file clerks who commuted to Wall Street from various neighborhoods in Brooklyn. One bleached blonde woman showed up in pin curls every day with a silk scarf arranged in the back of her head like half a Davy Crockett coonskin cap…you know with that tail hanging down. I still wondered about that. If she set her hair to go to work, when did she let her hair roam free? Maybe she let it down as she flirted and danced the night away at some Brooklyn dance hall. I never asked. Another woman, short and quite plump, figured out a way never to leave her chair while filing. She would just roll up and down the aisles, lean over the waste-high bins and file her papers. The only time I remember her getting out of her chair was for her morning ten-minute coffee/donut break, her lunch break, her afternoon break, this time consuming a package or two of Hostess cupcakes, and to clock out at the end of the day, all timed to coincide with her bathroom breaks. I admired her bladder control. She probably would have been a lot thinner if she actually stood up and walked around when doing her filing, but I thought it best not to bring it up.

I obviously didn't have much in common with these women. Though they were very nice to me, they didn't include me during their lunch hour which was usually in the company's cafeteria and that was fine with me. Instead, I explored the Wall Street area, still one of my favorite parts of the city. I sat in the beautiful Trinity Church eating a ham and cheese sandwich and discovered that Alexander Hamilton was buried there. But mostly, I took my brown bag lunch to the Exchange gallery so I could watch the commotion going on the floor. All the yelling and screaming as ticker tapes clicked away. I loved it! But it wasn't long before I realized there were no women trading on the floor. Even worse, I soon discovered that there wasn't a single female member on the Exchange and that women were actually barred from the floor. I bristled, as I remembered when I was about six or seven being told I couldn't try out for Little League because I was a girl. I was better than most boys back then and I was pissed. I went to my dad to make it right and painfully listened as he explained why he couldn't. I never went to another Little League game after that. It wasn't long that I realized that women were better at a lot of things, but I digress.

Back to my article. I wondered why a woman would actually want to work on Wall Street or at a brokerage firm since she would still be barred from trading on the floor. The floor was the cool place to be in my opinion, but unless she was a stock exchange runner or a quoting clerk or Muriel Siebert, women couldn't even step onto the floor. And no ladies rooms! Did Muriel run into a nearby coffee shop if she needed to go? Of course, all that was about to change now that she had bought into that ol' boys' club (whether those boys wanted it to or not)…but, I don't think she was going to buy her way into the old "George Washington drank here" watering holes like Fraunces Tavern that frowned on women drinking and eating in their establishments even with a male escort. Or bars and restaurants like McSorley's Old Ale House in the east Village were women were forbidden to enter—period. Of course, there were always those mediocre coffee shops for lunch, but they weren't going to cut it for a business lunch with mostly male clients. And what about having a drink after work? Nope, not happening downtown for women. At least not comfortably. And don't get me started on the clothes shopping. No Saks. No Bonwit's. No B. Altman's. No Lord & Taylor!! Just inexpensive, low-end women's stores like Lerner's. Fine for the average working girl working downtown and for striving reporters like myself, but definitely not the right "look" for a female stockbroker.

Muriel was a trailblazer and I really admired her, but it still seemed to me that the women stockbroker pioneers who would follow her would have to be very tough to get ahead downtown.

Besides, I was having my own female issues at the paper which was much more female-friendly to me than Wall Street would be, and mid-town had better restaurants and wonderful department stores which were embracing our money if not our gender...places where we could wine and dine ourselves and spend our money on ourselves. We were even welcomed into more and more bars, though some still insisted on a male companion as our entrance ticket.

Falling into a feminist funk, my mind wandered back to Vi. How did she do it back then? I wanted the day to end so I could get back to Schrafft's and talk more with MJ.

When I arrived at Schrafft's most of the dinner crowd had left. I found MJ sitting at a back table dressed in street clothes. To my surprise, Vi was sitting with her. My heart skipped a beat. There were so many questions I wanted to ask her. So much I wanted to know about living in New York before, during and right after the Depression.

MJ introduced us. I noticed both MJ and Vi had cocktails. It was late and I still hadn't had dinner, but I decided to join them when the waitress came over to take my order. MJ was sipping a Gibson, Vi had her perfect Rob Roy, and I opted for a gin martini, straight up with olives.

Vi started the conversation, "MJ told me that you're writing an article about Schrafft's."

"Yes," I answered. "My editor thought that Andy Warhol doing a TV commercial had an interesting twist on marketing restaurants not known for having an 'edge' or attracting a young crowd."

"How's it coming?" she asked.

"Fine. It's not a very in-depth piece. I think the paper just wanted to write something about Warhol, but I was able to sneak in some Schrafft history."

We sat silently for a moment as my drink arrived. I took a big sip. Perfectly chilled, it felt so good sliding down my throat. Here sat Vi, the woman I'd been obsessing about! I wanted to know everything about her, but where to begin?

"I don't know if MJ told you, but I would love to interview you. I want to know about your life and career. How you came to Schrafft's."

"Old and alone, you mean?"

My face flushed, but decided to answer truthfully. "Yes. Why Schrafft's? And why dinner here alone every Monday night?"

Vi stared into my eyes for a long time as if she were coming to some kind of decision. Neither of us said anything. I sipped more of my martini and popped an olive into my mouth just to have something to do.

It was Vi who broke the silence. "When MJ called yesterday morning and told me about you, I went to the library to read some of your articles and found them smart and quite refreshing."

I was taken aback. No one had ever researched me before. "Thank you," was all I could manage.

Vi drifted off in thought as she continued to stare into my eyes. Again, the three of us sat in silence.

"I have a long story to tell and if I tell it to you, it's off the record. You must promise me that you will never tell a soul, not until the rest of us are dead," Vi finally said.

"Rest of you?"

"Yes. I'm not the only old Schrafft's lady involved."

It was my turn to stare. I looked into her pale blue eyes and knew she had something big to tell. A secret. And, I wanted to know what it was.

I promised. A promise that turned out to be one of the most difficult decisions of my life. I didn't realize it then that this would not be an easy story for her to tell and that she would only dole it out in fragments, giving her the time to get to know me and trust me as we built our relationship,

CHAPTER 2

VIOLET — 1893-1937

Violet Rose Wilding was born in 1893 and at seventeen met Anthony Salvatore Natale, a nineteen-year-old construction worker who was working on a townhouse being built near her family's large home on 37th Street off Fifth, right around the corner from J.P. Morgan's mansion. She walked past the construction site one afternoon as Tony, sitting on a pile of lumber, was on a lunch break. He whistled as his eyes caressed her petite figure and blonde curls. He smiled. She smiled back.

"Ya know, you shouldn't be allowed to walk the streets," he said with a slight Jersey accent.

"And why is that?" she asked.

"Because you'll leave a trail of broken hearts. Starting with mine."

Vi laughed.

"I'm sure your heart will mend as soon as the next young girl walks by."

"Nope. Only way I see it mending is for you to run away with me to the Casbah," he smiled.

"Sorry, I hate travel."

"Come." He stood up, leaving his lunch pail and walked toward her. "At least have coffee with me. There's a diner just down the block."

She laughed. "You left your lunch?"

"Who can eat when their heart is broken?" He grabbed her hand and started walking.

She stopped short. "Wait. I didn't say I'd have coffee with you."

He smiled. "Sure you did, when you started talking to me."

Tony was unlike any boy she knew. He was smart and funny like some of her friends, but as she learned while sipping her coffee, he was burning with ambition and dreams for his future. He actually wanted to achieve something. Being a construction worker was not a goal, it was a means to a goal. Money for his education. His lunch break was over. He paid for their coffee and walked her out of the diner.

"Thanks for soothing my broken heart," he said as he walked back to the construction site.

Two days later, Vi went by the site again looking for him and soon they began dating. It wasn't long before they fell in love and got engaged. Tony scraped together enough money to give her a single pearl engagement ring set in gold. She loved it. Her parents, however, were horrified. It was one thing to go out with the boy to the movies, it was another to marry him, growled her father, Peter, a "son of the Revolution."

"He's an Italian, for heaven's sake, and Catholic!" Judith, her staunch *Church of England* mother stated with disdain.

Vi rebelled and continued to see Tony secretly, but eventually her father found out and threatened to monitor her every waking hour. She had no money of her own and no place to go. Peter had warned all her friends' parents that they were not to help or shelter her. She was basically under house arrest. Tony wanted to run away, this time not to the Casbah, but to elope and get a place of their own. As much as she loved him, Vi knew that that would be a horrible mistake. He'd have to give up his dream of a higher education. His hopes for the future would be cut off if he had to support himself and a wife.

After much arguing, begging and crying, her parents never wavered from their ultimatum. Vi knew she had to break off her engagement, but, before she promised never to see Tony again, she had an ultimatum of her own. She would only do so if she be allowed to go to work, something young ladies from good families rarely did. Vi was determined to become an independent woman and to never again be controlled by her father. This time Tony was truly heartbroken, but Vi had made up her mind.

Her father reluctantly agreed, but he, too, had conditions. As founder of Wilding Shipping, he would help her get a job as a secretary (or "typewriter" as they were often called), a profession that was only just opening up to a few well-connected women at one of the places he conducted business. He could keep tabs on her there. After making some calls, Peter secured Vi a position as a secretary to a senior vice president at his Wall Street bank, and there she would soon learn the real limitations placed on women. Though women controlled a great deal of money inherited from fathers and husbands, they really had limited power, having to rely on men to invest or co-sign any deals or real estate purchases they might want to make. She knew of no women bankers.

The Wildings were one of the few people in the city with a car and driver, but Vi announced she would be taking the trolley to work. Judith was horrified. People like them didn't travel on public transportation. They walked, rode in the family car if there was one, or took horse-drawn taxis. But Vi insisted. Her compromise was to take a taxi across town with her mother to Gimbel's, the new department store she had been reading about. She needed some practical business suits, dresses and accessories. Normally, she would have had her seamstress make her a few outfits, but she wanted to fit in. Store-bought clothes might help. Besides, she was curious to see the new store.

Vi had never been to a department store and this one block square, multiple-storied Renaissance-inspired building made her gasp. This is just a store, she thought?! When she walked into Gimbel's she was stunned by the interior's size and breadth. The beautiful pendant lighting made the display cases sparkle and showcased more merchandise than she had ever seen in one space. She found a plush settee and plopped herself down and just looked around trying to take it all in. The sales staff seemed so competent and knowledgeable. Everything and everyone were so modern. Judith, on the other hand, wasn't impressed by anything, especially by the store's merchandise. She grabbed her daughter's hand and pulled her up off the settee.

"We're going home. This place is an affront to good taste," she spewed in a huff. But Vi, though overwhelmed with it all, refused. She yanked her hand away.

"Go if you want. I'm staying."

She walked to a jewelry counter and stared at all the selections. A pair of tear-drop garnet earrings caught her eye.

A striking young woman about her own age was behind the counter and after finishing up with a customer she swooped over to Vi. "All these pieces were handcrafted in Paris and are made of rose gold and real gemstones. Beautiful, aren't they?" the salesgirl asked.

Vi just nodded.

"Would you like me to take a piece out for you so you can see it better?"

"No, she wouldn't," Judith snapped and dragged Vi away from the display case. "We're leaving!"

Again, Vi refused to be bullied and follow her mother out of the store.

"No, Mom, we're staying," she said. "I know it's overwhelming, but look around. It's exciting. You can come shop with me or not."

"And if I don't, how will you pay for anything?" Judith spewed.

"Obviously, I can't," Vi snapped, then played her "daddy's little girl" card. "But it doesn't mean I can't have some fun exploring and tomorrow I'll bring Daddy here and he'll help me find a business wardrobe."

Judith knew that Peter would give in to Vi on this, so she decided to let her win this skirmish.

As snootily as she could muster, Judith asked the salesgirl behind the jewelry counter where they could find women's attire.

As they made their way to the ladies department, Vi was taken aback by so many smart-looking women working as sales clerks. Her girlfriends were either in college, aiding their mothers in charitable causes or just languishing at one party or dance after another before marrying well. Though she sometimes regretted not going to college now that her engagement with Tony was over, she vowed she wasn't going to be like her friends who defined themselves by their social standing. She was not going to be paired off to some suitable boy and live in his shadow. She wanted to be like these self-assured women who were so business-like, yet friendly to the customers. She envied their poise and hoped that by becoming a working woman, she, too, would gain the self-assurance these women possessed, as well as some financial independence. She chafed at the idea that she would have to be dependent on some future husband or her parents' money for everything. What if they didn't like something she liked and wanted to buy it? As in the past, she wouldn't get it unless she used her feminine "wiles" on her father or made some kind of quid pro quo. Now that she had given up Tony, she was never going to give up anything else.

As Vi looked at various suits and dresses, the head salesgirl asked her if she wanted to see them on a model to get a better feel of how they would look on her. Vi's eyes lit up.

"Yes, I would love to see them modelled," she said to the salesgirl.

Judith agreed, thinking that once her daughter saw these inferior clothes on someone, she would see how common they were. But, as the models came out dressed in the various chosen outfits, Vi was thrilled and insisted that Judith buy them all and have them delivered that afternoon. And, just before they left Gimbels, Vi saw a smart beaver hat that would go perfectly with her new winter coat and cashmere gloves. At $5.95 it was one of the most expensive accessories she'd bought.

When the packages arrived later that day, Vi spent the entire evening trying and retrying on her new clothes, adding and subtracting accessories, picking out the right bags and the right shoes. She decided that shopping in a department store was so much more fun than having fittings at home with a seamstress for dresses her mother ordered for her. Today was Vi's first taste of independence. Even though her parents footed the bill, she was the one who chose the clothes. It was a start.

She arrived for her first day of work at James Ackerman's office at First Federal Bank of New York promptly at 9:00 A.M. As she made her way to the executive floor, she didn't see one woman working there. She looked around, totally lost and out of her element. It didn't matter what she had on, she thought, nothing was going to help her fit in. All the secretary-typewriters were men, one of whom noticed her confusion and politely directed her to her desk. She looked at it in bewilderment. Should she just sit down and wait until someone came over and told her what to do, or should she let her new boss know that she had arrived? She decided the latter and knocked on the closed door that led to her new boss' office.

"Come in," a man's voice boomed from inside. Vi took a deep breath, opened the door and entered a huge corner office paneled in dark mahogany with rugs from the Orient and sofa and club chairs upholstered in dark green leather. Sitting behind a large, carved cherry wood desk facing the door was a distinguished looking man at least two decades older than Vi, with dark brown hair, wearing a navy blue suit, crisp white shirt, and a red and blue striped tie. Vi assumed he was James Ackerman, senior vice president of the bank's business loan department. She felt she had entered a private men's club. And, in fact, she had.

Mr. Ackerman stood up from behind his desk. "You must be Violet Wilding. Welcome to First Federal. Please come in. Take a seat." He pointed to a chair opposite him on the other side of the desk. He continued to stand until she took a seat, then he returned to his chair.

He asked if she had any idea what was expected of her in her new position and she confessed that she did not. He explained that, to start, he would need her to do the filing, keep his schedule and type up the letters he would dictate for his signature.

"How fast do you type?" he asked.

Her heart skipped a beat. It was only at that moment that Vi realized that the problem with being hired as a secretary-typewriter was that she'd actually have to know how to type. She thought being a secretary would require all those other duties he mentioned, but it never dawned on her that she would really have to type letters. Oh, my God, she thought, I'm out of a job before I even start!

"I'm so sorry, Mr. Ackerman, I don't know how to type," she confessed embarrassingly. Convinced that she was totally unqualified for this job, she stood up to leave.

"Please sit down, Miss Wilding."

Her hands were now sweating underneath her white gloves.

"It seems we have a problem. But it's not one that can't be fixed."

"I don't know how, sir. My father should not have forced you to hire me since I'm incapable of performing one of the main requirements for this position."

"Don't give you father too much credit. My wife's been after me to hire a woman in the bank for years, and he gave me the perfect excuse to do so. His company's business with us is important and he wanted to make sure you found a job where you'd be safe."

"But if I can't do the job, there doesn't seem any point to my being here except to please my father."

Ackerman laughed. "I didn't need to please your father that much. You see, my wife's a suffragette, and quite frankly, I support that. She also feels that women should be allowed to work in business and banking, and I agree. Of course, this goes against the grain with a lot of my colleagues, so your father's request made it easy for me to bring a woman onto the executive floor. My colleagues are the ones who wanted to please him so I let them think that this was all their idea."

"Thank you, Mr. Ackerman. But I'm still not qualified and I'd be collecting a salary that I don't deserve."

"Then we're just going to have to get you qualified. That is, if you're willing to work at it."

"Yes, sir. Yes, I am. But how?"

"If you'll be here at 8:00 in the morning, I will arrange to have someone here teach you how to type and take stenography. And then again, during your lunch break. During office hours you will do the filing, make my appointments and do whatever else needs to be done."

"But what about your letters?" she asked, her expressive blue eyes filled with doubt.

"Don't worry about them. You'll be doing them soon enough."

And that was how Vi's career began in banking.

Once she mastered shorthand and typing, Vi loved being a secretary and she was good at it. She loved making her own money and the concomitant independence it gave her. But she still lived at home under her parents' ever-watchful eye. She made friends and soon started dating some of the young men she'd met at the bank. None, of course, became friends or boyfriends that passed muster with her mother so it was difficult to maintain those relationships outside the office. Her parents dragged her to country club dances and to weekends at their friends' estates outside the city, but now that Vi was a working woman, she had little in common with her well-to-do peers. Her old boarding school girlfriends were rapidly marrying and talked about nothing else and most of the boys she grew up were just as vacuous. The few other friends she remained close with, like her best friend Betsy, were away at college. And, the guys she did like in her crowd began working in their fathers' businesses as soon as they graduated and were busy trying to prove themselves. One of those boys from her old crowd whose father was President of First Federal, also worked at the bank. Vi never knew him that well, and thought he was nice enough, but she rarely saw him because he was "proving himself" in another department. Like the sons whose jobs were foreordained by their fathers' careers and companies, she was too young to see the irony of her achieving her position because of her father.

It was 1913 and her peers were the pearls in the world's oyster. But all that was about to change. By the start of World War I, Vi was a respected employee of the bank with increasing responsibility and a few salary raises, but, still, James Ackerman's secretary. Like everyone else, she and her childhood friends' worlds were rocked when WWI broke out and soon many of the boys volunteered for active duty. Because of their education and station in life, they were trained as officers and quickly sent to Europe. Wanting to help, Vi became increasingly involved with the war effort, and soon was volunteering after work at one of the city's hospitals where she rapidly learned to treat the wounded and dying who had been shipped to New York. Mr. Ackerman was proud of her service. At forty-four, he was too old to enlist, so he joined her at the hospital as a volunteer.

Being at the hospital opened Vi's eyes to a different world. The horror of war affected her deeply as she tended the wounded. Working with Mr. Ackerman for long hours at both the office and the hospital and often going out for supper together changed their relationship. Weeks went by when it seemed he was the only one she talked to. Then, late one night, he found her sitting on an overturned bucket in a supply room, weeping.

"Vi, what happened?" Mr. Ackerman asked.

"Daniel just died," she answered through her sobs.

"Daniel?"

"A sweet boy from Missouri who came in last week. God, he was only eighteen!" she managed to choke out, as tears streamed down her cheeks. "The gangrene just spread and spread and spread even after they chopped off his leg."

Mr. Ackerman turned over another bucket and sat down next to her. He took her hand and sympathetically listened as she continued to vent her emotions.

"Minutes before he died, he grabbed my hand and begged me to write his girlfriend back in Missouri and tell her he loved her. I promised. What am I going to tell her?"

She showed him a piece of paper with the girl's address that she had crumpled in her hand.

"Do I tell her that his last days were in a ward that smelled of rotting flesh? That he suffered and sometimes screamed in pain? Do I tell her that he also watched his friends suffer and heard their screams…that the sight of lost limbs and blood-soaked bandages was everywhere? That I couldn't help him?"

When she finished, Vi buried her head in her lap while Mr. Ackerman continued to hold her hand.

After that night, because she needed to feel needed and needed to unburden to someone about the war and the wounded, she turned to Mr. Ackerman. Their strong emotional bond turned to love. She knew it was wrong and after they made love for the first time, joy, guilt and a profound sense of sadness overwhelmed her. Those conflicting emotions during their lovemaking never left her as they continued to reach out to each other physically for solace and escape from all the pain they witnessed. She knew he loved his wife and would never leave her, but right then, at that time in her life she didn't care. "Mr. Ackerman" became "James," and James fulfilled her needs.

Being in a clandestine love affair gave her the courage to finally move out of her family home. She had saved quite a bit of money over the years and could afford to pay rent for her own apartment. However, finding a reputable building that would rent to a single woman proved to be a challenge. Landlords insisted that a man co-sign the lease. James offered to do so, but Vi felt strongly that that would put them in a situation where they could be found out, and neither wanted to hurt James' wife. It would be risky enough for him to come and go in her building. So she turned to her father. After many arguments, Vi finally convinced her father that she was independent enough and strong enough and old enough to be on her own. Of course, helping her had strings. He would buy her a suitable apartment in a building of his choice and put it jointly in their names. She would pay the mortgage. If, for some reason, she couldn't pay the mortgage, he would subsidize her. He also insisted that she come home for dinner one night a week and every Sunday.

After Vi agreed, they went to her mother, a united front. Judith was livid. No way was her daughter going to live outside their home and not be married. However, when she realized that fighting both Peter and Vi was a lost cause, she laid out her own demands. Chiefly, that she be allowed to help decorate. She didn't want to have her daughter scrimp on furnishings. If Vi had to live on her own, she would at least have a place her mother could brag about. Since Vi had no flair for decorating, she readily agreed, and eventually her father found a lovely, spacious two bedroom apartment with a large kitchen, a small library and terrace. As soon as the mortgage papers were signed, Vi moved out of the family mansion.

Vi had begun to grow close again to her childhood best friend, Betsy Howard, a direct descendent of Betsy Ross ("You know how we ol' WASPs are, always trading on our DAR status," she would tell people if anyone brought it up). Shortly after America entered the war, she left Mount Holyoke and returned to Manhattan to marry Bradley Howard. It was the wedding of the year. The reception was held on the roof of the St. Regis Hotel with its spectacular view of the surrounding skyline. Entrees of lobsters and steaks were served (pre-surf 'n' turf). Champagne flowed and the wedding cake was four tiers high. Vi was her maid of honor.

Shortly after, Bradley was shipped to Europe to fight the Germans. Betsy was five months pregnant with twins, but refused to sit home and worry. She wanted to be useful. To help in the war effort. She joined Vi as a volunteer at the hospital and their friendship became deeper and stronger. She admired Vi's independence, even envied her freedom. She loved being a wife and soon-to-be mother, but the thought of being out on her own with the accompanying freedom was something she longed for. She knew that that would never be her life, that she would never have adventures, so she lived vicariously through Vi. It wasn't long before she had figured out that Vi and James had much more than a working relationship.

One night when Vi had gone to Betsy's home for dinner, they were relaxing in the parlor sipping coffee when Betsy had interrupted Vi who had been going on about Betsy's cook and the miraculous way she had turned rationed goods into a gourmet meal.

"You know you're not fooling me, Violet Rose." Betsy had said with a smile. "You and James. If he weren't married and way too old for you, I'd mind my own business. But, Vi, what are you thinking?"

"Why?" Vi had asked. "Because women like us don't have sex outside of marriage?"

"Hell, we do!" Betsy had said, then laughed. "We just don't have it with men we work with."

"Ah, but 'we' don't work with men, so I'm forging a new path for women like us."

They both had laughed.

"I guess you are," Betsy had replied.

Vi was still working at the bank when the war ended, but she realized that she had to move on. Her affair with James had gone on long enough and she knew it had to end. For a week she made excuses not to see him after work as she tried to build up her courage to let him go. Not wanting to sit alone in her apartment for one more night, she went out to explore the city alone and eventually found herself outside a Schrafft's. She had never been in one, but she remembered some of the nurses at the hospital going to one after their shifts, because women were allowed to eat and drink there without a male escort even if she was by herself. She went inside and was seated at a small table near the back wall. She took off her white gloves and read the menu. The evening special was lamb hash and waxed beans. She told the waitress she would try the special and ordered a perfect Rob Roy. Never before had she gone out to dinner by herself. "Ladies" just didn't do that. She couldn't even remember ever ordering her own food in a restaurant. She always told the men at the table what she wanted, most often her father and lately James, and they would order for her. This simple act of ordering her own meal made her feel empowered. She liked the feeling. She sat up straight and, with head held high, she brazenly looked around the room at the other diners, mostly men. For the first time in her life Vi felt that she was their equal. As she sipped her drink and ate her dinner, she knew she had the strength to face life without James. She would tell him in the morning. She paid the bill and left a generous tip.

Vi arrived early, took off her hat and gloves and walked into James' office. He was on the phone. Her heart racing, she sat on the same chair where she had perched herself on the first morning she had met him. She put her hands in her lap while waiting for him to finish his call. When he hung up and looked at her, he knew.

"You're leaving me," he said, not a question, but a statement of fact.

She nodded. "I can't continue to work for you or we'll never be over."

They sat silently for a while.

"You do know every vice president and department head at the bank would love you to work for him," he finally said, resignation in his voice. "You pick which one and I'll see that you're transferred. We'll explain that you want to learn more about the banking business."

"I need to leave the bank," she whispered, afraid she was going to cry.

"Then I'll help you find a position in another bank or company."

"Thank you. I'd appreciate that."

"I do love you, you know," he said, his voice wavering.

"I know."

Vi stood up and left the office.

Within a short period of time, she was hired by Eli Rosen, the Chairman of Rosen & Steindler, a Jewish Wall Street brokerage house and a friend of James. Eli loved doing the unconventional, and having a female secretary was very unconventional on Wall Street. Not to mention, he was overjoyed with the prospect of having the society daughter of a prominent WASP business-man working for him.

With both the war and her affair now over, Vi threw herself into her new job. She continued to have dinner at her parents' home and attended many of the parties and weekend getaways at the country or beach homes of her childhood friends. The War had changed them. Some had been wounded. Many were struggling to recover emotionally, if not financially. They now viewed the world as it truly was. They became interesting peo-ple. The women still didn't seek careers, but many became more seriously involved in charitable work, which also opened their eyes to the world around them.

By 1930, Vi knew she was considered an "old maid," a "spinster," and she began to look at her life with a great deal more intro-spection than she'd ever previously mustered. Still close with Betsy, she doted on her goddaughters, Betsy and Bradley's twin girls, and envied Betsy's relationship with her husband who, after the war, decided to go to med school. Wanting to see Vi settled in a solid relationship, they were forever trying to fix her up with some doctor or another. It was on one those blind dates that her life dramatically changed.

Dinner was at eight. She was to meet the B's as she called Betsy and Bradley, at this very Schrafft's because it was reasonable, centrally located and didn't take notice of diners sipping from a flask…it was Prohibition, after all. She had no idea who the B's dragged out of the hospital this time. All she knew was that he was a heart specialist, a widower and his name was Tony. She liked most of the men the B's had introduced her to, but at thirty-seven, she wasn't looking to fall madly in love, or even un-madly in love. When she arrived and saw who was sitting at the table, she felt as if her heart stopped. There, talking to the B's was Tony…her Tony! Her first love! Her hands began to perspire and her knees went weak. She was embarrassed at her school girl reaction and wanted to run out of the restaurant, but it was too late. Betsy saw her and waved her over. If Tony was shocked to see her as she was to see him, he didn't let on. Betsy began the introduction as Tony stood to greet Vi.

"We're old friends," he interrupted, then looked directly into Vi's eyes and extended his hand. "You look beautiful, Vi."

Vi tried to casually wipe the sweat off her hand on her skirt before she took Tony's hand. She smiled. Bradley and Betsy didn't say a word. Entranced, they watched Tony and Vi stare at each other as Tony held onto her hand then pulled out a chair and led her into it. Vi had yet to say a word.

"Oh, my god!" Betsy gasped as if a lightbulb went off in her head.

"What?" Bradley asked his wife.

"It's Tony."

"Of course, it's Tony," he said.

"No! It's Tony, Tony!" Betsy said looking at her friend.

Vi finally broke her silence and laughed. "Yes, Betsy, it's Tony."

"Well, I'm glad we got that settled," Tony said as he smiled warmly at Vi.

"OK, what am I missing here?" Bradley laughed, then pulled out his flask. "Let's toast to whatever it is I don't know."

After that evening, she knew she had fallen madly in love with him all over again.

Tony courted her. Her parents, who had mellowed over the years, were thrilled that she had found someone who might actually marry her at this late date in their daughter's life. On New Year's Eve at 12:05 am, 1933, he gave her a beautiful three carat diamond ring from Tiffany when he proposed and she accepted. Eli threw them a huge engagement party with mountains of food and good bootleg liquor. Vi's life was perfect. Then it wasn't. Shortly after the party, Tony was about to leave the hospital to meet Vi for dinner when he suffered a massive heart attack. Doctors ran to help him, but they were too late. He died within seconds.

After Tony's funeral, Vi retreated into her work, retreated from her friends, retreated into herself, preferring her own company to anyone else's. After a long mourning period, she began to slowly re-enter the world. She started seeing a few friends now and again and went to Betsy and Bradley's for dinner with them and their girls, knowing the B's would no longer try to play matchmaker. As her emotional strength grew, she decided to dine out by herself once a week and chose the Schrafft's where she had found Tony again and where she knew a woman could enjoy a cocktail and dinner alone.

Four years later, at age forty-five, she met George Roman while sipping a perfect Rob Roy and eating her favorite Monday night special of pan-browned lamb hash with waxed beans.

CHAPTER 3

ASHLEY — 1968

At that point in her tale, Vi announced she was tired and needed to get home, but promised we would meet again.

"How about next Monday?" she asked.

I readily agreed. I knew her story had only just begun.

I rushed home, found a legal pad on top of my desk, and started scribbling down everything Vi had told me. My mind raced as I thought about the death of Tony and how lonely Vi's life seemed to become after that. Who were the other Schrafft women she referred to and who was George Roman? I had a million questions and imagined a million scenarios but instinctively knew that nothing I could imagine would come close to what Vi was going to tell me, *if* she told me. I had promised her that her story was all off the record, but that didn't stop me from writing it all down. As I got ready for bed and was brushing my teeth I realized that all I had had for dinner were the olives in my martini.

I don't really remember much of what I did till my next dinner with Vi. I know I wrote a lifestyle story on Ratner's and how the Fillmore East had changed the patrons of that restaurant from basically an older, Jewish crowd to a clientele of hippies, suburbanites and hip music lovers who often found themselves in Ratner's sharing cheese blintzes after a show at the legendary rock theater.

The East Village had turned into a mecca for flower children who littered the streets panhandling on show nights near and in front of the Fillmore and Ratner's, then invaded the restaurant for a cup of borscht. I loved going to the Fillmore for a rock 'n' roll music fix. One show I'll never forget took place the night Sly & the Family Stone debuted as the opening act for Jimi Hendrix. Few people had ever heard of the band but by the end of its set, the band had blown everyone away. As marijuana smoke wafted through the theater, we screamed and cheered and jumped to our feet begging for more. By the time Jimi was able to go on, I was wiped out. I often wondered if Hendrix was pissed that he'd allowed Sly to open for him. Following Sly wasn't easy, not even for the great Jimi Hendrix. Dwyre had liked my story, but once it was finished, all I could think about was Vi.

When I arrived the next Monday night, Vi was sipping her first perfect Rob Roy. MJ greeted me as she led me to the table and handed me a menu.

"Martini, rocks, olives, right?" she asked.

I smiled and nodded. "Thanks, MJ." It was nice going somewhere where the waitress knew your preferred cocktail.

"Hope you don't mind, Ashley, I started without you," Vi said lifting her drink.

"Of course not." I took a reporter's notebook out of my oversized, brown leather shoulder bag. "Do you mind if I take notes?"

Vi didn't answer right away. It was as if she were debating with herself then said, "No. I'm putting my trust in you, Ashley. But this is not for publication," she said, then repeated. "At least not while one of us is still alive. Can I have your promise?"

Again, I promised. What could possibly be so secret, I thought? A vision of female bank robbers dressed in long dusters like Jesse James and his gang robbing banks in the old west flashed through my mind. I made a note to check and see if there were any female gangs on J. Edgar Hoover's most wanted list.

MJ shook me out of my musing when she brought my martini along with some of Schrafft's signature cheese bread. "On the house."

I popped an olive in my mouth as Vi and I raised our glasses and took a sip of our drinks simultaneously. I opened my notebook. "I've been waiting all week to hear who George Roman is."

"Was, my dear. Was," she emphasized. "George was the last man I allowed in my life. He was a charming, handsome man with salt and pepper hair that formed a widow's peak at the top of his forehead. He wined me and dined me. Paid attention to me. Listened to me. Made love to me. And proposed marriage. But before we actually wed, he stole a great deal of my money and disappeared. But tonight's not about George, I need to begin telling you about the rest of us."

She waved MJ over. Vi, of course, was having her regular Monday night entrée. I glanced at the menu and couldn't decide between the lobster Newburg or the simmering Welsh rarebit on toast points. I love toast points. Makes me feel so "gourmet." I finally decided on the Welsh rarebit. MJ left to put our order in and Vi began to tell me the tale of Fritzie White, a woman who had dined on simmering beef with potato dumplings and vegetables at Schrafft's every Tuesday night since 1934. Her cocktail of choice was an old-fashioned.

CHAPTER 4

FRITZIE — 1890-1937

Eleanora "Fritzie" White, nee Buckley, came from even more money than Vi. She was born in her family's 15,000 square foot waterfront summer "cottage" in Newport, Rhode Island on August 4, 1890. Her mother, Annabelle Davis-Buckley (Belle for short) was a North Carolina tobacco heiress, attended to by Dr. Owen Hopkins, the family physician, two midwives and a bevy of servants. Her father, Edward Buckley, a railroad tycoon, was in Europe on business at the time.

By the time Eleanora was eight and sent off to join her older sister Lillian at a boarding school in Switzerland, she was known only as Fritzie Buckley. Years later she would explain that she was so nicknamed because everything she touched as a child went "on the fritz."

She was seventeen the summer she left boarding school for good. She returned to the bosom of her family, moved into their Fifth Avenue mansion and prepared for the debutante season and her debut in the Grand Ballroom in the Hotel Astor. Though Fritzie wasn't the most beautiful girl making her entrance into society that year, she was considered the "catch of the season." She was cute in a girl next door way with dirty blonde hair and gray eyes and had a warm and outgoing personality. Her choice of future husbands in their circle was limitless, but she was nothing like her sister, who at nineteen was in the midst of planning her wedding to Blake Barrett, a banking heir. How WASP is that? Fritzie thought to herself. But she liked Blake, he wasn't stiff or stuffy or full of himself, and she intended to have a jolly time at the wedding even in her poofy, pink maid-of-honor gown. (Lillian argued, "It's rose, Fritz. Rose!") Fritzie, however, wasn't quite ready to take her place in her parents' world. She wanted to go to Smith College, so off she went to Massachusetts.

In February, 1909 her parents brought Fritzie home to attend one of New York's events of the season, a formal, black-tie banquet hosted by the Peace Society honoring recent senator-elect from New York, Elihu Root, a former Secretary of War under Presidents William McKinley and Theodore Roosevelt and Secretary of State under Roosevelt. The event was at the Hotel Astor, the same hotel where Fritzie had had her coming out. Even President Taft managed to bring his nearly three-hundred-pound self to the festivities.

Her mother, wanting the new senator-elect and the President to know that their daughter had debuted, insisted that Fritzie wear her white coming out ball gown. Feeling a bit overwhelmed by all the dignitaries in tuxedos and their wives covered in more jewels than in all of Tiffany's, she meandered around the room trying to avoid the clouds of cigar smoke. She didn't see anyone her age, not even someone she might have nodded to once at some gathering or ball. In fact, there was barely anyone in the room younger than forty. After a while she found her seat at her assigned table where her mother soon found her sitting by herself. Belle dragged her out of her chair and across the ballroom floor, telling her there was someone important she wanted her to meet. As far as Fritzie was concerned, everyone in the room seemed important except the waiters. The next thing she knew she was standing in front of the President who was in conversation with her father. They stopped talking when Belle and Fritzie joined them.

"President Taft, I would like to introduce my daughter, Eleanora," Belle said in her sweet magnolia accent. "She came all the way down from Smith College just to meet you."

Fritzie gave her mother a look.

The President noticed it and smiled. "Stodgy, isn't it?" he said to her as he waved his arm indicating the people in the room.

"No, sir," Fritzie replied and curtsied, not having a clue how to talk or act in the situation she now found herself in.

"You don't have to curtsy, Eleanora." He laughed. "Save the curtsy for King Edward, he likes stuff like that."

Fritzie felt her face turn beet red. "Yes, sir."

The President resumed his conversation with her father, as she stood there wondering how one escapes the President of the United States without insulting him. At that very moment, she wanted to slap her mother silly.

Finally, dinner was announced and the President excused himself to find his table. Edward took his daughter's arm and escorted her back to her chair.

Her parents were seated on the other side of an enormous round table. On either side of her were men in their fifties who were in a heated political discussion about the new senator-elect with another gentleman sitting across from her next to her father. Edward winked at her and she smiled as he vigorously joined the political debate. Her mother was deeply engrossed in conversation with a heavyset woman wearing a diamond tiara, so Fritzie found herself staring at the white linen table cloth trying to name all the species of flowers in the over-sized, floral centerpiece. The gentlemen to her left broke her concentration when he asked her a question.

"I'm sorry," Fritzie answered politely. "I didn't hear your question."

"Just wondering how you're enjoying the evening," he said.

"Well, it's certainly more impressive than my debutante ball."

"Ah," he said.

"It was held here, too," she explained.

"Ah," he said again.

That was the extent of her dinner conversation for the entire evening. The next morning, she was on a train back to Smith.

In her senior year, it became clear that Fritzie's ambition to be a businesswoman was not realistic—women need not apply— so when she graduated and left Smith with her "MRS" degree, she threw herself into charitable work, most of which was spent fund-raising for New York hospitals.

Though popular, Fritzie discouraged serious suitors. She wasn't interested in giving up her freedom, such as it was. Then, in 1914, at the ripe old age of twenty-four, Fritzie met Benjamin White. A year younger than she, Ben was a handsome, outgoing young man with dark brown hair and mischievous green eyes. From a middle-class, New Jersey family, he had recently graduated from Princeton where he attended on scholarship. For the past year, he had worked for a Wall Street brokerage house and, by everyone's account, was reliable, hardworking and had a future in trading. Fritzie's parents, however, did not think he was right for their strong-willed, vivacious daughter. But, Ben was charming, funny and loved to take her dancing.

Europe had been at war for a year and Fritzie had become preoccupied with chairing her first big fundraiser for New York Hospital. She decided on a masked ball. The attire: black or white or both. She had chosen a white couture gown awash with white pearls that clung to her slender figure. Her pearl encrusted cat mask was made to match her gown. On the morning of the fundraiser, her hairdresser arrived at her house to weave strands of pearls into her long, "dirty" blonde hair. She had worked tirelessly for weeks on the event and on the evening of the fundraiser she just wanted to crawl into bed, pearls in her hair and all. She was exhausted and very nervous and the thought of putting on that slinky, heavy dress was the last thing she wanted to do. Begrudgingly, she knew she had to "stiff upper lip" it and was ready when Ben arrived to pick her up. The sight of him looking so dashing in white tie and tails with a black fabric mask that only showed his twinkling green eyes, filled her with renewed energy. She grabbed her white ermine stole and followed him to a waiting cab.

Guests were already arriving when they entered the ballroom and Fritzie immediately left Ben to fend for himself as she scurried about, checking on the caterers and the musicians. By the time she returned, the ball was in full sway. The sixteen-piece orchestra members, all dressed in white tie, were playing at the far side of the ballroom floor. Guests were dancing, ordering cocktails at the bar against a far wall, while others mingled or found their assigned seats. The tables were covered with black linen cloths and each had a centerpiece made up of white roses and white tapered, lighted candles in silver candlesticks. The napkins matched the table cloth and the white and gold china contrasted beautifully with the black linen.

Ben, who had been talking to a few men sipping champagne and smoking cigars, saw Fritzie walking toward him and his eyes lit up. He put his champagne glass on a nearby table, bowed, then held out his arms as he asked her to dance. She curtsied and moved into his arms. The men watched as they waltzed away then returned to their conversation.

"So what's for dinner?" Ben asked.

"Sole in a cream sauce and string beans with sliced almonds or filet mignon and asparagus with a hollandaise sauce. Both come with little roasted potatoes."

"What, no salad?"

She laughed. "Well, there were green leaves on little plates."

When the music stopped, Ben led her to an outside terrace. Fritzie shivered. "Ben, it's cold out here."

"Gives me an excuse to hold you in my arms," he said, then gave her a wink.

"You can hold me in your arms on the dance floor inside where it's warm."

Ben took off his jacket and put it around Fritzie's shoulders, then kissed her passionately, taking her aback.

"We won't be out here long," he said huskily as he got down on one knee and took out a small jewel box and opened it.

She looked at Ben, then at the lovely two-karat, emerald cut diamond ring set in yellow gold, and before he uttered a word, she said yes.

"You're not even going to let me formally ask, are you?" he smiled.

"Not when I know the question and my answer."

Ben seductively pulled off her long white glove and placed the ring on her finger.

"Then the deal is done. We can go in now before we catch pneumonia."

She laughed as he stood up and took her in his arms and kissed her again. "Sealed with a kiss," he said as he led her back inside.

It didn't surprise anyone except her family that they were engaged. At first Fritzie's parents objected because of Ben's family background. They were convinced he was after their daughter's inheritance. She could do so much better, they told her. But eventually Ben won them over and they accepted him with grace, if not warmth, after he readily signed a pre-nuptial agreement. The Whites' lawyers merely copied ancient Egyptian contracts which guaranteed a woman a modest income if her husband died or left her, but reversed the genders. As a wedding present, her parents gave the newlyweds a beautiful townhouse on Beekman Place, mortgage free.

Life was idyllic for Fritzie. She loved her home and was even learning how to cook. The nights their cook was off, she was proud that she could prepare a meal and the two of them could have an intimate dinner together by candlelight. They danced and laughed and made love with abandon, christening every room in their townhouse, even the kitchen. But as the weeks passed, Ben was becoming increasingly concerned with what was happening in Europe. The war was affecting the market, but as he read about the battles and what America's allies were going through his frustration grew. He knew it was only a matter of time before the country would be in the trenches, so he quit his job on Wall Street and enlisted. Fritzie was devastated, but understood that he felt it was his duty to serve. Because of his education and the fact that he had married into the White family, Ben was sent to officers' training school and, by the time America entered the war in April, 1917, he was a lieutenant in the army. Three months later, Fritzie was at a pier on the west side waving goodbye as his ship set sail for Europe.

At Belle's request, Fritzie eagerly joined her mother's women's charitable foundation using her fundraising expertise to raise more money for New York hospitals. She organized teas and luncheons and helped her mother on other fundraisers, trying not to worry about Ben, who initially wrote her every couple of days. But, his letters were now becoming less frequent.

At first Ben's letters were filled with news about his men, who they were, where they came from, those he befriended and those he took under his wing. He seemed to become very fond of Sal, a private under his command who grew up in a New Jersey neighborhood not far from Ben's. He described Sal as a skinny, awkward, seventeen-year-old Italian kid who made Ben laugh and she loved reading the funny little incidents and anecdotes Ben wrote about him. She chuckled when she remembered how he had described, in amusing detail, the time this city kid almost got bitten in the butt by a snake when he dropped his trousers to his ankles and was about to squat in the woods. But as weeks passed, Ben stopped writing about Sal and his letters became shorter and shorter, only serving to let her know he was still alive and unhurt. Reading between the lines she realized that Sal had been killed or wounded and that Ben was protecting her from his pain.

The longer Ben was away and the fewer letters she received, the more anxious Fritzie became. She tried discussing her feelings and fears with her mother, but Belle was of little comfort. Belle believed strongly in doing her duty, but avoided talking about anything unpleasant. Many of her old girlfriends were living with the same fear and they, at times, met for lunch to air their feelings, but it was Fritzie's sister Lillian, whom she sought out the most. Lillian's husband, Blake, was a Naval intelligence officer stationed in D.C. and though she'd go to Washington for long weekends once a month, she didn't want to uproot their year-old daughter and move there. So Fritzie spent most evenings when not working at Lillian's home playing with her niece, Bunny, and crying on her sister's shoulder. Lillian was warm and comforting, but she was also a strong woman who faced her fears head on and helped Fritzie do the same.

Lillian sat on the sofa holding Bunny, asleep in her arms, and asked her sister what her greatest fear was.

"That Ben won't come home," Fritzie answered.

"And if he doesn't?"

"I'll just die."

"You are *not* going to die, Eleanora," Lillian stated firmly, but quietly, not to awaken Bunny. "You'll be in pain. You'll grieve. Then you will move on. You know this."

Fritzie said nothing.

"You're my sister," Lillian continued, "I know you will find a way to survive and rebuild your life and I will be there to help you."

Fritzie, who had been sitting in an easy chair adjacent to the sofa, got up and put her arms around Lillian, bumping into Bunny and startling her awake. She began to cry. Fritzie took her niece out of her sister's arms and walked around the living room humming a lullaby till Bunny fell back to sleep. She sat down on an easy chair opposite Lillian.

"What if he comes home blind or paralyzed?" she asked.

"You tell me," Lillian said. "What if he does? What will you do?"

"I'll be heartbroken for him."

"I didn't ask how you'd feel, I'd be heartbroken for him, too. I asked what you would *do*."

Fritzie sat for over a minute, not knowing how to answer her sister.

"I'd love him and take care of him the best I knew how."

"You would do that? You would stay with him no matter what?"

"Of course, I would," Fritzie snapped. "As long as he comes home, I don't care *how* he comes home."

"Then you don't need to be anxious anymore, do you? You know what you'll do when the time comes, no matter how bad."

When the war ended and Ben came home, Fritzie was filled with joy. She was waiting at the dock when his ship landed and as soon as she found him in the crowd of GIs leaving the ship, she ran into his arms laughing and crying at the same time. He held her tentatively. She stepped back and looked at him. The mischief and twinkle in his eyes were gone, replaced with something she'd never seen before…anguish. He had lost a lot of weight and appeared frail.

As they settled into a new routine, she tried reaching him but it was like living with a ghost. His spirit was broken. No more dancing. No more funny stories. No more working on Wall Street. And, no more love making. He tried to be interested in whatever she was doing, but Fritzie could see that the effort was giving him even more emotional pain. She talked to him about things that used to interest him, but to no avail. She knew he still loved her. She could still see that in his eyes when he looked at her, and he knew she loved him. They both wanted what they had had, but slowly they realized that that carefree, romantic, happy time in their lives would never be recovered.

She continued to lean on Lillian for advice and for someone to unload on emotionally. Both Ben and Fritzie were trying to protect each other from their pain. Lillian encouraged her to be open with Ben about her own feelings and, perhaps, he'd then be able to open up to her.

"He won't make love to me, Lilly," she whispered. "My body just aches so much sometimes, I think I'm going to jump out of my skin. I want to feel that pleasure again."

"I know it's easy for me to say, but you can't pressure him. So much of a man's pride is wrapped up in his lovemaking. In the meantime, you might try pleasuring yourself."

"What?" Fritzie asked, startled at what her sister had just said.

"Don't look at me like that," Lillian said. "Don't tell me you never pleasured yourself?"

"Well…"

"Never mind," Lillian interrupted, "I really don't want to know. But if you haven't before, do so now, it will relieve a lot of body ache and tension."

Over the next few days, Fritzie tried to be honest with Ben about how she felt and what they were going through together but didn't have the temerity to mention their lack of sex. In a strange way, that seemed to comfort him and relieve some of the tension between them. They stopped walking on eggs around each other. After six months, his nightmares stopped, but he was still haunted and suffering from shell-shock. Fritzie was heartbroken and didn't know what to do to help him. He explained to her that his pain was something he had to work through on his own, and as much as she argued that he didn't have to do anything on his own, he never changed his mind and often locked himself away in his office for hours. He would then join her for dinner, trying his best to show interest in her day. When she asked what he was working on in his office, he would say he was just reading, but further questions as to what he was reading or if he enjoyed what he was reading, led to answers like "nothing in particular." At night, in bed, he'd hold her close, tell her how much he loved her and apologize over and over again before falling into a restless sleep. It pained him that he could no longer be intimate with Fritzie and knew that every night they lay together without making love her heart was breaking even more. Though she protested vehemently, he eventually turned a guest room across the hall into his bedroom.

One afternoon when Ben was out for a rare walk, Fritzie decided to snoop in his office to see if she could find what occupied his time hours on end, day in and day out. Piled on the floor by a club chair were dozens of legal pads filled with pencil drawings that Ben had obviously done. Many were of horrific battle scenes, but the pads on his desk appeared to be newer and had loving drawings of her and of the New York skyline. The skyline views he saw out his office window. Believing that these expressive drawings were the reason his nightmares had dissipated, Fritzie went to an art store and bought sketch pads, charcoal and pastels, watercolor and oil paints, brushes, canvases, and an easel and turned their top floor ballroom into an art studio. With ceiling to floor casement windows the views of the skyline, the East River, Blackwell's Island Bridge, and Long Island City were breathtaking. The light in the ballroom studio flooded the room and she thought how much more cheerful it would be for Ben's spirit than the dark, paneled office. When the studio was complete she prepared his favorite supper of meatloaf and mashed potatoes and waited for him to join her for dinner. She lit the candles (from the beginning of their marriage they'd always eaten by candlelight and she felt that continuing to do so showed her love and belief in their marriage), poured each of them a glass of red wine and sat down, catty-corner from his place at the head of the table.

He asked her how her day was.

"Busy. If you're up to it, I would like to show you what I've been working on this past week."

"Are you planning a new event for the hospital?" he asked politely.

"No, darling, I'm not."

"Then, I'm curious to see what's been keeping you so busy," he smiled, took her hand and kissed it.

After dinner, Fritzie led him up to the ballroom. Her heart was beating rapidly as she had no idea how Ben would react. Would he be angry that she invaded his privacy and found his drawings, would it bring him some joy, or would he not care one way or the other? She silently prayed that she had done the right thing and that in art her husband could express the feelings he couldn't share with her. That he could find some peace.

When they walked into the ballroom and Ben saw what Fritzie had done, he turned and faced her, his eyes filled with rage. She had never seen him angry, and seeing him look at her with such hate made her run out of the studio and out of the house. As soon as she was gone, Ben sat down on a stool in front of an easel and wept.

The streets were filled with happy couples coming and going to dinner as she wandered up and down city blocks crying, tears hampering her vision. She blamed herself for thinking she could give Ben some joy and now she destroyed the tenuous relationship they had built since his return. She berated herself for being so stupid, but as she calmed down, she got angry. She loved him and needed him. Why wouldn't she try any means she could to reach him? As she kept walking, fewer and fewer people were on the streets. She had no idea what she would do next, but she was determined to reach Ben or die trying.

It was after midnight when Fritzie returned home, cold and resolute. They would fight it out and get past it no matter how long it took. She ran up to his room ready to face him, but he wasn't there. She went back downstairs, but he wasn't in his office or anywhere else in the house. "If you think you can leave me, Benjamin White, you have another think coming," she said to the empty house.

She decided to check the studio, just in case he was still up there, and found him huddled in the dark on the floor, his face lit by the moonlight coming through the window. She knelt down beside him and put her arms around him.

"I'm so sorry. I didn't mean to cause you pain. Please forgive me, but…"

"No, I'm the one who's sorry," he interrupted. "I'm sorry I can't be the husband you need. That I'm no longer the man you married. I'll move out tomorrow. I'll…"

"Stop it," she cut him off. "You are not going anywhere. You're still the man I love, God help you," she said sharply. "When you hold me, my world is complete. No matter what, that will never change."

At first, Ben was startled by the tone of her voice, then let out a laugh. "You're not going to give up, are you?"

"Nope."

He looked around his new studio, overcome with all she had done for him…her stubbornness, her love. He smiled. "So you think I could be an artist, huh?"

"I think you could be a brilliant artist."

Giddy with relief, she took his face into her hands and kissed him passionately, which ignited a physical longing she could no longer control.

"I need you so much," she whispered in his ear while she reached down to undo his belt buckle.

He returned her kiss as he gently pushed her hand away, then gently eased her down on her back onto the floor. He slowly undressed her. He played with her breasts, teasing her nipples with his tongue as his hand caressed her thigh. He kissed her neck as he slid two fingers deep inside her. She arched her back and groaned with pleasure as he moved them up and down, then teased her by removing them.

"Don't stop," she moaned.

Ben slid his fingers back inside her and her breathing became faster and faster as he brought her to climax. Her body shuddered and she began to cry with joy.

Ben loved his studio. It made him feel alive again and when he wasn't painting, he sat by the window and watched the boats on the East River. Many of his paintings were of that view.

Ben still slept in his own room, but a few nights a week Fritzie would crawl into his bed. They would kiss and he'd arouse her and play with her body till she was physically satisfied, then they would fall asleep in each other's arms. Though Fritzie longed for children, she realized that might never happen and was content that they had found a way to be sexually intimate again.

The pain in Ben's eyes gradually disappeared and, at times, a glimmer of a twinkle seeped in. He started painting portraits of Fritzie. She'd sit for him, often posing in the nude and they'd talk and laugh. They never talked about the war or the horrors he experienced. He actively supported her charity work and was by her side at all the galas and events. They danced. He learned to cook and created elaborate and delicious French dinners for her and their friends. They had found peace and a new kind of happiness.

Fritzie felt she had finally found her happy ending. Ben was her soulmate and best friend, and she was his. She was his champion. She admired his art and hung many of his paintings around the townhouse. Friends began to notice and admire them as well. When they did, Ben would just take the painting off the wall and give it away. Eventually, a friend who owned a prominent art gallery invited him to do a show in his mid-town gallery. Its success caused a stir in the New York art world, and Benjamin White became a painter in demand.

Years passed, then a week before the stock market crashed, Ben was walking home from the gallery and stopped at his bank to make a deposit of monies he made from a recent exhibit when two masked men entered the bank waving their guns at everyone. One robber about ten feet behind Ben was pointing his gun at a very frightened young teller. Flashes of war time battle triggered a response in Ben and he rushed the robber, who panicked and fired. The bullet hit him in the throat. The robbers fled the bank, but by the time a medic arrived, Ben was dead.

Headlines in the newspapers called Ben a hero, but soon the story was replaced with the run on the banks and the collapse of Wall Street. The robbers were never found.

Edward and Belle were hit hard financially but they managed to sell their Manhattan mansion and moved to their summer house in Quogue, New York. Fritzie saw how badly her parents were hurting, but was dealing with her own grief and felt they would be fine because they still had the house on Long Island and enough money to take care of themselves. They would survive. Fritzie, however, had no idea how she was going to survive without Ben, but was relieved she didn't have to sell their townhouse. The thought of moving out of the home where they had struggled and loved would have been too much to bear. But, thanks to her parents all those years ago, she was mortgage free and was able to maintain their home on the monies made from Ben's paintings. Rather than sell her stocks for rock bottom prices, she put the certificates in the safe in her bedroom hoping to weather the storm and rebuild her finances once the world markets settled down. But she saw many of her friends' families lose everything, some having to abandon their beautiful homes and apartments in Manhattan because they could no longer afford them. Few buyers were left. They had fled the city. Lillian and her family had been living in Washington D.C. since the war ended and were doing fine since Blake had decided to make a career out of Naval intelligence. So, with her friends and family gone from the city, Fritzie was totally alone for the first time as she approached her forty-second birthday. Her parents were getting on in years so she made sure she spent one weekend a month with them in Quogue, but on Tuesday night while Prohibition was still law, she would make a double old-fashioned, pour it into a flask, put on her white gloves and go to Schrafft's, where a lone woman could surreptitiously sip her drink with her favorite dinner of simmering beef.

It was during one of those lonely Tuesday night dinners in 1937, forty-seven year old Fritzie, who had more or less recovered financially, met a sophisticated and charming man in his late forties, early fifties with warm brown eyes and salt and pepper hair that formed a widow's peak at the top of his forehead. His name was Ransom Fiske. He wined her and dined her. Paid attention to her. Listened to her. Made love to her. Asked her to marry him, but before they tied the knot, stole a good deal of her money and disappeared.

CHAPTER 5

ASHLEY — 1968

It was nine o'clock when our dinner was over. I had filled my reporter's notebook and Vi was ready to leave, but now I had even more questions…specifically, who was Ransom Fiske? It had to be more than a coincidence that he did the same thing to Fritzie that George Roman had done to Vi. I asked her if I could interview Fritzie, but she told me that Fritzie had passed away in 1959. I wanted to know more, but Vi was done for the evening.

I walked her outside and helped her into a cab, but not before I made her promise to call me and set up our next meeting. Now that she had begun, I had to know the whole story.

As the cab drove away, I went back into the restaurant to see if I could get some answers from MJ. What I had so far was something I could only label as a weird coincidence and, if Fritzie really was dead, who are the other Schrafft ladies Vi made me promise not to expose until after they were all dead? I ordered a B&B and went over my notes while I waited for MJ to finish her shift. Two wealthy women who ended up dining alone one night a week at this very Schrafft's. Two wealthy women who met a man with a similar descriptions who courted them, made love to them, proposed to them, and then stole their money.

What were the odds?

Now in street clothes, MJ carried a pony of crème de menthe to my table and sat in Vi's seat.

"Ya know, every once in a while I just love treating myself on Schrafft's dime," she smiled. "My reward for being on my feet all day."

"To rewards," I said. We clicked our pony glasses.

I showed her my notes and briefly told her about Fritzie. MJ listened closely as she sipped her liqueur. My mind racing, I ordered another B&B. If this kept up, I'd be in A.A. before I was able to get Vi's whole story.

I pumped MJ for more information. Who else was in Vi's story? Who were these men who bilked them of their money? Did she know the whole story?

She nodded. "It's not my story to tell, Ashley, it's up to Vi."

I could tell by the firmness in her voice that she wasn't going to be persuaded, but I was in hyper-mode and didn't want the evening to end, so I decided to find out who MJ was.

Freckled and red-haired, sixteen year old Mary Jane O'Brien, nee Slattery, landed in Manhattan in the steaming summer of 1927 and soon was working as a waitress at Schrafft's. And though she lived in a four-room, fourth floor walk-up with her Aunt Mary and Uncle Mickey who sponsored her immigration to America, along with their two daughters, she was thrilled to be in New York. She was pretty and outgoing and had a healthy share of "stage door Johnnies" who waited outside Schrafft's to take her dancing or to a show after her shift. She was escorted to some of the best restaurants and speakeasies in New York.

She was nineteen when she met twenty-two year old Ian O'Brien at a dance at Sacred Heart, the neighborhood church. He had black hair and green eyes and was quite handsome in his NYC policeman's uniform. Ian loved his outlawed beer and dancing, in that order, and their courtship was fun and carefree. She was enchanted by his Irish charm and good looks. His parents approved of MJ and encouraged the match. MJ stopped going out with other men, but after about five months of dating, Ian started pressuring her to sleep with him, but she was a good Catholic girl and told him no. She was going to stay a virgin till she married no matter how often he professed his love and desire for her. One night, frustrated after much kissing and petting, Ian proposed. MJ was thrilled and a month later they said their vows at Sacred Heart. The reception was held in the church's basement and about a hundred friends from the parish, from Ian's precinct and from Schrafft's attended. Her aunt made a slew of Irish meats and casseroles, as did many of the parishioners, her uncle provided the bootleg whiskey and her new mother-in-law made soda bread and the wedding cake.

They ate, they danced and they got drunk, then Ian took MJ's hand as they snuck out of the reception and went two blocks to their new one-room apartment. She was excited and frightened at the same time and had fantasized about her wedding night, but when she woke up the next morning she was sore, no longer a virgin and depressed. Though she had nothing to compare her experience to, she knew that love making had to be more than her being a vessel for Ian to relieve himself over and over again. She realized pretty soon after the wedding that she had made a terrible mistake. Ian was neither caring nor tender. He wasn't mean or disrespectful, but her feelings were really of no concern to him. He was the food and shelter provider and she was there to service all his needs. That's how he saw marriage. She didn't even have the joy of going to work and being with her Schrafft's friends since Ian insisted on her quitting her job.

"I'm not having a wife who works!" he bellowed, after the first time she broached the subject. When she brought it up again, she tried to explain how much she enjoyed working and meeting new people, but he would have none of it. "I'm not telling the world I can't provide for my wife. Don't ever bring it up again!"

And MJ never did. Her whole life was about taking care of Ian. She cooked his meals, cleaned their apartment, washed and ironed his clothes. He even taught her how to clean his gun. At six o'clock Ian would come home, strip off his uniform shirt, have a couple of his bootleg beers, and eat the dinner MJ prepared. He never asked her about her day. It didn't interest him. He'd just talk about his day and gossiped or complained about his fellow cops. When dinner was over, on most nights, he'd finish undressing and take her to bed. After exhausting himself, he'd fall asleep. MJ would then get out of bed, put away any leftovers and do the dishes. When Ian was at work, she spent what little time was left after finishing all her chores with her Aunt Mary and Uncle Mickey. They knew she was unhappy even though she never complained. Mary tried to explain to her niece that this was the life women were born to, but MJ saw how close and loving she and her uncle had been and wanted that kind of marriage. They were tender with each other, often holding hands even after years of being together.

Then, six months into their marriage MJ broke her leg in two places after falling down the stairs of her tenement building. She could no longer cook for him or do his laundry. He was angry that sex had become cumbersome for him because of her cast. He did try to be careful when he learned that it was painful for her because of her broken leg, but his pleasure was his main objective so they still had sex almost every night. As the days passed, Ian became resentful having to tend to his wife, help her to the hall bathroom shared by the tenants on their floor, bring her food and tidy the apartment. He tried to persuade his mother to come and take care of him and MJ, but she was too busy caring for her own husband and Ian's three siblings.

Within two weeks Ian packed his bag and left MJ stranded without help or the ability to go the grocer for food. She often couldn't even get to the bathroom and used a chamber pot she was unable to clean. After two days, MJ was ravenous and filthy.

When Uncle Mickey showed up he was heartbroken to see her so helpless. He had heard from a neighbor that Ian had abandoned his niece and came over to see if that was true. The apartment smelled from the uncleaned chamber pot and MJ's face was tear stained, her eyes vacant. She was in pain and appeared to be in shock. He picked her up, grabbed her crutches and practically carried her back to his family's apartment three blocks away so that Mary and the girls could bathe and feed her and help her recuperate. After the cast came off, she underwent serious physical therapy and prayed that when it was over, Schrafft's would take her back. As a nice Catholic girl, divorce wasn't an option. But eventually, because she was rehired at Schrafft's, MJ was able to move out of her aunt's and uncle's apartment and into a one room studio with a bathtub. The shared toilet was out in the hall just a few feet away from her front door. She vowed to herself that she would never depend on a man again.

Reunited with her friends and some of her regular customers, she loved being back at work in Schrafft's. It had a nice, middle-class clientele, who tipped well and her meals were free. She met many successful and interesting men at the restaurant and her social life became very full. When Ian learned she was well and working again, he showed up at Schrafft's and demanded, as his wife, she move back with him. She refused. She was never going to go back with him.

Ian was furious and went to Mickey to make the same demand, but her uncle would have none of it. They fought, but eventually Ian let it go. He really hadn't like being married and paying for another person, he just liked the easy sex. He had moved back with his parents, so his mother was again doing all the other things for him that MJ had. He didn't need a wife. Soon he was out dancing and drinking in speakeasies, and sleeping with as many women as he could.

"Whatever happened to him?" I asked.

"What's the difference between ignorance and apathy?"

I looked at her, puzzled.

"I don't know and I don't care," MJ said with a big smile on her face.

After I finished my second B&B I knew it was time to go home and type up my notes before going to bed.

While I waited to hear again from Vi, Dwyre decided it was time I wrote a column of my own. He told me I had earned it because of the spin I gave my lifestyle articles…a little history mixed with a little humor.

"Letters to the editors show that you make fluff interesting and fun for our readers," he said.

I didn't quite know if I should take the "fluff" part as a compliment, but decided to follow my mother's advice, something I rarely did, and not bite off my nose to spite my face. It was my own column, such as it was, since it was only to be once a month in the back of the Sunday magazine section, but it was going to be all mine. It could be about anything lifestyle-y… well, he didn't say "lifestyle-y," but he might as well have. It was a start. I would try to make it something that was different and more than "lifestyle-y."

My first column was due in two weeks and it was a challenge. How would I write a relevant piece about "lifestyle" just months after the assassinations of Martin Luther King, Jr. and Bobby Kennedy? I decided to take a wry, tongue-in-cheek approach which would set a tone that wouldn't butt heads with serious world events. Columns which would talk about lifestyles in a "this isn't serious, folks" winking manner. For my first piece, I settled on a story about P.J. Clarke's, the old tavern on 55th and Third. I checked in with Dwyre and he signed off on the story.

It was getting late and I hadn't heard from Vi, so I thought it was a good time to start my Clarke's research. I called my girlfriend, Kate Rockwell, a junior exec at Revlon and part-time runway model, to see if she wanted to meet me there for dinner. Might as well have the paper pay for a burger or steak Diane while I do my research.

P.J. Clarke's, Clarke's or PJ's, no matter what you called it, was one of my favorite restaurants/saloons in town. I first heard about the place when Kate and I went to see the 1945 classic black and white movie *The Lost Weekend* at a revival movie house in the Village. After the movie, we went to get a bite to eat to talk about it. We were both blown away by Ray Milland's heartbreaking performance and couldn't *stop* talking about it. Over BLTs, Kate told me that the bar they used in the movie was Clarke's. Legend had it that Johnny Mercer wrote the song "One for My Baby" for the movie on a napkin while sitting at the bar. I thought that was cool and now that I lived just a few blocks east of Clarke's, I made it my neighborhood hangout.

The famous, the un-famous, and probably the infamous rubbed elbows every night at Clarke's. I, of course, was one of the un-famous, but being in the restaurant or having a drink at the bar, I liked to pretend I was part of the "in" crowd, especially the writer "in" crowd that frequented the place. I imagined what it would be like to sit and talk shop. To be asked how my new book was coming. And, unlike many bars and taverns in New York, it didn't refuse to serve women who came to drink or eat *sans* (I love that word) a man. I felt comfortable in Clarke's. I didn't have to worry about being mistaken for a call girl (a story for another time) or be hit on the way I often was in singles bars like Maxwell's Plum and Fridays. Besides, Clarke's made the best burgers and sweet potato fries.

One night while sitting alone at the bar waiting for a friend, I asked the bartender why Clarke's willingly catered to women.

He laughed. "Why not? Your money's as green as mine, right?" I laughed. "Right."

I walked past the mahogany bar in the front of the tavern and got a table in the back room with its red and white checkerboard table cloths, brick and dark wood paneled walls, black & white photos (many of which were of baseball players and boxers) and chalk board menus. Schrafft's it wasn't.

Clarke's had been operating in its brick building since 1884. Over the bar were human bones…an Irish talisman for luck. According to one of the bartenders, they'd been there forever, but no one had a clue whose bones they were. Whether true or not, it added to Clarke's legend.

The Lavezzo family owned Clarke's and ran an antique and furniture restoring business on the second floor. When a developer last year planned to tear the old brick tavern down and build a skyscraper, the Lavezzos said "nope, no way." Instead, the parties quietly (at least as far as most New Yorkers knew) negotiated a deal where the developer would build around Clarke's, securing the old building (and Clarke's) and the air above it indefinitely. David had beaten Goliath.

Kate, all five feet ten inches of her, rushed in a little past eight.

"Am so glad you called," she said breathlessly as she took off the tan trench coat she had bought in Paris last year and threw it over the back of her chair. She put her Vuitton shoulder bag on the floor by her feet. Kate had hair most women would kill for. Thick, bone straight, and a rich toffee brown she wore in a shoulder-length version of Sassoon's "Nancy Kwan" geometric, longer-in-the-front cut. Parted on the side and always falling over one eye, it was sexy as hell. I coveted the cut, but with my unruly curls, that style would not be wash and wear as advertised. I'd have to spend an hour every day under my portable dryer straightening it with Dippity Do to keep the humidity from turning it into an afro.

"What are we drinking?" she asked as she ran her fingers through her hair trying to get it out of her left eye, a futile effort as it always fell dramatically back into place.

I went with a scotch sour on the rocks (some vitamin C can't hurt) and so did Kate.

"You're not going to believe this, but I was offered a runway gig for Mary Quant's spring collection in London and Revlon wants me to go even though I'll have to wear Quant cosmetics."

"Of course I believe it. They'll figure out a way to promote this for Revlon," I said, laughing. "You know, girl, you could be a superstar like Twiggy if you wanted to, right?"

"No way. But even if I could, it's only fun once in a while. I couldn't do it all the time. I like working in advertising and marketing."

"Well, I'll never be able to say 'I knew you when' if you refuse to become rich and famous."

Kate laughed. "Let's order, I'm starved."

So was I and I knew what I wanted. I loved Clarke's pan-fried steak Diane with its mix of sautéed onion, mustard, lemon juice, Worcestershire sauce and butter that just melts in your mouth. That seemed the perfect comfort food dinner for a cold, November night. I had no idea who Diane was, but I loved her steak. Kate ordered a rare cheeseburger, a double order of sweet potato fries and a side of sautéed spinach. I had no idea how she stayed a size four, she ate like a truck driver.

"To celebrate your new modelling adventure, dinner's on me," I told her. "Well, actually, it's on the paper. Expense accounts are my friend."

"Thanks. I should have ordered something more celebratory." She smiled.

"Get dessert. I'm doing a piece on Clarke's so dessert is research."

"Research?"

"Well, not really since I'm not going to be writing about the food. Don't want to step on any of the paper's food writers' toes. But I am going to write about the tavern—then and now—who hung out and who hangs out."

Kate laughed. "Are you going to include a mention about how this place has become a mecca for divorced, "weekend" fathers and their kids on Sunday for breakfast or lunch before they have to be returned to mom?"

I laughed. "I just might. It is a 'lifestyle.'"

Over dinner, Kate regaled me with her latest horror date.

"You won't believe the guy I went out with last night. A surgical resident at Mount Sinai," she said. "Jane, my boss' wife, fixed me up. He sounded great on paper. Anyway, when he shows up at my door, he comes into my apartment, pulls out a wallet from his sports coat breast pocket, flips it open then throws it on my coffee table.

"'I'm a narc. Have to search your apartment,'" he announced. "Needless to say I was a bit stunned and just stared at him as if he had just been released from Creedmore."

"Oh my god, what did you do?"

"Well, that's it, I certainly didn't want to go out with him, but I had no idea if he was *really* crazy or if he was only socially maladjusted. I did know I wanted him out of my apartment, so I got my coat and left with him."

"You left with him?"

"It was the only way I could get him to leave."

"Well, obviously you survived intact. Where'd you go?"

"Actually, it was cute little Italian place a few blocks from my place, but the evening only got worse. I don't think I've ever gone out with a more conceited ass in my life. He even bragged about smoking a joint before going into surgery. God, who does that?"

"Sounds delightful."

"Wait, you haven't heard the kicker. When the bill came, he couldn't pay it. He left his wallet on my coffee table. He looked at me to bail him out."

"Did you?"

"Are you kidding? No way. I told him I only had a few bucks and didn't own a credit card."

"What happened?"

"Since the owner wasn't going to let us leave without paying, I offered to go and get his wallet and bring it back to him. Humiliated, he agreed. When I came back, before he had a chance to pay up, I thanked him for an interesting evening and walked out of the restaurant. By the time I got back to my apartment my face was covered in tears I was laughing so hard. I must have burned off at least a hundred calories."

Outside the tavern, Kate took off in a cab and I walked the two blocks east to my building. It was still fairly early so I turned on the TV to catch the latest episode of *The Mod Squad*.

After the show was over, I crawled under the covers and tried to sleep, but Vi's story came rushing forward and I began obsessing about why she hadn't called me to set up a new meeting. I didn't want to get out of bed and turn the TV back on, so I grabbed Arthur Hailey's *Airport*, resting on my night table. It certainly was my night for pop culture. I had loved *Hotel* and, at one point, thought that if the reporting thing didn't work out, I'd go work as a desk clerk in a hotel like The Plaza. When I was a kid, I thought it would be so cool to be Eloise, so when I first moved to Manhattan, I would walk through the beautiful, old-world lobby and breathe in all the history emanating from that hotel as I looked for Eloise in the Palm Court. Having drinks at the Oyster Bar is still one of my favorite things to do. Though, I had to laugh, the last time I had to meet someone there, I was early and women were discouraged to sit at the bar alone, so I waited in the lobby. Sitting on a sofa, I was skimming though a newspaper left behind when a man, dressed in a nice three-piece suit sat down next to me and asked, "How much?" Startled, I hadn't a clue what he was talking about, but when it finally dawned on me that he thought I was a hooker, I just started to laugh…loudly… uncontrollably. Scared him right off. Still laughing, I hoped he was from Oklahoma or somewhere where men aren't used to seeing women alone in hotels or restaurants rather than some New York businessman who didn't know any better.

Two days later, after almost three weeks of silence, I got a call from Vi at the paper inviting me to her home for dinner. When I asked for her address on Beekman Place, she replied, "Oh, no darling, I don't live there. Fritzie did. I now live in a stable in Sniffen Court." She gave me the address.

I had no idea what Sniffen Court was other than it was on East 36th, placing it in Manhattan's Murray Hill district. I knew the area because I had done a piece on old New York gilded-age homes. Robert Murray's mansion on Park and 36th named Inclenburg was there, as well as the old J.P. Morgan mansion on 36th and Madison. I wondered if Vi's family had hobnobbed with the Murrays and Morgans back in the day. I could not imagine regal Vi living in a stable, so I asked a reporter friend who sat at the desk next to mine if he knew anything about Sniffen Court. He didn't know much, just that it was a dead end cobblestoned alleyway that consisted of a row of brick stables on each side built in the 1800's that had been converted into automobile garages sometime in the '20s. Intrigued, I decided to go to the New York Public Library at 42nd and Fifth on my lunch break and see what I could find.

I could live in that library. It's gorgeous. I always notice the details, learn the design history then feel compelled to write about them. The same with food, decor and fashion as you might have noticed. If not, you will. I am a lifestyle writer, right?

The massive beaux arts building was built in the late 1800s when Gov. Sam Tilden died and left his money to the city specifically to build a public library. It was a public space fit for royalty. I wondered again if Vi's parents knew the governor… if they were friends. As I walked up the wide front steps past the two large, cement stone lions guarding the entrance, I felt the excitement I always felt when I entered the interior and saw its dark woods, huge museum quality murals on the walls and ceilings, carved stone and marble archways, stairs, walls, floors and pillars, the converted candle chandeliers and sconces—like I said, I could live there.

I made my way to the microfilm room and started my Sniffen Court research by reading old newspaper accounts. A few papers even included some photos of the alleyway that stood behind a black wrought iron gate with small iron horse head decorations, indicating that these buildings were private stables. Built in 1863-64, the Romanesque Revival style exteriors of the ten brick stables with potted trees and bushes lining the cobblestoned alleyway were stunning. I could envision a dashing young man in tight "breeches" riding through the gate, past the gas lanterns, dismounting gracefully in front of one of buildings and handing the reins to a stable hand before heading to his nearby townhouse or mansion. At the end of the alleyway were two large plaques of Greek horsemen sculpted by artist Malvina Hoffman who had a studio in the Court during the first half of the 20th century. One article told of the Amateur Comedy Club and theater also housed in one of the former stables since 1884. Way cool, I thought. Another told of one of the building's conversion to an architect's office and home, another mentioned that others were converted into private carriage house homes. The alley that served as the communal courtyard looked as it might have been built pre-American Revolution. I loved it. I couldn't wait to see Vi's home.

I arrived at Vi's promptly at 7:30, a bouquet of white tea roses in hand. Walking into her carriage house was like walking into a design magazine. Though it was filled with lovely antiques and paintings, there was nothing stuffy or old lady-ish about it. In the living room family portraits dating back to Adam and Eve (well, not quite, but you get the picture) in carved wood frames hung on interior brick walls painted flat white. Faded floral area rugs were layered on the old, whitewashed pine floors. Her pale green velvet sofa and pink and white striped linen slipcovered easy chairs were stuffed with down and her coffee table was a thick piece of glass, thirty-six inches square, sitting atop criss-crossed chrome legs. I recognized it immediately as a table I'd seen at the Museum of Modern Art by Mies Van Der Rohe. An imposing chrome floor lamp that arched its thin pole majestically toward the sofa I knew to be a Robert Sonneman design. Old, perfectly mixed with mid-century. I was impressed and nervous. I was out of my element.

Vi put my roses in a modern, uncarved crystal vase and placed them on the coffee table next to a matching crystal bowl filled with caviar sitting in a larger silver bowl of ice. Next to the bowl was a silver platter with a row of butter pads, silver butter knives and toast points. Have I mentioned, I love toast points? I'd only had caviar once and I loved it. She poured me a glass of sherry.

"Please help yourself," she said, indicating the caviar as she buttered a toast and spooned some caviar on top. I'd only had caviar served with sour cream, chopped egg and chopped onion, so I didn't know how I'd like it with just plain butter. I mimicked Vi and buttered a toast, put caviar on top and took a bite. The salty black eggs on sweet butter was a revelation. I could eat this every day. It almost made me forget Vi and her story. Almost.

As I sipped my sherry, the doorbell rang and Vi excused herself to answer it. While she was gone, I was tempted to pick up the caviar spoon made of horn (caviar tarnishes silver I was once told) and scarf down the caviar before she came back. My better nature prevailed just as Vi came back into the room with a tall, thin, elderly woman with platinum hair pulled back into a chignon, pale hazel eyes and the posture of a dancer. She towered over petite Vi.

"Ashley, I'd like you to meet Lynne Davis, one of the ladies I mentioned. Lynne, this is Ashley Wilkes, the reporter I told you about."

We shook hands as Vi poured another glass of sherry and handed it to her friend.

Lynne started the conversation by stating that she had been reluctant to come tonight, but Vi told her that this was all off the record and that it was time for them to share their story with someone who could tell the world after they're gone.

CHAPTER 6

LYNNE DAVIS — 1889-1937

Pauline Lynne Demarist a/k/a Lynne Davis, was born on a potato farm on the North Fork of Long Island in 1891 and, with irony that did not escape her, she was chosen "Miss Long Island Potato" in 1908. The potato farm girl dubbed Miss Potato. She found that amusing. She was seventeen. At her coronation her father told her that she had achieved the highest goal a pretty girl could possibly attain and that she now must get serious and pick a husband from her many beaus before her beauty faded. Her mother and two older brothers agreed. With pale, hazel eyes and long, almost white hair framing her beautiful face, boys followed her around like sheep and she was little Bo Peep. But the thought of settling down to a drudgery existence in rural farm country horrified her. Her hands belied her face. They were rough from working the farm with her parents and brothers and helping her mother with the housework. No amount of vinegar could get them totally clean and she hated that. She owned two dresses. One for church and one for school. Pauline's education was not a priority for her parents, but their daughter was smart and insisted on finishing high school.

At school she could escape her life. She had access to books where she learned about the great world cities…Paris, Rome, London, Athens, St. Petersburg, Tokyo, but especially New York. The only book in her house was the Bible, but in school she devoured books by Jane Austin, Dumas and Tolstoy, loaned to her by Mrs. Cole, her English teacher. And, after reading *Washington Square* by Henry James she knew she had to live in Manhattan. She dreamed of a genteel life described in the novel. The clothes, the sophisticated conversations, the fine dining, horse and carriages with drivers who wore top hats. She knew she would never have that on the North Fork. But, Pauline also knew instinctively that the world wasn't a welcoming place for single women and they were not afforded the same opportunities as men. Mrs. Cole picked up on Pauline's longings for a different life and encouraged her to go to a women's college and become a teacher, but her parents could not afford that, so with Mrs. Cole's help, Pauline was offered a scholarship to Hunter College in Manhattan. Thrilled, she rushed home to tell her parents, but they flatly refused it. If their sons didn't go to college, neither would she.

"College is for men, daughter," her mother told her. "The Good Book teaches a woman's place is to care for a husband and rear his children. That is God's law!" Angry, Pauline began to formulate her escape from the farm.

She knew that if blessed with it, beauty was the one commodity a woman could use to get what she desired. And she was blessed. If her father taught her nothing, he taught her that beauty faded, so the minute she graduated high school in 1909, she set her plan into motion. She chose unwitting Silas Vanetsky as her target because his father, who owned Vanetsky's, the town's dry goods store, was the wealthiest man in town. He even had his own car. Silas' father had bought his Model T the minute it came off the assembly line, and young Silas would often chauffer him to the Huntington train station so he could easily go into the city on buying trips.

Silas was the high school heartthrob, star athlete and very vain. Girls flocked to him and he reveled in it. He often bragged to Pauline that he could bed any girl in town and was clearly challenged when his "charm," athletic prowess and good looks never had any effect on her. She was the prettiest girl in school and he wanted her, but she practically ignored him, preferring to bury her nose in a book. He saw how the boys flocked around her and he wanted to best them all and claim her as his own. She knew that if she played him right, she would have him eating out of her unsmooth hand.

Pauline began to flirt with Silas shamelessly. She would tease him, leading him on, then pull back "shyly." And, when she finally agreed to actually date him, he preened like a peacock when he showed her off as "his girl." She was a Long Island beauty queen, after all. She was pleased. She went with him to the church socials, spent Saturdays going for walks after her chores or having a picnic under a big oak tree on her parents' farm. He couldn't get enough of her and she was growing fond of him. She was surprised how much she enjoyed her own physical, sexual awakening as she let him take more and more liberties with her body. But she put her foot down and refused to "go all the way." Hormones raging, Silas fell madly in love with Pauline and it wasn't long before he proposed. Pauline had achieved what she had wanted. She was going to get away from the farm. They set a date for early fall.

After one of their long petting sessions in the tall grass on her parents property, she gently pushed his hands away and told him how she envied his trips to Huntington, part of Long Island's "Gold Coast" filled with gorgeous homes and estates... how she longed to see them, have lunch or dinner in one of the town's fine restaurants. But he barely heard her at this point. All Silas wanted to do at that moment was have sex with her.

"You know how much I love you. I don't want to wait for the fall," he told her as he tried to fondle her breasts. "Let's just find a justice of the peace. Then you can move in with me."

She sat up and firmly held his hands.

"Where would we live?"

"With my parents. The house is big and will be mine when I take over the store."

Pauline thought eloping was a great idea and was surprised she hadn't thought of it herself, the sooner the better.

"Okay, but, let's make it romantic," she said as she hugged him. "We can elope to Huntington. I'm sure we can find someone there to marry us, then spend our wedding night in a hotel."

The thought excited him.

"We can leave the car at the depot," Pauline continued, "and take a train into the city the next day for a little honeymoon. Even if it's only a day. Please."

She lay back down on the grass as he put his hand under her skirt high up on her thigh. At this point, feeling her soft skin, he'd do anything to get Pauline to sleep with him. And, since his father wanted Silas to settle down and become serious about taking over the store and had encouraged the match with Pauline, Silas knew he'd be able to borrow the car for the day. If it turned into a few days, so be it. He had never been in the city. It might be fun.

Later that afternoon in the Vanetsky kitchen, Pauline discovered a train schedule to New York. She slipped it into her purse and took it home to study. She memorized the schedule, then seductively suggested they plan their elopement for July 11th, just two days away. Silas agreed.

Pauline was excited that she would be finally moving out and away from the farm. She practically skipped home to ask her parents' permission to go to Huntington for the day. She knew they'd say yes. She was engaged to a man "with prospects" and they were relieved. They wouldn't have to be concerned about her anymore. She also knew that they were probably counting on her to help them financially after Silas took over the store.

The night before she was to go to Huntington, while they and her brothers were asleep, she snuck downstairs and found the coffee tin where her parents kept their life savings. She counted one hundred and twenty three dollars. Contingency money, she thought, but decided to take only fifty. She didn't want to leave them with nothing. When morning arrived, Pauline put on her church dress and rolled up her school dress into a tiny ball and shoved it into the oversized purse she had made from fabric remnants she had found at Vanetsky's. She didn't want her parents to see it just in case they came onto the front porch where she waited anxiously for Silas. She prayed nothing would go wrong.

It was a beautiful sunrise as Silas drove up the long dirt road to Pauline's house. She waved and smiled brightly. This was going to be a glorious day. Her new life was about to begin and she was very excited about her future. When he pulled up, Silas jumped out of the car and opened the passenger door. Pauline impetuously gave him a kiss on the cheek as she climbed in. This would be the first time she would ride in a car. The first of many firsts to come.

When they arrived in Huntington, Pauline checked her watch as they drove by the new train station to the courthouse. It wasn't even noon yet. Inside, they filled out the marriage certificate and were soon standing in an office in front of a judge. Her heart was beating so rapidly, she barely heard what he was saying and needed to be prompted to say, "I do." The judge pronounced them "man and wife," then smiled as he told Silas he could now kiss the bride. Silas hurriedly kissed his new wife, then took her hand and rushed her out of the judge's office. Now that they were married, Silas didn't want to wait a minute longer. He wanted to go directly to the hotel, but Pauline pleaded with him to show her some of Huntington's grand homes first. Not wanting to seem like a boor, he relented and gave her a tour around the town, stopping the Model T where she wanted, so she could linger in front of a house and soak up the architecture. She asked him questions about the people who lived in them, what they did for a living...anything she could think of to kill time. He filled her in on the little he knew from his father. He didn't notice that Pauline kept checking her watch.

After a while, she flirtatiously asked him to take her to the beautiful hotel they had passed. She'd smiled seductively as she told him it would be the perfect place to spend their first night. She caressed his thigh. She watched his pants as Silas became aroused and knew he was no longer thinking clearly. As he parked the car, she slowly removed her hand from his thigh. She again checked her watch. She gave Silas a passionate kiss before they left the car.

When they entered the lobby, Pauline was very nervous and barely noticed her surroundings. She took Silas' arm and looked longingly into his eyes, then in a husky whisper told him to go to the desk clerk and ask if he could check out one of the rooms to see if it was suitable for him and his wife. All Silas could think of as he showed the clerk their new marriage certificate, registered and hurriedly followed the clerk to a room on the second floor, was Pauline lying naked on a bed, her legs parted and her arms reaching out for him. But, as soon as they were out of sight, Pauline slipped out of the hotel and ran as fast as she could to the train station. She had less than five minutes until the train arrived. Her heart was beating wildly as she said over and over to herself, "Please be on time. Please be on time." If it was, she knew by the time Silas started searching the hotel for her, she'd be on her way to New York.

The train arrived promptly and she quickly got on board, never looking back. She had escaped. But, escaping successfully was all that she had planned. Pauline had no idea what abandoning Silas on their wedding day would do to his ego. Would he tell anyone they eloped and she ran off, or would he make up some lie? And, she had no idea what her running away would do to her family. She just knew at seventeen she wouldn't survive to twenty if she stayed. But, she also had no plan beyond this point. She had no idea how she would actually survive once she reached Manhattan. She knew that it could be a dangerous place, so she carefully hid her money in her undergarments, leaving a few dollars in her handmade purse to pay for the train ticket and something to eat once she arrived in New York. She didn't know where she would live, or even stay the night, but she was smart and had the long train ride to figure it out.

Nervous, she carefully looked over the people in the train car and saw an empty seat across from an expensively dressed older woman. She felt she would be a safe with her and sat down. She smiled demurely when the woman took notice of her. After some minutes, the woman introduced herself as Alice Holmes, a widow with a home in Manhattan and one in Oyster Bay. As far as Pauline was concerned, Pauline Demarist no longer existed. Before she had a second thought, she introduced herself as Lynne Davis, taking her middle name as her new first name for her new life. She had no idea where "Davis" came from, it just popped into her head and seemed to go with Lynne. Not wanting to confess that she was running away from her family, a new husband and a life she hated, the newly born Lynne spun a sad tale to explain why she was traveling alone into the city. She lowered her eyes when she told Alice that she, too, was a widow, though just recently, and had lost her farm on the North Fork to a bank foreclosure. She scraped up a few dollars and was headed to New York City to see if she could find a job. When Alice learned she had no friends or relatives in the city, she insisted that "Lynne" come and stay with her in her large home until she found employment and could settle somewhere. Pauline hesitated, but "Lynne" instinctively knew that this was an answer to her prayers. She would have someplace safe to stay until she could figure out what she would do next. It also meant that she didn't have to spend her money on room or board right away. She accepted Alice's offer.

A car and driver waited outside the Manhattan train station to take Alice and her new house guest home to her brick townhouse on W. 4th Street. Lynne was overjoyed when she learned she would be living, however briefly, only a stone's throw from Washington Square Park. The inside of the townhouse was everything she imagined it would look like, including a library filled with rows and rows of books in dark mahogany bookshelves. Her new life was already a wonderful fairy tale. Then it wasn't.

As she looked for "genteel" employment, she was turned away from one office job after another because she had no office skills or didn't even rate an interview because she was a *woman*. The shops where she sought sales clerk employment weren't hiring or weren't hiring *women* and she knew that Alice's generosity might soon end. Though their relationship had grown close in the two months she'd live with Alice, Lynne was pragmatic enough to know that eventually Alice would tire of paying for her. She went out every morning to look for work, but when home she tried to be as helpful as she could. She got along with the staff, made her own bed, cleaned her own room and assisted the cook in the kitchen. Lynne even taught her how to make rabbit stew, which they proudly served Alice one night for dinner, along with a loaf of braided bread that Lynne had made at dawn before going off to find a job.

Alice became quite fond of Lynne and one evening surprised her with two new dresses she bought for Lynne's job search. Finally, at the end of September, out of desperation, Lynne took a job at the Triangle Shirtwaist Company, a garment making factory in the Village where she worked on a sewing machine and made button holes by hand. The factory occupied the eighth, ninth and tenth floors of a building in walking distance from Alice's home.

Lynne arrived shortly before seven A.M. the time her first shift started and she discovered the elevator being loaded up with crates to be taken to the seventh floor. Not wanting to be late, she climbed up nine flights of a dimly lit stairwell to her assigned floor. Out of breath, she entered a huge, cavernous room encompassing the entire ninth floor, with rows and rows of women working on sewing machines and a few men standing over machines in the back pressing on what appeared to be fabric. Even though the room had a wall of windows, it was badly ventilated with only a few panes cranked open to let in a bit of fresh air. The stale air, smelling of years of sweat, was overwhelming and the noise from the machines was deafening. Lynne had no idea if she would be able to stand working there without going insane. Her male supervisor led her to an empty chair in front of a sewing machine in the middle row in the middle of the room. She was surrounded by women peddling away on their machines like robots.

The young woman working next to her introduced herself and gave Lynne an extra pair of earplugs.

"I'm Vera Zahler. You're gonna need those or go deaf."

"Thanks. I'm Lynne Davis."

Lynne was about to say "nice to meet you," but Vera had turned her attention back to her sewing machine.

They worked in silence but for the constant roar of the sewing machines. At ten thirty, a loud horn went off in the room. Vera immediately stopped her machine and jumped up out of her seat.

"Break time. Follow me, Lynne Davis."

Lynne followed her to a locked door and watched as Vera took a nail file from her apron pocket and used it as a key, opening the door onto a landing in a stairwell near a half-open window. Vera went over to the open window and took a breath, then pulled a cigarette out of the same apron pocket and lit it. She inhaled deeply. A few moments later, two other women joined them.

"Rachel Klein, Marsha Hertzberg, meet Lynne Davis," Vera said waving her cigarette at them.

Everyone said "hi" to each other as Vera offered the two women cigarettes.

"Want one?" she asked Lynne.

Lynne shook her head. The women seemed quite comfortable with each other as they used the tip of Vera's lit cigarette to light their own. She noticed a tiny gold star on a thin gold chain hanging around Rachel's neck.

"That's lovely," she said. "I've never seen a star like that."

"It's a Star of David," Rachel replied.

"Star of David?"

"You know, David from the Bible," Rachel answered.

"Oh, yes."

"You're not Jewish are you?" Vera asked, smiling.

"No," Lynne replied. She looked at the three women quizzically. She had never met a Jewish person before.

"We're all Jews," Marsha piped in as she exhaled a cloud of smoke.

"Well, most of us here are," Vera said, "if you're not Italian.

"The Star of David is to us Jews what the cross is to Gentiles," Rachel added.

"Gentiles?"

"What we call you Christians and other non-Jews," Vera remarked.

"Oh."

The horn blared again. This time it sounded much louder since all the machines were quiet.

"Back to work," Vera said, and the three women stamped out their cigarettes on the floor, picked up the butts and threw them out the window. When they left the stairwell, Lynne heard the door lock behind them.

"Why's this door locked?" Lynne asked Vera.

"All the doors are locked after a shift starts."

"Why?"

"So we don't steal stuff or sneak out for extra breaks."

"Oh."

When the horn blew again, ending Lynne's first twelve hour shift, she was exhausted. She grabbed her purse and headed out when Vera caught up with her.

"Hey, wait. Where'ya living? I'm heading downtown. It's getting dark, maybe we can go home together."

"Thanks, but I'm heading east," Lynne answered

"You got a room?""

"Right now I'm staying with a friend, but I'm looking for a place."

"Didn't see a ring. You married?"

"No, I'm not," Lynne said, and didn't feel she was lying. Pauline was married, not Lynne.

"Well, good luck in finding a place" Vera said. "Landlords don't like renting to women alone."

"I heard."

"Hey, I have an idea. Move in with me. I could always use the extra money. I gotta warn you though, it's pretty awful, but it's got a stove and the bathroom in the hall is just steps from my front door."

Lynne decided to take a chance. Vera was so self-assured and seemed to know her way around. Besides, she really didn't have any idea how to find a place to live in Manhattan.

"Sounds great."

Though the shifts were long and the pay was abysmal, Lynne told Alice she found a nice factory job with good pay, made some new friends and would be moving out over the weekend. She told Alice about Vera and her invitation to live with her.

"I'll have a roommate," Lynne said cheerily.

Alice was sad to see her leave, she liked having her around, but told Lynne how proud she was of her and relieved she would not be living alone. She knew how tough it was for a woman without money or a man to rely on.

Calling Vera's room in a lower eastside tenement dingy would be an understatement. But it was clean. Lynne could see that Vera had washed away years of grease and grime off the once white walls because of the scrub marks made by a brush, but the white muslin curtain Vera had made and put over the room's one window only highlighted how gray the walls had become. A cot made up as a bed was against one wall and a tired sofa draped with colorful hand-knit afghans was on an adjacent wall. A nicely made cherry wood table with two matching wooden chairs near the two-burner stove served as a dining table. Vera had even found a few flowers she'd put in a water glass and displayed in the middle of the dining table. She caught Lynne looking at the flowers.

"Tried to brighten the room for your arrival," she said.

"They're pretty."

"So, welcome! The cot is your bed."

"No, I'm not taking your bed, Vera."

"You aren't. The couch may be old, but it's comfortable. I've been sleeping on it since I took this room. I got the cot from my parents for you."

Lynne smiled. "Thank you."

Vera grabbed Lynne's arm and opened the room's front door and pointed to a door about ten feet down the hall.

"The floor's bathroom."

Lynne just nodded. Though she had loved having a private bathroom at Alice's, Lynne grew up sharing a privy with her parents and two brothers. Any indoor bathroom was a luxury as far as she was concerned, especially in winter.

"It has a lock," Vera said, "and we all do our best to keep it clean and sanitary."

Back inside the room Lynne searched for something positive to say.

"I like your table and chairs. And the afghans are pretty."

"Thanks. My dad made them."

"The afghans?" Lynne asked, surprised.

"No," Vera laughed, "the table and chairs. My mom made the blankets."

The pungent smells of poverty were overpowering at times, but after Lynne settled in, she was usually too exhausted after her shift to care. She and Vera ate dinner together most nights. They made omelets when one of the peddlers on their street had fresh eggs, but most of the time they just had oatmeal or beans as that was all they could afford after paying their living expenses. Lynne had always been a good eater. There was never a lack of food on the farm and at Alice's house, but after having only a sandwich for lunch and a sparse dinner, she was losing weight rapidly. Her dresses were becoming increasingly looser. When the girls felt "flush," they splurged and bought a chicken, a few carrots and an onion which they made into chicken soup, giving them something more substantial to eat for a few nights. Neither girl had time to date, but Vera would go to her synagogue a few blocks away for Friday night services and to see her family and old friends. On one Friday night, Vera dragged an exhausted Lynne to the service and Lynne was so glad she did. She was completely taken with the strangeness of the temple's interior, strange because it was so different from the stark Methodist church where she was raised. She was totally mesmerized by the service ritual. When it was over, Vera grabbed Lynne's arm and pulled her toward a group of people standing outside. She knew they must be Vera's family and was nervous to meet them as Vera had told her that they were not happy that their daughter was living with a "goy." But, Vera's parents were friendly and told her they were impressed that she had made the effort to come to temple. "Maybe you'll convert," Vera's mother said hopefully.

During the weekends Lynne and Vera washed clothes in their room's sink and hung them to dry on a clothesline that Vera had rigged across the room, and took turns with the other tenants to clean the bathroom. It was a dreary existence. Not how she thought it would be when she fled the North Fork. But she clung to her "Washington Square" dreams and never admitted to herself that the life she was now living was worse than living on a potato farm. If it wasn't for Vera, Lynne would have cried herself to sleep every night.

In November, the women at the factory went on strike and she was out of a job. It was a sign from God, or at least that was how Lynne took it. A sign telling her she had to leave the factory and Vera and try to find something better. In just the few weeks she had lived with Vera, Lynne had become rail thin and under-nourished. Vera was just the opposite. Though she was naturally thin, she appeared healthy and strong even though she ate the same food Lynne did, except for her dinners on Friday night with her family. She suspected that Vera's mother gave her extra food, but she never saw Vera eating anything other than the food they bought and made together. She knew Vera now relied on her for half of the expenses, but Vera had managed before without a roommate and Lynne knew she'd manage again or move back home with her family, something Vera's mother really wanted. "It's not kosher you living, unmarried, by yourself," she would tell her daughter every time they were together.

Vera paced their room the day Lynne packed up the satchel she had bought from a street vendor. Lynne knew Vera was hurt, but once again she knew that to survive she had to leave.

"Where you gonna go?" Vera asked.

"I don't know. Hopefully to my friend's place on the eastside until I can figure it all out."

"Then just stay here."

"I can't, Vera. I'm so sorry."

"No you're not!" Vera snapped angrily, holding back tears. "I thought you were my friend!"

"I am your friend!"

"No you're not! I took you in. I even got you a cot for God's sake and now you leave me hanging!"

"I know and I can never thank you enough for that kindness. But we're on strike!"

"No, I'm on strike! You quit your job."

Lynne put five dollars on the table. "To tide you over till you reorganize your money situation."

"Where'd you get five bucks?" Vera asked suspiciously.

"I robbed a bank," Lynne flippantly answered which wasn't far from the truth, then she grabbed Vera and hugged her tight.

Vera kept her arms to her side, but Lynne continued to hold her until she finally returned Lynne's hug.

"I promise once I'm settled, I'll come down one Friday night and go to service with you."

"My mother would love that," Vera said with tears in her eyes, all her anger gone as they let go of each other. They hadn't been together that long, but they had formed a strong bond. Having Lynne as a roommate eased her loneliness as Vera tried to make it on her own.

"I'm going to miss you," Vera whispered.

"I'm going to miss you, too."

"Maybe I'll ask Rachel to move in," Vera said, trying to find a positive spin as Lynne walked out the door.

When Lynne showed up on Alice's front door, Alice was shocked to see how thin she had become in just a matter of weeks. She took Lynne in with open arms. Lynne still had most of the fifty dollars she had stolen from her parents and was relieved she wouldn't have to spend it to house and feed herself while she looked for a new job. Her factory wage had been pitiful, but because she shared the room and meal expenses with Vera she hadn't needed to spend any of her parents' money except for the five dollars she gave Vera. When she had stayed with Alice, Alice had given her money for transportation when she was out job seeking and, of course, fed her when she got home.

Lynne was so relieved by Alice's kindness she flopped on a couch and began to weep uncontrollably. Alice rushed over to her and took her into her arms as Lynne told her all about the factory and Vera and the room they shared in that rundown tenement. Alice was appalled and told Lynne that no matter what job she got next, she insisted that Lynne continue to live with her. Lynne, who had stopped crying, broke down in tears again because she had been terrified of being forced to move back into another filthy, smelly tenement or even worse, she'd have to give up her dream of a life in Manhattan and go back to the North Fork, though she was pretty sure she'd be a pariah if she ever showed up at home again.

The holidays were approaching and Lynne was finally able to land a job in an upscale men's haberdashery because the owner, a friend of Alice's, had just lost one of his salesmen and Alice had challenged him to "experiment."

"Let's see who sells more expensive merchandise to a man...a beautiful young woman or your standard male sales clerk."

Because he could pay a woman much less than a man, he agreed and after a few weeks, his experiment proved fruitful. Lynne was selling more merchandise than anyone else at the store. Though she was paid less than her fellow sales clerk, it was more than she made at the factory and enough to augment the two nice dresses Alice had bought her. She even offered to pay rent. Alice refused. She had no living family and Lynne's presence in her home eased her loneliness. That was all the rent she wanted.

Lynne was content. She loved her job. She met many wealthy men. Some, taken by her beauty, took her to dinner, but most nights she spent with Alice. A strong mother-daughter bond was beginning to form. Alice decided to throw a Christmas party to introduce Lynne to society. She hadn't decorated the house in years, but found all her old ornaments in the attic and sent Lynne out to buy a tree. Together they decorated the tree with Alice recounting stories about some of the ornaments. She held up a beautiful hand painted glass Santa.

"My mother bought this for me in Paris one autumn when she and my father went on holiday to France," Alice said wistfully.

"You didn't go with them?" Lynne asked.

"No, I stayed here with my governess. They were on a ship on their way home in time for Thanksgiving when my mother became ill. She died a week before Christmas. I was thirteen years old."

Lynne didn't know what to say as she watched Alice lovingly hang the ornament on a tree branch. Alice then picked up a silver-framed photograph from her grand piano that was cluttered with them and showed it to Lynne. It was a picture of a pretty young girl and a stunning, elegant woman of about thirty-five.

"My mother and me," Alice said.

"She's beautiful."

"Yes. She was."

Changing the mood, Alice went over to a sideboard and poured two glass of red wine from a crystal decanter and handed one to Lynne, then raised her glass.

"To our first Christmas!" she smiled.

When they finished decorating, Lynne thought the house looked like something out of a fairytale. Wreaths and garlands adorned every corner. The party was to be on Christmas Eve and more than fifty guests were invited, with thirty-two accepting the invitation.

Alice's cook brought in a few kitchen helpers and they made plum puddings, gingerbread men and butter cookies, and prepared multiple geese for roasting, a red snapper fish course, and various potato and vegetable dishes. Christmas with Lynne's family had been nothing like this. There never had been any real joy, even though they would chop down a tree and decorate it with pine cones and candles. After church, they'd sit at the long wood table in the kitchen eating whatever game her father or brothers had shot for dinner. Then off to bed and back to farm work the next morning. Alice brought joy and beauty to the holiday.

The night of the party, Lynne dressed in a lovely pale blue silk peau de soie gown from Paris, a present from Alice. She put on her new, long white gloves that went past her elbow and walked down the staircase to the first floor feeling like a queen. At that moment, Pauline had truly died and the Lynne Davis that Pauline had dreamed about was born. But she still wasn't prepared for what greeted her when she entered the front parlor. She gasped when she saw all the women dressed in magnificent gowns, their arms, ears and necks dripping with pearls, diamonds, sapphires or emeralds. Even the dumpiest man in the room looked elegant in black-tie. The fire in the fireplace warmed the room. Lighted candles in tall candlesticks were strategically arranged in a thick garland atop the mantel. Their flames bounced off the large gold framed mirror hung above the fireplace, adding to the room's glow. No party scene in any book she had read lived up to the reality she was now experiencing. A tuxedoed waiter balancing glasses on a silver tray offered her some champagne. Though she had never tasted champagne, she accepted and took a sip. The bubbles surprised her. For some inexplicable reason she couldn't figure out, they tickled her nose. She enjoyed the bubbles affect.

A stunning woman in her forties, dressed in a form-hugging gold satin gown with a daring décolletage and holding a cocktail in a white gloved hand approached Lynne. The woman was wearing the most elaborate ruby necklace and matching teardrop earrings Lynne had ever seen and she'd actually seen a few while meandering in various jewelry stores in town on her lunch breaks. There were so many large stones in the necklace that it nearly formed a neck plate. She looked like a warrior woman in rubies, Lynne thought. The woman clinked Lynne's glass.

"Merry Christmas, dear," she said. "You must be Alice's young friend. I'm Maude Cooke, one of Alice's *theatah* friends, though 'theatre' might be stretching it."

Lynne didn't have a clue how to respond, but she needn't have worried as the woman barely took a breath before continuing.

"I'm sure you haven't heard of me, so I'll fill you in before all the gossips do." She waved her hand to indicate the guests in the room.

"I'm Maude Cooke, formerly Maude McKeon back in my day when I was quite the burlesque queen. Still in my prime I married Mr. Cooke over there, an oilman," she said as she pointed to an attractive, tall, silver-haired man talking to a few people not far from them. "Retired, and lived happily ever after."

In a conspiratorial tone, she continued. "Of course, the swells weren't too happy to bring me into their refined circle, but Alice thought it would be perfectly grand to have a stripper for a friend and, if Alice likes you, the world likes you. You're a lucky young lady."

Lynne still hadn't said a word when Alice rang a little bell and announced.

"Let's all head up to the ballroom where I've set up a banquet table. Dinner's served."

Lynne followed Maude up the stairs and into the ballroom that had been transformed into a Christmas wonderland. Wreaths hung from long red ribbons on the walls. Greens had been woven into the crystal chandeliers. Three tall silver candelabras with lighted red taper candles adorned the table. A long garland of holly served as a centerpiece runner on top of the green damask tablecloth on the very long table. Since Lynne had last checked the dinner table earlier that day, someone had put name cards atop the white and gold china at each place setting. She looked for hers and found her seat in the middle of the table. On her right, her dinner partner was Maude's husband, whose full name she learned from the place card was Jay Cooke. To her left was Taylor Jackson. She had no idea who he was but, during the course of their dinner conversation, found out he was a judge. Maude sat across from her and smiled.

"Now Jay, darlin', you be nice to Alice's young friend. But not too nice," Maude said as she winked at Lynne. Lynne blushed.

As the first course was served she looked at all the silver utensils lined up in front of her and remembered Alice's golden rule, "Start from the outside, Lynne dear, and work your way in." She watched as the other diners grabbed the outside fork and began to eat. She did the same. As she listened to the various conversations about business, the arts or just local gossip going on near her, she tried not to be intimidated and was grateful that both Jay and Taylor included her by often looking at her when they spoke. She listened and learned. At least when the subject was books, she felt she could contribute, and did, but she was uncomfortable when anyone at the table asked about her past. Though the past she had made up for Lynne Davis felt more real to her now than Pauline's, she knew she was lying and hated that she had to continue the lies she had started with Alice.

After dinner, everyone retired downstairs to the various parlors and sitting rooms. Another theater friend of Alice's played Christmas carols on a piano in the sun room and many of the guests gathered round and sang enthusiastically. Food had been eaten, wine had been drunk and Lynne had made her "debut" into New York society. She had finally landed a million miles away from the potato farm. She did, however, have a score to settle. After she saved a bit of money, she travelled into Brooklyn on her day off, found a Western Union office and sent her parents fifty dollars, anonymously. She knew they would know it was from her, but if they were inclined to look for her, it wouldn't be in Manhattan. With the money safely sent off, she walked out of the Western Union office feeling totally free from her past for the first time. As far as she was concerned, all connection to her family was now severed.

On March 26, 1911 Lynne came home late from a dinner date with one of her occasional beaus and was surprised to discover Alice still up and sitting on the settee in the parlor. The fire in the fireplace was ebbing and on Alice's lap was the day's newspaper.

"Sorry I'm home so late, Alice," Lynne said as she entered the parlor still in her coat, "but you needn't have waited up for me." She automatically took a log out of a basket on the hearth and placed it in the fireplace.

"Yes. I did, dear. Please, come, sit next to me," she said and patted the empty space on the settee next to her.

Lynne took off her coat and tossed it on a nearby chair. As she sat down she noticed that Alice looked so serious, and felt something terrible must have happened. The first thing that flashed through her mind was that she found out who "Lynne" really was. She tried not to panic and took a deep breath to slow down her racing heart.

They sat in silence for a few moments, then Alice handed Lynne the paper.

"I don't know how to tell you, so please just read this," Alice said as she grabbed hold of Lynne's hand.

Lynne saw the headline: "Over 100 People Perish in Factory Blaze." As she read further she realized the factory was the Triangle Shirtwaist Factory. She let out a piercing wail, then began to shake violently. There were no names of the dead listed, just a retelling of what had happened the day before and how the locked doors had prohibited the mostly female workers from escaping. More remains were expected to be found. Alice wrapped her arms around Lynne to try and stop her shaking.

"I never went back. I promised her I'd go to temple. Why didn't I go back?" Lynne cried.

A bottle of bourbon was on a side table. Alice got up and poured some into a shot glass and handed it to Lynne who was still shaking.

"Drink this, dear."

Lynne drank it all in one gulp. "I have to know."

"I know you do."

"How do I find out? Vera? My friends? How do I find out?"

"I'll find out for you, sweetheart," Alice said. "I'll call the Mayor and I'll find out."

Three days later, Alice was able to tell Lynne that Vera Zahler was not listed among the dead.

The next Friday night Lynne stood outside the Jewish temple that she'd gone to with Vera, waiting for the service to end, hoping to catch a glimpse of Vera. It had turned cold, but Lynne didn't notice. She scanned the congregants as they filed out of the synagogue. She has to be here, she thought. Then Vera's mother spotted Lynne. She turned to Vera who was coming out behind her. When Vera saw Lynne standing in the dark, she rushed over and threw her arms around her.

"I knew you'd come," she said.

Vera's mother joined them and invited Lynne back for Sabbath supper.

"Please come, it would mean a great deal to our daughter."

"Thank you, yes, I'll come," Lynne answered.

Vera hooked her arm into Lynne's as they walked the few blocks to the Zahler apartment, a decent size second story walk-up with three bedrooms and its own bathroom.

After eating dinner in the large foyer that doubled as a dining room, then helping with the clean-up, Lynne and Vera went into a slightly shabby, but homey living room. Vera's father, an in-demand carpenter, had made a wall-to-ceiling bookshelf that was filled with old and tattered books and a beautiful menorah he and his wife had brought with them when they left Europe for America. The comfortable sofa and upholstered easy chairs were covered in worn, faded floral slipcovers. Two reading floor lamps were on, as well as a table lamp on a dark wood sideboard that Vera's father had also made.

The conversation at dinner after the Friday night Sabbath ritual did not include any talk about the fire and, now that Lynne was alone with Vera, she didn't know what to say.

"I'm sorry I never…"

"Forget it. No regrets," Vera said cutting her off.

"You seem to have escaped our little hovel nicely," she continued, indicating Lynne's attire.

"I have."

"Tell me all about it. Where have you been all this time?" Vera asked.

"I promise I'll tell you everything, but first you have to tell me about the fire. I was so scared for you."

At first Vera didn't want to talk about it, she wanted to hear all about Lynne's good fortune, but she soon relented. Tears flooded her eyes as she described the fire's horror, the smells, the screams as workers on the floor rushed to the doors trying to get free, and how she was able to pick the same lock she picked every day during breaks to have a cigarette and opened that one door. Marsha and a few others made it out with her, but not Rachel.

Vera grabbed a knitted afghan draped over the sofa and buried her face inside it, muffling her sobs. When she stopped crying Vera continued her story, saying that after Lynne had moved out, Vera decided to return home and live with her parents. She could pay them rent which would help them financially since her last brother living at home had married and had moved out to set up house with his new wife. She didn't want her parents to struggle, so she moved back home and was happy about cooking and eating real meals again. She didn't know what they would all do now, now that she didn't have a job and could see no prospects of finding one soon.

"Okay, I've told you my sad tale, now it's your turn, Lynne Davis, to brighten my day."

Lynne told her just about everything. How she met Alice on the train and how Alice had turned her life around, gave her a home and brought love into her life. She did not tell Vera her real name or what she had done to escape the North Fork, she just repeated the lie she told Alice when they first met.

"So you're a widow?" Vera asked.

"Yes, though I was barely married a minute." Lynne embellished the lied, then changed the subject.

It was late when Lynne finally made her goodbyes. Vera's father insisted on walking her to the trolley, but when they got outside, Alice's driver was there waiting for her. She thanked the Zahlers for a wonderful dinner and, as she hugged Vera goodbye, she promised she'd keep in touch, and this time she knew she would.

When she got home, Alice was once again waiting up for her in the parlor. Lynne joined her and told her about her evening and about Vera's fear that without her measly income, her parents would struggle financially. Alice thought about it for a while.

"Is she smart?" she asked.

"Yes. Very. Why?"

"Maude is looking for someone to organize her life. Keep track of her appointments, make sure her staff does what it's supposed to. Jay's out of town a lot and I think Maude just needs a bright young companion to keep her company. The female kind. And, she'd be thrilled to help out a friend of yours. She doesn't live far from here, so it wouldn't be much of a change in commute for Vera."

"She won't care if Vera's Jewish?" Lynne asked.

Alice laughed. "Maude? Ha. Are you kidding?! She'll love it! And she pays well."

Maude felt that Vera was a kindred spirit the minute they began the interview. Vera was forthright, pragmatic and self-assured and reminded her of herself at that age. A survivor. She hired Vera on the spot. Lynne was thrilled and she got to see her friend more often as Alice insisted that Vera come for dinner at least once a week.

Lynne was twenty-three and was about to start her first fifteen minutes of fame as "Lynne Davis" a Ziegfeld girl in the 1912 Follies. Still working at the men's haberdashery, Lynne waited on the soon-to-be-cast 1912 Follies choreographer, Oscar London. Taken by her beauty, he insisted she audition. She sweetly explained to him that she would be happy to but for the fact that she had no talent. She couldn't sing or dance. He pooh-poohed her. "All you have to do is walk around the stage, head held high and look as beautiful as your costume."

After talking it over with Alice who encouraged her to take advantage of this new adventure, she decided to take him up on his offer and Alice, Maude and Vera made sure that Lynne was the toast of uptown and downtown when she opened in her first Follies. Oscar reveled in her beauty and in her standing in society and took her everywhere with him. He doted on her and granted her every wish, whether it be a walk in the park or a dinner at one of her favorite restaurants. If she admired a piece of jewelry, he bought it for her, and the tabloids and society columns ate it all up by taking pictures of their comings and goings as often as they could. Lynne's appearance had changed so dramatically from the girl she was on the North Fork of Long Island, she never worried that someone from her past would recognize her, if anyone there actually read the society pages.

In less than a year they married in a beautiful wedding hosted and paid for by Alice at The Plaza Hotel. Vera was her maid of honor. The ceremony and reception were written about in every society page and show biz gossip columns. And, though Lynne was a virgin when she married, nine months later to the day, she gave birth to a daughter on the first day of May 1914 making all scandal sheet writers in town count the months on their fingers and speculate in print. Lynne didn't care. She had a gloriously healthy, beautiful little girl. She named her Spring.

But at twenty-five Lynne's Follies days were over and Oscar soon became bored with his wife's desire to stay home with their daughter and not continually be an ornament on his arm at fancy restaurants, theater openings, and society salons and parties. Spring was only a few months old when Oscar packed his bags and abandoned them in their palatial apartment for his latest Follies discovery who was younger and more than willing to fulfill Lynne's role and flatter his ego. The tabloids and society pages again had a field day, photographing Oscar and his new companion as reporters and photographers plagued Lynne for pictures of her and her baby every time she left her apartment building.

A few days after Oscar moved out, Alice had to actually push through a mob of reporters to get inside Lynne's apartment building. She insisted that Lynne, with Spring in tow, move back in with her.

"They'll move on to greener gossip pastures soon enough," Lynne told her.

"Maybe so, but Spring will be safer from prying eyes in my home," Alice declared. "Besides, you'll be happier back home with me."

Lynne relented and moved back to W. 4th Street. Alice turned one of the bedrooms into a nursery fit for a princess. Oscar had no paternal instincts so, when Lynne asked for sole custody of Spring during the divorce proceedings, he didn't contest. When he was working, he'd send some child support, but Lynne never pressed for more. She didn't hate him, he had been a fun companion while it lasted, but she realized after their marriage was over that she didn't really love him, either.

Even though Alice was again supporting her and now her daughter, Lynne missed the hustle and bustle of working and meeting new people. She had no desire to pursue anything in the theater, didn't want to go back to the haberdashery and after the Triangle Shirtwaist factory fire, she swore she and her daughter would go back to the farm before she'd ever go back and work in a sweatshop. But, acceptable positions for women were still scarce. Finally, she landed a job as a waitress at Childs Restaurant which had recently started hiring more women. She loved it, met interesting people, the tips were great and her hours were flexible. Though many of Alice's friends thought her waiting on people was inappropriate for someone in their "crowd," Alice was proud of the example Lynne was setting for Spring.

Lynne didn't date, but occasionally, she went dancing with Vera and the friends she had made at the restaurant. With beautiful long legs and a face to match she was often stopped in the street by photographers and modelling agents who wanted to take her picture or have her pose for artists' fashion illustrations for *Vogue* magazine. She enjoyed the attention, but never seriously considered it. Her second fifteen minutes of fame happened when she finally said "yes" and did a shoot for one of the early *Vogue* photographers she met and took a fancy to. He stuffed her in gowns and made her pose in the cold in front of fountains and foliage in Central Park. The pictures were stunning and a modelling career would have taken off, except Lynne wanted nothing to do with it. She saw how the world treated fading beauties and at nearly thirty, she also knew she was too old to last more than a minute as a model, nor did she have any desire to be poked and prodded in semi-freezing weather. "I'll be dead before my daughter graduates from kindergarten," she told Alice. Happily, she stayed at Childs and never modelled again.

It took three months for "Blackie" to track Lynne Davis down. When he saw her pictures in *Vogue*, he had to meet her. And, when he found out she worked at Childs he casually walked into the restaurant, sat in her section, ordered a cup of coffee and asked her to marry him. She laughed, said no, but did accept an invitation to the theater and a late dinner. The date was perfect. He made her feel like she was the only person in the world. She knew she could fall madly in love with this tall, dark, handsome man. A few of Blackie's friends joined them at that late dinner in Delmonico's, the tony restaurant on Fifth and 44th Street. During conversational banter she learned that her black-haired suitor was the well-known society playboy, Bryson Hill, an Oklahoma coal baron. One of the women at their table laughingly warned Lynne that he would woo her then stomp on her heart if she wasn't careful. Everyone at the table laughed, including Blackie. She wasn't too sure exactly who "Bryson Hill" was, but she decided that Blackie and his friends were way too fast a crowd for her and she was swimming in water above her head. If she didn't get to shore soon, she would drown. Though he pursued her for weeks, she refused to go out with Blackie again, but still cherishes the picture of them sitting at the table in Delmonico's.

Lynne continued to work off and on at Childs, coordinating her hours so she could be home most nights with Spring and Alice. Most nights except Friday. Friday was the night she reserved for herself. After a long week of waiting on other people and sharing dinners with Alice, Spring and, at times, Vera, it was the night she wanted to have dinner alone and anonymous. She chose Schrafft's, a restaurant where she knew she could sip a gimlet, her cocktail of choice, and eat dinner without being bothered. Both Alice and Spring hated fish, so she never had it at home. She loved fish and Schrafft's Friday special, designed to bring in Irish Catholics, was filet of sole, mashed potatoes and peas.

When Alice passed away from natural causes in 1922, she left her entire estate to Lynne. Spring was ten years old and Lynne was thirty-five. Lynne was now a very wealthy woman. Life changed. Vera married a young rabbi and was living in an apartment near his synagogue and, though she was still working for Maude, the two friends weren't able to see each other that often. Even though Spring had the same live-in governess she'd had since she was a baby and was close to her, Lynne left Childs to be home for her daughter more often, now that her "grandmother" was gone. But, on Friday night she would ask her daughter's governess to babysit so she could continue having her quiet dinners at Schrafft's. Prohibition didn't stop her Friday night ritual, she just savored a gimlet at home before going to dinner.

Even after the stock market crash, Lynne's holdings remained strong, but she went back to work at Childs to augment her income—just in case. Everything was as it should be, but as the years passed, Spring had married and moved to St. Louis. Though they spoke on the phone often, Lynne saw her daughter only a few times a year and she missed her.

Middle-aged and lonely, Lynne dined alone at home most nights if she didn't have dinner at Childs or had an invitation to dinner at Vera's or other friends. But her Fridays were still reserved for Schrafft's. With her white gloves folded neatly on her regular table, she would sip her gimlet and relish the Friday night special even though she had started making fish for herself at home.

On one of those Friday nights she met Hayes Walker. Handsome, with brown eyes and salt and pepper hair that formed a high widow's peak, Hayes had all intentions of wining and dining her, even making love to her before conning her out of her money. But, Lynne knew him, she recognized him immediately, so he blackmailed her instead.

CHAPTER 7

ASHLEY — 1968

OK, maybe taking notes while dining on rack of lamb and a poached pear salad while sipping a rich Bordeaux wine was gauche, but I did it anyway. I wanted to make sure I was accurate and didn't want to trust anything to my memory. Lynne's detailed descriptions of the places and parties she'd been to and the people she'd met filled my reporter's notepad, and as a lifestyle reporter I cherished every word. By the time Lynne got to Hayes Walker, Vi had just brought out demitasse cups of very strong coffee with rock sugar on little sticks to swirl in the hot liquid.

I begged Lynne to tell me more about Hayes, but that topic was over. We drank our coffee and ate a few pralines as Vi veered the conversation to a new subject. Me.

"Why Ashley Wilkes?"

A question I'd been asked a million times. I started to repeat my rote answer about my mom's love of *Gone with the Wind*… hated the name Scarlett, didn't like Melanie, liked Ashley and decided a female Ashley Wilkes thanks to my father's last name would be just fine. But as I looked at Vi and Lynne, I thought I owed it to them to give them the whole story, boring as it was.

Aleksandra (Sandra) Nurmi Wilkes, my mom, was a first generation Finn. Her parents, Johanna and Emil, emigrated from Finland as newlyweds at the turn of the 20th century and moved to a farm in the Cape Ann area of Massachusetts. Johanna made ends meet as a seamstress while my grandfather, Emil, tended to their apple orchard and took odd jobs as a handyman. Johanna also was an active suffragette and marched in Boston. Though their home was a fairly large clapboard farmhouse, to escape the hustle and bustle of her ever present siblings, my mom would go deep into the orchard and climb one of the apple trees where she'd gaze at the sky and ponder the world from her very own perch. When she discovered books, she'd take one with her and curl up on a cluster of branches she used as a chair in her favorite tree and fall in love with the Count of Monte Cristo or dream she was Anna Karenina destined to die for love. Then she discovered "Jo" in *Little Women*. Louisa May Alcott had lived in a town not far from my mom so after finishing the book, Emil took her to see the Alcott home. My mom couldn't decide if she wanted to be Louisa or Jo. She started writing poems and stories in her tree and as soon as she graduated high school, like her sisters before her (and Jo), she moved to New York City. She rented a room in Brooklyn's "Finntown" where two of her siblings lived, and found a job as a clerk for the Civil Defense Department in Manhattan.

Mom continued to write her stories, but fear of failure kept her from submitting them. She met my father, matinee idol handsome Jack Wilkes when one of her sisters nagged her to get involved with a little theater company in Brooklyn. Jack, a Manhattan boy originally from upstate New York, was an actor in the play that was currently running in the theater. They fell in love. WWII broke out and Jack enlisted in the Army Air Corps. On leave, they married in Atlantic City and a year later, while Jack was stationed in Guam, Sandra delivered a daughter at the Scandinavian Hospital in Brooklyn while her sisters and mother-in-law paced in the waiting room. At first she wanted to name her newborn daughter—that would be me—Johanna, after her mother who died when she was ten, because then she could call me Jo, after Jo March. But eventually, her love for *Gone with the Wind*, a book she had just finished, won out. Hence, I became Ashley.

Unlike my grandmother, Johanna, the card-carrying suffragette, my mom had no interest in politics, not even current events. The war terrified her. She moved to the town where Jack's parents lived, leaving behind her sisters in New York and all news of the war. She spent her days writing letters to Jack, writing poems and romantic stories and taking care of me. I got my love of writing from my mother, but my desire to be a journalist and write about things that matter, even fight for them, came from my grandmother. Some family traits really do just skip a generation.

"Your mother must be very proud you've become a writer, Ashley," Lynne said.

"I think she is now, but when I was growing up she never encouraged me to write."

"No?"

"No. She claimed she just wanted to protect me from being disappointed. She wanted me to go to Katie Gibbs, learn to type and take shorthand with precision and become a professional secretary even though I had already learned to do both these skills in college as electives to my journalism courses."

Vi looked at me curiously. "So you went against your mother's wishes," she said as a statement not a question. "Do you think she was afraid you would fail or that you would succeed where she hadn't?" That was a question.

I thought about it for a minute. I didn't know how to answer that. I didn't want to paint my mother as someone jealous of her own daughter, at least jealous of her drive, but it was a question I often asked myself. My mother had always been afraid to make waves, yet she was the most loving mom on the planet and could be fierce when it came to protecting me from any kind of pain. But if I wanted to do something "out of the norm," she would discourage me if she thought I'd be hurt or that people wouldn't approve, but once I made up my mind and plunged forward, she didn't interfere. She'd learned to accept my desire to be a reporter and when she saw I could support myself at writing, she started to clip my articles and brag to her friends.

"My mom was a romantic and a dreamer. She loved getting lost in a Daphne du Maurier novel or Edith Wharton or the Brontes and adored Walt Whitman. She believed that there were certain roles for men in this life and certain roles for women. Me. I loved those writers, too, well, du Maurier and Wharton, anyway. But I'm more of a pragmatist. *Wuthering Heights* makes me so angry. Heathcliff? Please. He's just a cruel man in a continual temper tantrum. And I could just slap Kathy. What a poor excuse for a heroine."

Both Vi and Lynne laughed.

"So, a brooding hero wandering the moors isn't romantic to you?" Vi asked with a smile.

"Nope. If he's brooding, give me Sidney Carton any day. 'It's a far, far better thing I do than I've ever done before.' Now that's romantic!"

"What about your father?" Lynne asked.

"Oh, he's pretty cool, a sort of pre-feminist male. He even made hot dogs and beans for Saturday dinners or waffles for Sunday suppers when we had a big meal after church. My friends' fathers couldn't boil water and wouldn't be caught dead in the kitchen."

Vi and Lynne laughed again.

"What was so great about him is he didn't buy into my high school guidance counselor's advice that women, if they must work, should just aspire to be nurses, teachers, stewardesses or secretaries. He truly believed I could be anything I wanted and encouraged my writing and interest in politics. One day, and I remember this so clearly, I was barely out of diapers when the McCarthy hearings were going on. He was home from work for some reason and I sat on his lap while he watched the proceedings on television. He kept yelling at the screen and when it was over, he explained what an awful thing McCarthy and his committee were doing and that he was ashamed that Congress was allowing it. I had no idea what he was talking about at the time, but that moment always stayed with me. Later, when I learned about the hearings, I felt so proud that my dad stood against them."

"What kind of work does he do?" Vi asked.

"Before the war he was studying acting, but after it was over he went to Columbia and got his law degree. He's now a partner for a big law firm in mid-town. He and my mom still hold hands when they watch TV."

We sipped some more coffee. "OK," I continued with a smile, "you deflected my questions by asking about me, but you're not getting off so easily. I want to know about the men who stole your money."

"I promise, we'll tell you, but not tonight. It's late and I'm tired," Vi said.

Out of nowhere, a uniformed butler who hadn't made an appearance all evening came into the dining room, whispered something in Vi's ear, and began to clear off the dishes. "Will you walk Lynne outside?" she asked. "There's a cab waiting to take you both home."

Lynne had already gotten her coat and purse and was ready to leave. I grabbed my reporter's notebook and shoved it into my bag, threw on my coat, then impulsively kissed Vi good night as she walked us to the front door, promising we would meet again soon. There was still another Schrafft's lady I needed to meet.

While I waited to hear from Vi, I began to see more of Marty Lambert, an old high school boyfriend, who had resurfaced in my life. We reconnected a year earlier at a black-tie affair at The

St. Regis Hotel that Mayor Lindsay was attending. Marty, who had made a name for himself as a New York City homicide detective after law school, had been assigned that night to protect the Mayor along with a few other elite New York detectives. The city was in the midst of a long garbage strike, with tensions running high and death threats hurled at the Mayor. Of course, I never got to write about any of that because Dwyre had sent me to cover the charity event for the lifestyle section.

Since then, we would have dinner a couple of times a week in one of my favorite New York Italian red sauce restaurants that wasn't in Little Italy. Il Vagabondo was on East 62nd, a stone's throw from the Queensboro bridge exit into Manhattan. I discovered the restaurant when I was writing a fluff piece on Epic Records, a division of CBS, about how a record is made. I reached out to Joe Lombardi, a friend I'd met at a party and who worked as an A&R producer at Epic. He suggested we meet at the restaurant for the interview and promised he'd buy me the best veal parmigiana I'd ever eaten. I walked down a few steps to the entrance of a brownstone and entered a dark, long barroom packed with a clientele that looked like the guys who were questioned in the televised Kefauver mafia hearings some years back. I think I was the only female in the room who didn't have overly teased, overly hair-sprayed hair and a tight angora sweater. With my little mini-skirt, sweater set, pearls, white knee socks and little stacked heels, I was so out of my element.

The bartender looked at me questioningly. I bet he was wondering what the hell I was doing in his bar, but when I told him who I was looking for, he just smiled and pointed to the back of the room and told me to turn right. I found a large main dining room and a partially open kitchen. The aromas coming out of the kitchen were mouthwatering. I spotted my friend Joe sitting a table for four with another guy. Dressed in a black silk shirt opened at the neck to highlight his chest hair and three long gold chains, he couldn't be more of a cliché—the boy from

"Jersey" who made it big in the record biz. But he was smart and funny and I liked him.

"Welcome to Il Vagabondo," Joe said as I reached the table. "Meet Pete Walsh, or as I call him, Mr. Preppy."

Pete was dressed like a banker on his day off in a blue oxford cloth, button down shirt most likely from Brooks Brothers or Rogers Peet, and faded jeans. He handed me a glass of Chianti then took my hand and showed me around the restaurant which included a smaller dining room with tables for two and a bocce court. Pete told me that this was one of the very few indoor bocce courts in the entire city.

The interview went great and afterward, Pete and Joe "off the record" filled me in on a little gossip about Simon & Garfunkel's *Bookends* album recently released by Columbia Records, also part of CBS, and causing quite a stir.

It seems that though there had been no new Simon & Garfunkel album released in 1967 and other artists were garnering the music headlines, Mike Nichols was a huge fan of the duo and had obsessively listened to their previous three albums over and over again before, during and after directing *The Graduate*. So, while editing the movie Mike decided he had to have some of their songs on the movie's soundtrack. He also wanted to hire Paul to write an original song for the movie. He went to Clive Davis, who had recently become President of Columbia and convinced him to let him use a couple of Simon & Garfunkel tunes and asked Clive to set up a meeting with Paul about a new song. According to the grapevine, Paul wasn't all that interested in writing music for movies, but finally agreed to deliver three new songs to Mike, the first two of which Mike didn't like. The third was "Mrs. Robinson."

"The rest is present music history," Pete said. "*The Graduate* soundtrack is a huge hit. Simon & Garfunkel's fame has reached the stratosphere. And, as you probably know, *Bookends* which included 'Mrs. Robinson,' came out in April on the heels of *The Graduate* soundtrack to great reviews, better than great sales and is still the talk of the industry. Clive, of course, is now rock'n'roll's golden boy." I had both albums and loved this "insider" story.

As we were leaving the restaurant, I noticed for the first time that, unlike the mostly male crowd in the front bar, many of the people in the dining rooms were people like me, twenty-something professionals. When I remarked on the difference in clientele, Joe told me that it was also a big hangout for people in the music business, Madison Avenue types as well as the "connected" who seemed to be all in the front room bar. Dwyre loved the Epic piece and I had loved the veal parmigiana. Win, win.

But no veal parm tonight, Marty was taking me dancing at Arthur, the club Sybil Burton opened in the city after she was dumped by Richard Burton. To get into the club you either had to be a movie star, royalty *or* drop dead gorgeous. When we arrived, the bouncers guarding the door waved us in past all the people outside waiting on line. We weren't movies stars, royalty or drop dead gorgeous, though Marty, with his tall, lanky, yet muscular body and his huge blue eyes and shaggy light brown hair bordered on silver screen handsome. I was impressed. A little table for two by the dance floor was waiting for us. Ari Onassis sat two tables away. Now I was really impressed.

I looked at Marty, suspiciously dressed in a beautifully tailored Brooks Brothers blue blazer I'd never seen before, expensive gray flannel trousers and Gucci loafers as he guided me into my chair and sat down. "OK, how'd you pull this off? Cute as you are, and you *are* cute, you're a cop, not a millionaire playboy."

I had read about cops getting preferential treatment for doing "favors" and I didn't want Marty to be one of those cops. I liked him too much. And his outfit was definitely not from Alexander's or even Macy's.

He smiled. "I'm working."

"Working? How can I get a job where all I have to is dance and drink expensive booze at Arthur?" I asked disbelievingly.

He took my hand and pressed it to his lips. "Trust me. It's all good."

I didn't like that answer. I'm not one who trusts people easily, even old boyfriends I've known since high school and who are currently my lover, but I decided Arthur was not the place to get into it.

We drank very good scotch, danced, and even made out on the dance floor, but I still wondered how he was paying for all this. By three in the morning, I told him I needed to go home. So we made our way to the door.

"What about the check?" I asked.

"It's taken care of."

Now I was *really* suspicious.

In the cab ride home, I pressed him for an explanation, but all he would say was to trust him. I couldn't, so when we got to my apartment building, I told him to stay in the cab, I could make it to my door on my own.

Inside my studio apartment, I took off my white, sleeveless, shimmery disco mini dress and paced back and forth in my tiny one room. I may be falling in love with Marty, but I needed an explanation or I couldn't continue to see him.

I had obsessed about Marty all night and barely got an hour's sleep so wasn't surprised that I kept making typos as I tried to finish up a story for my new column. I was pleased when Dwyre had told me that the response had been good to my Clarke's piece and that the publisher liked the idea of having a woman's take on people and places in New York City, but right now, as

I looked around the newsroom, I just wanted to sleep and not have to meet another deadline.

By noon, after five cups of strong coffee and a can of Tab, I finally finished my column and was about to go to lunch when I saw Bobby, one of the copyboys, escorting Vi to my desk. It had been a month since I'd had dinner at her house and I was beginning to worry that she was regretting opening up to me. I had transcribed all the notes from our meetings and was startled to discover that the descriptions of the men who stole from "my" Schrafft's ladies all were the same. "My" was how I was beginning to feel about them. I was anxious to hear the rest of the story. Seeing her again made me forget my concerns about Marty.

She thanked Bobby for showing her to my desk, then looked at me, tears in her eyes. "Is it possible for you to take the rest of the day off and come with me?"

I asked her to sit in my chair. I grabbed my column and went into Dwyre's office and put it on his desk then headed back to mine, gathered my things and left the newsroom with Vi. Thankfully, I was researching a new lifestyle story so if I didn't come back to work, Dwyre would think I was out working on that.

When we left the building Vi led me to a black Lincoln Continental double parked in front. We got in the back. I hadn't asked a single question since she came to the newsroom. I just knew that it was important to her that I go with her. But now I needed to know why. As the driver took us out of the city toward Westchester County, Vi told me one of the Schrafft's ladies was very ill and that she hadn't called me all these weeks because she and Lynne had been spending time with her at a nursing home. They had told her about their confessions to me and now that this woman was dying, she wanted to tell me her story.

When Vi and I entered a private room in a tony nursing home in Tuckahoe, Dorothy "Dot" Pierce, nee Kimmel, was propped up in her bed with an IV in her arm. Lynne was sitting in a chair pulled up next to the bed. Though frail and under-weight, with most of her white hair gone from lengthy bouts of chemo, Dot's voice was strong. After our introduction, Vi repeated to me that she had told Dot about our meetings and that Dot wanted to confess what she had done.

CHAPTER 8

DOT KIMMEL PIERCE — 1892-1937

Born in June, 1892, Dot was raised in Brooklyn. Her father, Ezra Kimmel, had a pushcart business which he turned into a moderately successful deli in Flatbush, a strong working class Italian, Irish, Jewish community. Her mother, Ruth, worked side-by-side with her husband making all sorts of sandwiches and cooking various dishes like brisket, matzo ball soup and kugel, a delicious noodle pudding. When Dot was twelve, her parents moved her and her sister, Sarah, out of their one bedroom tenement flat into their own newly built two-bedroom row house three blocks away. The girls no longer had to sleep in the living room and the toilet in the bathroom didn't need to be plunged every other flush. Ezra bought each girl her own bed and a dresser, wholesale, from their Uncle Yehuda who owned a furniture store in the lower east side of Manhattan. Life had improved and Dot did well in school. She was cute in a bookish way with curly dark brown hair and big chocolate brown eyes. Vivacious and funny, she was popular with her classmates, but two days after she graduated from high school in 1910, she took the Brooklyn Bridge trolley into Manhattan and applied for a job as a sales clerk at Macy's. Jobs for young ladies were few and far between, especially Jewish "young ladies," but her best friend, Fanny Friedman, had gotten a job in the store after she had graduated the year before, so that's where Dot saw her future. Macy's hired her.

At first she worked as a salesgirl in the women's lingerie department. Fanny worked in ladies' hats. The girls would have dinner together whenever they could in a nearby Schrafft's before heading home to Brooklyn. By now Dot had moved out of her parents' row house and shared a room with Fanny in a Jewish women's boarding house in the Bay Ridge section of Brooklyn…just far enough away from her parents to keep them from "dropping in" all the time, but close enough to keep them from complaining. The two girls were closer than sisters.

A couple of years later, Dot was transferred to the men's shoe department. After two short months in her new job she met Sidney Schuster, an extremely wealthy, but married, book publisher and fell madly in love with him. They began an affair, with Sidney promising to leave his wife, telling Dot he loved only her and that he didn't sleep with his wife…the usual. She kept her affair a secret from everyone including Fanny, from whom she was slowly distancing herself. But lithe, raven-haired Fanny didn't mind because she had fallen in love with Ira Levitt, a nice Jewish boy…a law student her parents had fixed her up with. The girls became ships that passed in the night. Or, in truth, two girls who just shared a place to sleep.

After a year, Sidney moved Dot into a small apartment in Manhattan that he paid for. Her parents were horrified that she would move into the city and live on her own and wondered how she could afford it on her Macy's salary. They had no idea that Dot had become a "kept" woman, but Fanny did. She had suspected Dot's boyfriend was a married man for some time. Fanny had never met him and Dot never told her his name, so when Ira invited Dot and her "boyfriend" for dinner in Manhattan, his treat, and Dot showed up alone, Fanny was livid. Dot was her closest and dearest friend. She wanted to tell Dot before anyone else that she and Ira were engaged and she wanted to share that news with the man Dot loved.

"Why did you accept Ira's invitation to both of you if you knew you would be coming alone?"

Dot, having lived a double life for so long, became defensive and cruelly snapped back that her boyfriend didn't want to have dinner with a kid in law school and his girlfriend. He had more important things to do, but as soon as she said that, Dot regretted it instantly.

"I'm so sorry, Fanny. I didn't mean that," she said. "That's not true, it's just…"

Fanny wasn't having it. Ira saw how hurt and angry Fanny was and put his hand on hers as she coldly said, "I think you should leave."

Dot looked at her best friend and realized that Fanny knew, and that she should have been truthful with Fanny from the beginning. She had betrayed their friendship.

"I'm sorry," she said as she got up and left the restaurant. When they saw each other in the store, Fanny was perfunctorily cordial, but their friendship was over.

Dot tried to rebuild the closeness they once had, but Fanny wasn't having it, and a few months later, Fanny left the store. Almost a year later, when Dot was visiting her parents in Brooklyn, she saw Fanny and Ira's wedding announcement in the *Brooklyn Daily News*. Fanny was now a married woman and, as her mother told it, she and her husband were living not far from Columbia University where he was going to law school.

Dot missed Fanny even though her affair with Sidney was going strong. He came for dinner every Wednesday night and they arranged to meet often in her apartment or a hotel room near Macy's for afternoon trysts during Dot's lunch hour or on her days off. This went on for a couple of years, Dot always believing that Sidney would eventually leave his wife and children and marry her, but when she read in on the society page that his wife gave birth to a third child, a little girl, Dot realized that he was obviously still sleeping with his wife and had no intentions of marrying her. Dot was heartbroken and cried herself to sleep every night until he showed up that next Wednesday as if nothing was new in his life.

Sidney sat at the small dining table she had set and talked about the latest writer he had discovered and complimented her on her brisket. She still hadn't decided whether to confront him or not.

"How are Ruth and the children?" she asked, giving him an opening to be honest with her.

"The kids are thriving," he answered.

"And Ruth?"

"I guess she's fine. We barely speak to one another. She lives her life and I live mine." He reached across the table and took Dot's hand. "And my heart is here with you."

At that moment, Dot knew she wasn't going to say anything. She loved him and, now that her friendship with Fanny was dead, she had no one she felt close to. Determined not to cry, she pulled her hand away and started clearing the dishes.

Over the years, Sidney had given Dot expensive gifts and money, which she invested carefully, building a small nest egg for herself. She also worked hard at Macy's and had moved up to become one of the few female Assistant Buyers in the entire store. Her department was men's ties.

Then, without warning a few months after the birth of his daughter, during the height of the Christmas season, Sidney disappeared from her life. He stopped calling and she was too timid to call him at his office. When the January rent wasn't paid, she paid it. She began to worry. She checked the hospitals, went to the library and read all the obituaries for the past month. Nothing. She began to wait in the cold, outside his office building after work and finally spotted him. She followed him onto the train to Long Island, carefully keeping out of his sight, then watched as he got off at the Great Neck station and ran into the arms of his wife and children waiting to take him home. He smothered them all with kisses and tossed his five-month-old daughter in the air as she laughed with glee. Devastated, Dot went home.

She managed to keep the apartment and a year later was dining out with Sanford, "Sandy" Pierce, a friend she met while working at Macy's, who had his own fledgling brokerage house. They talked about the possibility of America entering the war that was raging in Europe. It was only a matter of time. Sandy told her how he had tried to enlist, but was classified 4F because of flat feet. "Nobody's perfect," he laughed, but she could tell he was disappointed he'd been rejected. As their waiter brought menus, Dot spotted Sidney in a dimly lit corner booth, holding hands and looking romantically into the eyes of a younger version of herself. She slowly got up from her chair, walked over to his table, picked up his glass of red wine and poured it over his head, then ran from the restaurant in tears leaving Sanford alone and confused. He threw some money onto their table and ran after her.

At first she refused to talk about what happened and just cried on his shoulder outside the restaurant, but as she calmed down they began to walk and eventually found themselves outside a Schrafft's. Hungry, Sandy convinced her to go inside with him. He ordered a Manhattan and when he asked her what she would like to drink, she had no idea. He ordered another. Realizing she was in no shape to decide on something to eat, he chose two breaded veal cutlets with tomato sauce, the Thursday night special. Over two cocktails and her partially eaten dinner, Dot opened up about her affair with Sidney and how he broke her heart. Sandy listened without judgment.

Soon after, they began to date and Sandy fell hard. Dot wasn't beautiful in the traditional WASP sense (blonde, blue-eyed), but to him, with her tight brown curls twisted into an unruly bun, full red lips and large chocolate brown eyes, she was gorgeous in an "exotic" way. She was also Jewish, something his family would frown on. He didn't care. She was smart, caring and was making a name for herself in the retail business, an accomplishment few women had made. He was proud of her independence and ambition, but so far she was his little secret.

A month later, his secret was out when he spotted a picture of the two of them in an intimate pose at an out-of-the-way restaurant published in the society section of the New York Journal. The story's writer wanted to know who the dark-haired mystery woman was with Sanford Pierce III, heir to the Pierce real estate fortune. So did his parents. Sandy had no memory of any photographs being taken at the restaurant and rushed to Macy's to warn Dot. He did not see that a reporter followed him. He found Dot in her tiny office and showed her the article as the reporter asked Dot's fellow Macy's employees who she was. The next day the headline in the Journal's society page. "Jewish Cinderella or Conniving Gelt Digger?"

Sanford II was furious and summoned his son and Dot to his Manhattan neo-classical mansion on 66th Street and Fifth Avenue. His wife, Gloria, waited impatiently in the front parlor to confront her son and his "paramour," but when he arrived, he was alone.

"Where is she, Sandy?" Gloria demanded. "Is she too afraid to meet your father and me?"

"I doubt it. I never extended the invitation," he replied.

At that moment, Sanford II entered the room.

"It wasn't an invitation. It was an order," he boomed.

"Exactly!"

Sandy stood his ground. There was no way he would have subjected Dot to an inquisition.

"Don't be smart with me! I was prepared to offer your little Jewish shop girl quite a bit of money to get out of your life," Sanford continued.

"She's not for sale," Sandy snapped.

"You don't think so? You don't think that if I offered her ten thousand dollars she wouldn't take it?"

"No, I don't."

"You're naïve!" Gloria chimed in. "Sleep with your Jewess then, but don't ever be seen in public with her again. It's embarrassing the family."

Holding back his anger, Sandy glared at his father and mother, "You make me ashamed. I love her and I am not sleeping with her," he said steadily. Then he smiled. "But, I will when I marry her."

"You do that, Sandy, and you won't get a dime," Sanford II threatened. "And I will make damn sure not a single one of my friends will use your brokerage house."

"First, you can't cut me off, my money is in a trust grandfather set up even you can't break," Sandy spit back. "Second, if your friends are that bigoted, fine. There are plenty of people out there with a checkbook who don't live by your prejudices and class distinctions." He turned and walked out of the room.

Furious, Sanford II yelled, "You won't last a year without my connections and when you're ostracized from your family, friends and our society, we'll see how long it will be before your little tramp divorces you and takes you for every penny she can get." The front door slammed shut.

Impulsively, Sandy took a street car downtown to Tiffany and bought Dot the largest diamond ring the store had to offer. He was going to ask Dot to marry him that night.

It was a beautiful summer evening as they dined al fresco on the Champagne Porch, the Plaza Hotel's outdoor café. Sandy had calmed down, but he was still set on marrying Dot. The sun had set when he opened the jewel box and took her hand in his and proposed. Looking into his eyes, Dot realized that she did love him. Not the youthful, naive way she had loved Sidney with all of that relationship's ups and downs, but with a steady, mature love. He made her feel safe. She said yes. When she asked when she would meet his parents, he told her the truth, that he had cut ties with his family and that their wedding should be a private affair with only her family and friends. When she pressed him about how he would feel separated from his family, he convinced her that his love for her was all that mattered.

Dot couldn't believe how happy she was, but when Dot told her parents who she was marrying, they were furious. Ruth collapsed into tears.

"You're pregnant?" she cried. "I knew it. Living on your own you're *so sophisticated* you can sleep with a gentile?"

"I'm not pregnant."

"Then why're you marrying him?" asked Ezra, his voice raising. "You think being with him you're better than us?"

"Of course not. I love him."

"You don't know what love is," Ezra yelled. "If you did you'd never betray your family! Look at your mother—look at her," he continued at the top of his lungs, "You're making her sick. We will never accept this."

"She's making herself sick! And I'm not betraying you," Dot said, holding back angry tears.

"You are," her mother said. "You think he's better than Sarah's Joel?"

"Of course not..."

"Why are you doing this?" Ruth pleaded. "Find a nice Jewish man..."

"I did, Mom!" Dot said. "He was married and lied to me for years and years that he'd leave his wife, and I believed him…this nice Jewish man…but all he wanted from me was sex!"

Ruth cried even louder.

"It was Sandy, a good, loving Christian man who helped me pick up the pieces of my life," Dot continued. "Not some nice Jewish boy."

"We know who his parents are and they're never going to let you into their rarified world," her father bellowed, ignoring everything his daughter had just confessed. "They will never accept you!"

"Well, it seems you have a lot in common with them, don't you," she shot back.

After that night, Dot's parents turned their backs on her. Even her sister Sarah who had married Joel Shlisky, a nice Jewish doctor, abandoned her. Joel was nice, Dot thought, but not because he was Jewish. Like Sandy, he was just a good man, and religion had nothing to do with it. Joel tried to bring Sarah around, but she wouldn't budge. Dot was hurt that her parents and Sarah could be so closed-minded and cut her out of their lives, but that didn't change her mind. She was going to marry him, with or without their approval.

A month later, Dot married Sandy at City Hall with a girl-friend from Macy's and Sandy's best friend and roommate from college as their witnesses. An enterprising reporter for one of the New York tabloids discovered they had applied for a marriage license and showed up at City Hall with a photographer. The picture of the newlyweds as they left the building was plastered on the front page of the tabloid, "Jewish Shop Girl Marries Gentile Millionaire." The press was relentless. They interviewed Sandy's friends, employees, and partners. They accosted his mother on the street for a comment and followed Dot everywhere taking pictures. They even invaded Macy's, flashbulbs flashing, as they tried to take pictures of Dot at work. And when

Sanford II showed up at the store waving a fifty thousand dollar check in the middle of the tie department, calling out her name, demanding she take the check and divorce his son, the powers that be at Macy's let her go. She was devastated. Her career meant everything to her. She loved what she did and it allowed her to be self-sufficient and independent. She didn't want to be totally reliant on Sandy, but now she'd be forced to.

Dot had moved into Sandy's beautiful Fifth Avenue apartment not far from his parents' mansion and one afternoon as she was coming home, Gloria accosted her on the street, screaming she was a whore and should move back to Brooklyn where her "kind" belonged. After that incident, Sandy and Dot decided to leave the city and go to Europe, hoping that when they returned, the furor would be over. They were right. By the time they returned, the press had moved on to another scandal. Dot settled into married life and redecorated the apartment. Slowly, some of Sandy's friends other than his college roommate came around and Dot began to give small dinner parties for them and business friends of Sandy's. A few years after their elopement, the tabloids and society pages were writing about her as one of New York society's premier hostesses, but since she hadn't become pregnant, Dot yearned to go back to work.

After discussing it with Sandy, she decided to go see Aaron Hirsch, her old boss at Macy's, now the overseer of every department in the store. She hadn't a clue how she'd be received. The door to his office was open. He was sitting behind his desk talking on the phone. She knocked tentatively and he waved her in. She sat on a chair facing Aaron's desk.

"OK, OK, don't disappoint me. I expect delivery tomorrow," he said into the phone. "Gotta go. Tomorrow!"

Aaron hung up the phone and looked directly at Dot. "Well, if it ain't High Society herself perched right here in front of me. What can this ol' working stiff do for you?" he said, then gave her a big smile.

"You can give me my job back," She smiled back.

"What, Mr. Wall Street not providing for you?"

She laughed. "You know me, Aaron, I'm just not cut out to eat bon bons all day and party all night, it goes against my rag picking, retailing, Jewish roots," she answered. "Besides, you need me."

"I need you?" Aaron asked in mock astonishment. "Now why would I need the great Dot Pierce nee Kimmel?"

"Ladies' hats. I just walked through the department and there wasn't a single hat I wanted to buy. That's not good, Aaron. If I don't want to buy your hats, my friends won't want to buy your hats."

"I should fire Harry, the buyer?"

"No, of course not, but I'm sure you'll figure a way to transfer him and make him think he's getting a big promotion."

"You're sure, are you?"

"I'm sure," Dot answered with a smile. She knew by the amusement in his eyes, she was getting the job.

"Should I give him a raise while I'm at it?"

"Couldn't hurt."

"Say I hire you. There's going to be press you know?"

"This time I think it'll be press you'll relish."

"I think you're right," he said, then winked. "Be here 7:00 a.m. a week from today and you better sell a lot of hats."

Dot bolted up and headed for the door and was almost out of the office.

"By the way," Aaron said. "I missed you."

"I missed you, too," she said not looking back as she walked out of the office.

When she left the store, Dot practically danced on the sidewalk as she headed home. She knew Sandy would be happy for her. *She* was happy for her!

Dot and Sandy were married for fifteen years when he was diagnosed with cancer. He died within the year, leaving Dot his entire estate, making her one of the wealthiest women in the country with substantial shares in Sandy's brokerage company. Sandy's parents did not attend his funeral. Neither did Dot's.

She remained at Macy's and lost herself in her work, withdrawing from her friends. She stopped entertaining, ate lunch in the store and dinner at home…except on Thursday…that was the day she would put on her best white gloves and take herself to Schrafft's for the breaded veal cutlet with tomato sauce special. Once Prohibition was overturned, Dot again ordered two Manhattans with her meal.

On one of those Thursday nights, years after Sandy died, she met Sy Levy with his flashing brown eyes and his salt and pepper hair elegantly coiffed to show off his widow's peak. He wined her and dined her. Paid attention to her. Listened to her. Made love to her. Asked her to marry him, then stole a good deal of her money and disappeared.

CHAPTER 9

ASHLEY — 1968

Ashley stifled a gasp when she heard Sy's description. "It seemed I always fell for men whose first names began with 'S,'" Dot said, as Ashley tried to put all the pieces together mentally.

Vi interjected. "I think we should stop here, Dot, and let you get some rest."

Dot seemed willing to continue, but her eyes looked relieved. She thanked me for coming and made me promise I'd come back soon to hear the rest of her story. I promised, as I bent down to give her a kiss good bye. Vi gave her a hug then left the room with me. Lynne had come in her own car and was going to stay a little longer.

While driving back to the city in the Continental, we talked about Dot's story, but I had a question. It may not mean anything, but it was something that was bugging me.

"OK, you were Monday night. Fritzie was Tuesday night. Lynne was Friday night and Dot Thursday. Who was Wednesday? Is there a Wednesday Schrafft's lady?"

"Yes."

"Will I be able to meet her, too?"

"No, dear, she was murdered in 1936." Vi turned away from me and gazed out the window.

"You can't just leave me hanging, Vi," I said after a few minutes. "Who was she and did her murder have anything to do with her eating at Schrafft's?"

"She was Fanny Friedman, dear, Dot's best friend. After their falling out Dot lost touch and had no idea Fanny was eating alone at Schrafft's on Wednesdays until after she died and MJ told us."

"Did they find the person who did it?"

"No, the police called it a suicide."

The way Vi emphasized *police*, I had to ask, "but you know she was murdered?"

"Yes."

Though I kept asking questions as we headed into the city, Vi refused to talk further about it, again promising me that I would learn it all in good time.

It was almost seven o'clock when we reached Manhattan so Vi dropped me off in front of my apartment building before heading to Sniffen Court. When I opened the front door to my studio apartment it was almost completely dark. Only the lights from the street below kept it from being pitch black. My first thought was that the light bulb in the lamp on my desk must have burned out, as I always left it on when I went out. I went into my galley kitchen and switched on the ceiling light and walked into the little alcove where my bed was and turned on my night table lamp. I let out a mini scream when I saw the drawers to my dresser empty on my bed, their contents scattered all over the floor. The doors to my closet were open and my clothes had been piled on top of my only easy chair. I looked around my tiny one room apartment, my heart beating rapidly.

The door to my bathroom was open and, though I knew better, I cautiously walked over to it and flipped on the light switch. I debated with myself as I stared at the pretty Liberty print shower curtain I had made and prayed that no one was hiding behind it with a butcher knife ready to stab me a billion times. Trembling, I held my breath and yanked it back. No one. Relief flooded my entire body as my legs gave way and I slid to the bathroom floor. I was still terrified and felt totally violated. I held back my tears and called Marty.

"Don't give in to your impulse to straighten up," he cautioned. "I'll report it to your precinct and they'll send someone right over. I'll be there as soon as I can."

Within a half-hour, Vince Fariello, a uniformed cop from my local precinct was at my door. After I let him in and he checked out my apartment which took all of thirty seconds, maybe less, he asked me to go through my things to see what was missing. I didn't own much expensive jewelry, but what I did have was gone. My 14K gold studs and gold hoop earrings were gone. So were the graduated pearl necklace my grandmother had left me, a gold bangle, and my gold charm bracelet filled with charms my parents and others had bought me over the years.

Marty arrived and the tears I was holding at bay flooded my eyes. He comforted me as he tried to remain professional. Finally, he put his arms around me and I cried, but only for a moment. I pulled myself together. I was more angry now than frightened.

Marty looked at Vince. "How'd they get in?" he asked.

"Probably with a key. The door doesn't seem to be picked or jimmied and since she's on the eighth floor and has no fire escapes, I doubt anyone came in through the windows."

"Does the super have a key?" Marty asked me.

"Yes, but Marty, he and his wife are really good people. They would never do anything like this."

He asked what was missing and I filled him in.

"If you can describe the charm bracelet, that might help," Vince said.

"It was a large, chunky link, fourteen karat gold bracelet with charms my parents had given me, including a gold cross when I was confirmed, a paint palette for when I took art lessons, a gold toe shoe I got during my dancing school days and a megaphone."

I looked at Marty. "It was the one you bought me when we were dating in high school and you played against Boys High in Madison Square Garden for the city basketball championship and I was kicking and cheering you on as co-captain of cheerleaders." I knew I was rambling.

"I remember," he said softly and tenderly kissed me on the cheek.

As Vince took notes, he asked me if anyone besides me and the super had keys to my apartment.

"Only my old roommate. When she lost her job, she gave up our old apartment and slept on my couch for a few weeks until she found a new one."

"She never gave you back your keys?"

"No. She only lives six blocks away, and I thought it would be a good idea to let a friend have a set of my keys, just in case."

"How do you know her?"

"She was at Skidmore with me. I didn't know her well then, but when I moved into the city, I knew she was already living here. I didn't know anyone, so I gave her a call. She was looking for a roommate, I needed a place to live, so I moved into her one bedroom apartment."

"How long did you live together?"

"Only about a year, then I found this place and, since the rent was cheaper than the half I was paying her, I took it."

"What's her name?" Marty asked.

"Why?"

"So Vince can have someone ask her a few questions, that's why."

"She's a bit of a flake, Marty, Skidmore aside, but I don't think she'd steal from me."

"You're probably right, but humor me."

"Eileen Gillingwater."

As Vince wrote all that down, he said he would check up on Eileen. When he finished, he showed his notes to Marty and me to make sure he had all the items listed correctly, then left.

"Have you eaten?" Marty kindly asked.

"No."

"Come on, get your bag, I'll buy you a burger at Clarke's."

I didn't want Marty to stay over, but I didn't want to be alone in my apartment, either, so I agreed. I'd transcribe my notes on Dot later.

The restaurant was jammed, so after Marty gave the maître d' his name, we decided to grab two stools and wait at the bar. We'd been silent walking the long two blocks to the tavern and I still didn't want to talk. I think I was in shock as my hands began to shake. What if the burglar had still been in my apartment when I had returned home? What if he'd had a knife or gun? I needed a martini! I held onto Marty's hand like it was a lifeline. Though I hadn't seen him since our night at Arthur and I had been barely civil to him when he'd call, I was grateful that he was here for me now.

"We need to talk," he said as the bartender put my martini in front of me and gave Marty a draft beer.

I let go of his hand. I needed both of mine to lift the glass steadily. I took a huge sip. "I don't want to talk about the break-in. I'm freaked out and pissed and upset and a million other feelings I can't describe."

"Not about the break-in. About us."

"What about us?"

"I know how your mind works, Ashley. You think I'm dirty or doing something underhanded. I'm not."

"And I'm just supposed to take your word for it?"

"Well, yes. It would be nice to know that the woman I'm involved with trusts me."

"I want to trust you, but I can't think of a single legal reason why you can afford outrageously expensive clothes and expensive dinners at places like Arthur. We grew up together. I know your parents. They're middle-class at best. You make a detective's salary which is a nice living, but not that nice. Look at the watch you're wearing, for God's sake. It's a Cartier tank! No way you can afford that and I doubt the mayor paid for it."

"No, I bought it, but he did pick up the tab at Arthur."

"Why?"

"Because he has me checking up on some things there. You can't write about this, Ashley, but you know that there are private lockers there, right?"

"No."

"Well, there are. They're there so that rich people like Ari Onassis can keep their expensive, private scotch or cognac or whatever there."

"So?"

"Well, I know you'll be shocked! Shocked, I tell you!" he said, trying to lighten the mood. "But it seems there may be illegal whatevers in one of those lockers. I've been asked to find out if that's true and who owns that locker."

My martini was gone and I indicated to the bartender to make me another one as I chewed an olive.

"OK, I get it. You did say you were working, so I gather you've made friends with the bouncers and bartenders and they think you're a rich playboy or something, right."

"Or something. They know I'm a cop but, like you, they think I'm dirty. I've been there quite a few times with various undercover female cops on my arm throwing money around and playing a role."

"That doesn't explain your clothes and that watch."

132

"No it doesn't. My own money bought it all. Money I inherited two years ago."

"Inherited from whom? Your family can't afford expensive Brooks Brothers blazers and Cartier watches."

"No, but a great, great uncle in Germany could. When he died, the German Embassy tracked me down and told me that I was his heir. He had no wife, no children and no living relatives except my mother and her sister. He was old school. I was the only male Gerber left in his family so he left everything to me, and let's just say he didn't die insolvent."

"Who was this rich great, great uncle anyway?"

"I have no idea and neither did my mother. His name was Kurt Gerber, my mother's maiden name. That's all we really know. But my inheritance is legit, though I don't know if my uncle was."

My second martini arrived as we were told our table was ready. Marty finished the last of his beer and carried my drink to the table. We both ordered burgers and decided to share a spinach salad. I popped another olive in my mouth.

"What are the odds of having an unknown rich uncle leaving you a lot of money? About the same as winning a jackpot in Las Vegas?"

"Probably. But it happened. And people do win bundles in Vegas."

"Not people we know."

"Ashley, why can't you believe me?"

"I'm a pessimist."

Marty reached across the table and took my hands in his, then kissed them.

"Good things do happen, sweetheart. They do. Call my mom, she'll tell you. She had to find my birth certificate and sign documents for the German government attesting that I was her son. She knows it's true."

I could feel tears welling up again as the tension in my body slowly slipped away. I felt relief. I believed him. Our burgers arrived.

Marty went home with me that night and we've been together most nights ever since. Vince called and told me that there seemed to be no link to my break-in with Eileen or anyone else. No other break-ins were reported in my building or neighboring buildings. When I asked him what else the police were doing, he answered "not much" unless they get lucky and the jewelry shows up at a crime scene or in the possession of someone they arrest for another crime.

"Sometimes, if a pawn shop owner suspects an item is stolen, he'll call us, but frankly, Ashley, there's really nothing special or unusual about your jewelry that would wave a red flag," he said. "I'll keep checking for you, though."

I thanked him for all he was trying to do, but after I hung up I began to dwell on pawnshops. Since my jewelry wasn't all that valuable and, like Vince mentioned, "nothing special"— well, except to me—what would a thief do with it? My guess, pawn it. So, as I once again waited to hear from Vi, I thought, hmmm, a serious column on buying jewelry at pawnshops because of the misfortunes of others might be an interesting piece for the lifestyle section. Why do people pawn jewelry and heirlooms? I pitched it to Dwyre who agreed.

Vi finally called. Dot had passed away and she felt I should know.

"I think Dot would have liked it if you came to say goodbye. She was sorry she never got to finish her story, but talking to you and knowing Lynne and I will tell you the rest of it helped ease her conscience. The memorial's Thursday at five o'clock at Riverside Memorial Chapel on West 76th."

"I'll be there," I whispered, a lump forming in my throat.

I hung up the phone and cried. How ironic that her memorial service was to be on Thursday, her regular night at Schrafft's. And ease her conscience? What was that all about? All I knew was *my* conscience wasn't eased at all. I had promised Dot that I would go see her again and I didn't. Why didn't I? I knew where she was! I knew she wanted to tell me more! I felt terrible!

When I told Marty a little about my Schrafft's ladies and how upset I was that I hadn't gone to see Dot before she died, he made it a point to come with me to the memorial. I didn't tell him about the story they were confiding to me or my promise never to reveal it until they all had died, but I did tell him how I met Vi and the others because of my Andy Warhol article.

The viewing room was filled. The lighting was low. At the far end of the room, dark drapes hung behind the casket which was covered in a blanket of white flowers. Vi and Lynne stood nearby, greeting many of the mourners as they filed by. Dot was only seventy-six, so many of her friends, some older, others younger were still alive. I saw MJ sitting on a bridge chair against a wall talking to an elderly man. There were two empty chairs by her so I sat next to her. I introduced her to Marty. When Vi was able to break away and join us, I asked her if Dot's sister, Sarah, had come. She hadn't. They had never reconciled.

I listened to the eulogies and learned that Dot had been an advocate for single working women and their healthcare. She seemed loved by her friends and I wondered why, when she was only forty-five, she was such easy prey for Sy Levy. I also wondered why all my Schrafft's ladies fell for men who stole from them. I realized that a single woman in her forties in the Depression era 1930's was considered old, but it still puzzled me.

After the funeral Vi asked me to dinner the next night. She and Lynne wanted to finish sharing Dot's story.

To make my day go faster, I decided to drop in on a pawnshop near the paper at lunch time to research my next article. Though the local newscast had predicted showers, the sky was blue and the temperature was a brisk, but not cold, fifty degrees. Traffic was at a standstill, but, then, when was it not? I zigzagged across the street in the middle of the block and made my way to the pawnshop. I peered in the window that seemed to be showcasing a display of classical composer marble busts and an ornate "Erte-style" bronze lamp, but no one seemed to be inside. The front door was locked, so I rang the bell. An invisible person buzzed me in.

The shop was big and had two long, waist-high, glass display counters at ninety degree angles filled with jewelry, watches and all sorts of small artifacts. I recognized some Native American beaded bags, tomahawks and pewter gunpowder holders. The walls were covered with guitars, tapestries, paintings, belts with silver and turquoise buckles, even a musket. Sculptures, lamps, antique music boxes and other large knickknacks were displayed on the floor or on tables in front of the store window. I thought the shop would smell musty like most thrift stores or some cramped antique stores because of all the old merchandise, but its smell was clean and fresh.

As I waited, I could hear voices coming from a back room, then familiar music. It stopped, but the chords played over in my head as I continued to look around. Finally, an overly muscular man pushing seventy, with long white hair tied in a ponytail came into the shop from behind a black curtain. He was dressed in a white button-down shirt with the sleeves rolled up, baggy, black flannel trousers and a slew of love beads hanging from his neck.

"Sorry, couldn't miss the ending of *Search*," he said.

"*Search*?" I asked.

"*Search for Tomorrow*," he answered. "Got a little TV in the back. Usually close up shop when it's on. I'm addicted."

"Oh, wow." I smiled. "I knew that music was familiar. My mom watches that soap."

He nodded knowingly. "What'cha got?"

At first I didn't know what he was asking, then realized he thought I was there to pawn something. Reasonable assumption. I introduced myself and told him that I was doing an article on pawnshops and, if he was the owner, I would like to interview him. He said he was and told me his name was Gus Gronroos, but that he didn't want to be interviewed. He looked at me with weary, "I've heard everything" blue eyes as he listened to my spontaneous, embellished sob story about having to prove myself to my editor. I'm sure he didn't believe a word of it, but he relented anyway. Not my greatest feminist moment.

I pulled out my trusty reporter's notebook as I looked over the fine jewelry and watches and got their prices which were significantly less than in a jewelry store, but expensive enough for Mr. Gronroos to make a very nice profit. I spotted a pair of Tiffany platinum wedding rings in the original robin's egg blue box and wondered who would sell them? Were they rings a son or daughter had inherited and didn't want to keep? Were they sadly pawned by a widow who needed money to buy food? If he knew, Mr. Gronroos refused to tell me, no matter how much I tried to coax it out of him.

"Basically, I'm in the loan business and like any loan officer at a bank, I maintain my customers' privacy," he explained. "I negotiate with them…how much the loan and interest will be based on the merchandise they're pawning. If they agree, they leave the merchandise with me as collateral. I give them a time frame to repay the loan, if they don't, I'm free to sell the item in my shop."

"How long do you hold the merchandise before you offer it for sale?" I asked.

"About two weeks."

"And that's a law for all pawnshop owners?"

"No. Some owners hold stuff for ten days, others less, others longer. It's all pretty arbitrary. Hell, if I'm in a bleeding heart frame of mind, I've been known to hold an item for three weeks before putting it out for sale."

"What about stolen items? How do you check everything that comes in to make sure they're not stolen?"

His eyes took on an "ah, this is really what this is all about" look. "So, you're not just another pretty little liar, huh? You digging up dirt on pawnshop owners?"

Embarrassed, I could feel my face turn red. "No, honest, really," I answered. "I was just robbed and sort of have a personal interest in what may be happening to my stuff."

"What'd they steal?"

I filled him in on the robbery of my jewelry and how the police told me there was little they could do unless the jewelry surfaced and they were notified.

"And you think whoever stole it was stupid enough to pawn it?"

"I don't know. Maybe. My jewelry isn't worth all that much. I think the thief might have just wanted to make quick cash."

"Well, to answer your original question, it's a pain in the ass for us in the business to evaluate whether something is stolen. Impossible really. All we got to go on is our gut. Mostly we just refuse to loan money to someone if we think the merchandise is hot. Sometimes we do our civic duty and just buy it, then call the police to see if anyone reported it stolen," he explained. "We're not a bunch of shysters."

"Oh, no…no, I never thought that," I sputtered. "In fact, I never thought anything. That's why I wanted to talk to you."

I realized the chances were slim and none that my bracelet or pearls would show up in a pawn shop and the owner would think they were stolen and call the police, but I'm an optimistic pessimist, so hope lingered.

Mr. Gronroos and I chatted a bit more then I thanked him for being so helpful. I just had one more question before I left.

"You filled me in on all the different types of people who come here and sell their stuff, but what kind of people actually shop here?" I asked.

"All kinds. Kids like you looking for cheap. Subway guitarists thinking they'll find Les Paul's Gibson. Guys looking for flashy engagement rings to impress their girlfriends. Young couples looking for antique wedding rings or just plain gold bands. All types of people looking for bargains. Last winter I had a woman in here shopping for Christmas presents who showed up in a stretch limo, wearing a mink coat down to her ankles. She bought over two thousand bucks worth of stuff."

We laughed. I thanked Mr. Gronroos again, shook his hand and left to go back to the paper to typed up my notes and work on a rough draft of my story until it was time to go to Vi's.

As I came out of the subway station in Murray Hill at Park and 33rd, the skies opened up. This was not the time for the weathermen to be right. I had no umbrella! I ran up Park holding my purse over my head to keep my hair dry, a futile effort as I dodged in and out of doorways and under apartment entrance canopies. I turned down 36th Street and headed to Sniffen Court and almost crashed into a rat the size of a bulldog scurrying across the sidewalk to get to a sewer opening and out of the rain. Shudder. Even the toniest parts of town have rats as neighbors. Finally, I made it to Vi's. This time her silent butler opened the door and helped me out of my drenched London Fog. I was beginning to think it was time to find a more repellent raincoat. He handed me a towel as he left the entryway, taking my coat to drip somewhere else. I squeezed the rain out of my hair and walked into the living room.

A fire was blazing, so I zoomed in on it like a miserable, cold, wet kitten seeking its heat to get rid of the damp chill. I stepped out of my soggy black leather heels and placed them on the marble hearth to dry out. Lynne, dry as the sherry she was sipping, sat on the sofa. Vi poured a glass and handed it to me. To my surprise, sitting next to Lynne was MJ, also dry as the sherry. Again, there was caviar, sweet butter and toast points on the glass coffee table. I took a sip of sherry and felt its welcomed warmth slide down my throat, then sat down on the yellow and gray striped occasional chair opposite the sofa. Between the fire, sherry and caviar, I was warming up just fine even if my hair was soaked and would frizz from here to Times Square when it dried.

"We were just talking about Thanksgiving and were wondering what you're doing to celebrate," Lynne said, as she buttered a piece of toast and piled on some caviar.

"I usually go home to my parents, but this year they're finally doing a long-saved-for 'grand tour' of Europe and will be in Paris, so I haven't any plans," I answered trying not to talk with my mouth full of caviar.

"Good!" MJ chimed in.

Vi laughed. "What MJ means is 'good' you're available, not 'good' you'll be alone for the holiday," Vi explained. "I'm planning a big black-tie Thanksgiving dinner for a few of my friends in town and would love it if you and Marty would join us."

"When she says a few, she means a few hundred." Lynne laughed.

"Well, not quite that many," Vi smiled, then continued. "The Deputy Mayor and his wife are coming. I'm sure Marty knows them. Also, some journalists and magazine editors I'd like you to meet."

I didn't know what to say. This seemed a bit out of my league.

Sensing my hesitancy, Vi continued, "It'll be fun, Ashley. I promise. Lynne and MJ are coming. I'm tenting up the courtyard, setting up banquet tables, and all my Court neighbors will be there. I'm even hiring a string quartet. And the food will be magnificent. The chef from Lutece is cooking."

"Let me talk to Marty and see…"

"And don't you worry about Marty," Vi interrupted. "He's a Cornell boy. He'll love it."

I smiled. She obviously had a longer conversation with Marty at Dot's funeral than I'd realized. "I don't know if he's free, but I promise I'll be there," then thought, what the hell does one wear to a black-tie Thanksgiving dinner?

We continued to talk about the party till dinner and I wondered if the ladies were ever going to get around to the rest of Dot's story. Finally, Vi's butler motioned us into the dining room and the four of us gathered around the table. A white wine had already been poured into our wine glasses. Vi lifted hers, "To Dot."

We did the same. "To Dot."

As a hot carrot soup was served, Vi began. "It really all started when Dot's friend, Fanny, died and MJ saw a picture in the newspaper."

CHAPTER 10

1938

It was January, 1938 when the front pages of the New York papers reported the story that the widow of prominent New York State assemblyman, Ira Levitt, was found dead by her housekeeper, hanging from a beam in her eastside co-op. The safe in her bedroom was open and empty of any contents. The police's initial statement called the death "suspicious." Though on the surface it appeared to be suicide, Patrick O'Conner, the lead homicide detective, felt the need to investigate. The story went on to tell that after a career as a high-powered defense attorney, Ira had run for state senate in 1928 and won handily. He died of heart disease in his second term and his wife, the former Fanny Friedman, was appointed by the governor to fulfill his term. She became a popular politician in her district because she was instrumental in getting extra funding for healthcare. But, when she finished Ira's term in 1936, the party refused to back her run for his seat. They wanted a male candidate and they were concerned that because she was female *and* Jewish, the political atmosphere pervading Europe and parts of America would lead to her defeat. Nazi Bund rallies were becoming commonplace in New York and throughout the country. Nothing was left for her in Albany, so she moved back to their Fifth Avenue apartment.

A week later, the papers reported that Fanny's death was declared a suicide after all, even though no note was found. It was discovered during the investigation that her bank accounts had also recently been depleted of all cash. Her stock certificates, however, were still safely locked in her safe deposit box. Fanny's investment banker told Detective O'Conner that her savings account had been closed by a man named Morton Katz.

"Mr. Katz just showed up early one morning waving a power-of-attorney signed by Fanny. I was suspicious, of course. Fanny had never mentioned him to me before, so I tried calling her a couple of times while Mr. Katz nervously paced my office, but she never answered. Now I know why. According to newspaper accounts, I realized his appearance here was the morning *after* Fanny died," the banker said sorrowfully, then continued. "Mr. Katz insisted that Fanny instructed him to close her accounts. Not knowing she was dead, my hands were tied. But when he demanded that I open her safe deposit box, I refused. He didn't have a key, nor did the power-of-attorney say anything about access to her safe deposit box. There was nothing more he could do, so he left the bank with all her cash in his brief case. I had no legal authority to stop him. When I read that the police said Fanny had committed suicide, I was more than just suspicious and wanted to call them immediately, but the president of the bank said no. We hadn't done anything wrong, so he wanted to avoid the bank getting involved in a society scandal."

"Well, the bank's involved now," O'Conner said.

"Yes, it is."

Further investigation by O'Conner revealed that nothing was left but her stocks, which were still of some considerable value, and her expensive co-op which might be difficult to sell in the continuing depressed real estate market. Her son David, and daughter Myra, wanted the investigation pursued. Who was this Morton Katz? Where is he? Where did all their mother's cash go? Detective O'Conner was at a dead end in his search for Morton Katz, but appeared adamant that Fanny committed suicide.

"You know women," O'Conner said, then continued as if he were reading from a prepared text. "Perhaps your mother eventually found her finances too taxing and, therefore, needed a power-of-attorney to pay creditors from her bad investments and the bills she accrued by buying expensive clothes and jewelry which are all still in her bedroom." He even implied that she might have been depressed because her children abandoned her after their father had died.

David was incensed at the detective's insinuations and said so, and tried to explain that their mother was far from a frivolous woman. "She was a serious state senator, for God's sake, and wouldn't piss away a fortune," he practically yelled, his anger growing. "And, this Katz guy? He just happens to clean out her bank accounts the day *after* she dies, then falls into an abyss?! Really? That doesn't rankle your detective's brain?"

Furious that O'Conner refused to even consider the possibility of foul play, both children tried pleading with him to at least continue looking for Morton Katz. Myra tried flattery, telling the detective how smart she thought he was by initially believing that her mother's death needed to be investigated and that she thought his suspicion was correct. She had no idea that he secretly agreed. Myra believed everything she said fell on deaf ears. She and her brother argued that Morton Katz should at least be a suspect in what they were sure was their mother's murder. "Our mother was very savvy about money. That kind of cash just doesn't disappear."

"Perhaps she just gave it to Mr. Katz," O'Conner shot back, frustrated that they just wouldn't drop it. "You know how women are with money."

"Are you fucking kidding me," David yelled. "Do you know what kind of money we're talking about here?"

"*You people* are all alike," the detective snapped. "Money, money, money."

Enraged, David lunged forward, but Myra grabbed his arm, stopping him from assaulting a police officer.

"Come on David, either someone bribed this man, or he's an anti-Semite," she said quietly.

O'Conner faced turned beet red as he stood very still. "The case is closed. Get the hell out of here."

After making a few phone calls, David learned from a friend who was a New York City ADA that it was someone in the police commissioner's office who forced O'Conner to shut down his investigation. His friend told him that O'Conner had, in fact, argued with his superiors that Fanny was murdered and that the police should keep the case open, but was accused of being a "Jew lover" and that if he valued his career, he'd stop the investigation. His friend didn't give David the name of the person who ordered the shutdown, but when David asked why it was ordered at all, he was told that that "someone" had problems with the Levitts, their position in society, their wealth, and refused to spend police resources on "uppity Jews" who were better off dead. David's friend also said he learned that this "someone" had a specific beef with Ira stemming from Ira's days as a defense attorney. David had faced anti-Semitism before and let it slide, but this time he was angry. He told his friend that he was going to the papers and tell them what he just learned.

"We're talking about the murder of my mother!" he screamed.

"I'm sorry, I really am," his friend said, "but let it go, David. Let it go."

From the tone in his friend's voice, he realized he was giving David a real warning. Morton Katz had walked away with almost a quarter of a million dollars and probably murdered his mother to do so and there was nothing he could do. In the political climate of the day, he would find no allies.

While all this was still front page news, one enterprising tabloid had even scored some recent photos found by a police reporter in a desk drawer in Fanny's library showing her looking lovingly at an unidentified man at what appeared to be a social gathering in a banquet room. Another photo showed them dancing. No mention of where the pictures were taken, but both parties seemed unaware they were being photographed. MJ recognized the man as a one-time Schrafft's semi-regular and remembered he had dined with Vi one night a year or two ago. She remembered him because Vi had never dined with anyone before (or since) and seemed to really enjoy herself that evening. MJ even thought she caught Vi flirting a little. It was then that Vi stopped coming to the restaurant. When she finally returned a few months later for her Monday night special and two perfect Rob Roys she told MJ that a large amount of her money had been stolen by a man she had recently been involved with. MJ couldn't believe anyone would prey on someone as lovely as Vi. She decided to save the paper and show it to Vi the next time she came in to see if this was the man who had stolen her money.

Vi knew him immediately. It was her George Roman. Because MJ knew that Fritzie was also bilked out of a good deal of money, she showed her the picture on Tuesday, Fritzie's regular night. It was her Ransom Fiske. MJ followed through with Dot and Lynne because each woman had confided in her a similar tale. They each confirmed that the man in the picture was the same man who stole from them. MJ felt she had to do something, so the following week as each woman came in on their regular night, MJ told them she knew of other women who had been conned by the same man and she thought it was time they all met. Fritzie volunteered that they meet at her home on Beekman Place on Sunday afternoon, MJ's day off.

All the women arrived promptly at Fritzie's and MJ made the introductions. They gathered in the cozy, dark walnut paneled library with floor-to-ceiling bookcases filled with hundreds of books, photos and Chinese blue and white vases and ginger jars. A fire was aglow in the marble fireplace. As they sat down on the tufted, maroon leather sofa and matching club chairs, the talk centered on Fanny, but soon the questions were flying, prompting MJ to take the lead in the conversation.

"I honestly had no idea that the man I recognized in the picture from his time in Schrafft's was the man who had bilked you," she told them. "All I remembered was that, for a few months he was one of my regular customers. I don't ever remember him sitting with any of you other than Vi. He usually ate dinner alone, but every now and then had a male dinner companion. He never talked to me other than to give me his order."

"What made you suspicious when you saw the newspaper pictures?" Dot asked.

"His widow's peak. I didn't put it together when each of you told me how you were betrayed. I just remembered how happy you had been when you found love again and how hurt you were afterward. But seeing his picture with Fanny, one of my Wednesday night regulars, made me remember your descriptions of the man who stole from you. Not even when each of you gave me his description did I put it together with the man who ate at my station when he came in or that you all had described the same man."

"Do you know his name?" Vi asked.

"I've been trying to remember, but no. He always paid in cash. And, like I said, he never chatted with me about anything. Not even about the weather."

"Do any of his dinner companions ever come to Schrafft's? Maybe they know his real name," Lynne interjected.

"If they do, I haven't recognized them. Sorry. But, after seeing those photographs in the newspaper, everything you ladies told me came rushing back. Fanny was so happy the last time I saw her, but like you, when she started dating the new man in her life she stopped coming to Schrafft's for dinner. Because I was as happy for her as I had been for you, I didn't see a pattern. What happened to all of you never crossed my mind. But I don't believe in coincidences. And I just knew it wasn't a coincidence that after being connected to the same man Fanny's money disappeared and she killed herself."

"She didn't kill herself. I know she didn't," Dot exclaimed.

"How do you know that?" Fritzie asked. "You said you hadn't seen her in years."

"I just do!" Dot was adamant. "We may not have reconciled but my parents kept me up to date with her life and I always read any articles about her or her husband. I watched her campaign for him and saw what she did in Albany. She was a warrior. The strongest woman I'll ever know and losing love and all her money to a con man would never break her. It would only make her angry. She would not kill herself!"

The other women remained silent.

"I don't care what the police think," Dot continued, "Fanny was a strong and positive woman and had friends and family who would have stood by her and help her financially if needed. And, unlike me, she was too bright to fall for any con."

"But she did," Lynne said sympathetically.

"Or maybe she didn't and that's why she was murdered. Either way, we have to find him and confront him," Dot proclaimed.

"Maybe we should go to the police or her children and tell them what we know," Fritzie said.

"No. The police won't believe us," Dot said. "They'll look at us as lonely old biddies who want attention. And I don't want to tell her children until we find out who he really is, confront him and get the truth out of him."

Lynne looked uncomfortable as she sat listening to the other women.

"Dot, do you think he murdered her?" Vi asked.

"Hell, yes!" she answered.

"I think it's a real possibility," MJ chimed in. "And I'll keep an eye out for him at the restaurant."

"If we can't go to the police, should we hire a private detective?" Fritzie asked.

"Maybe as a last resort," Lynne finally chimed in. "Personally, I'd rather keep this among ourselves. Let's see if we can be our own detectives."

They all agreed.

It was then that they confided their stories to one another.

Vi went first, recounting how she and George met. Tony, the love of her life, had been dead for seven years and for all intents and purposes so was Vi. She was alone and lonely. She realized being alone was her choice, but being with friends seemed only to add to her loneliness. Her work was no longer fulfilling and, though her friends tried to revive her, they couldn't. She had lost Tony twice and was filled with regret. If she hadn't kowtowed to her parents she would have had all those lost years with him. After four years, she no longer wallowed in self-pity, but she had no idea how to restart her life. Her only reprieve from her loneliness was her dinners at Schrafft's. It was the one night she looked forward to. Not just because it was the place where she and Tony had found each other again, but because she enjoyed talking with MJ when MJ had a free moment between waiting tables.

New York was having an Indian summer in the fall of 1936. Vi arrived that Monday evening at 5:30 and sat at her same small table for two that MJ had reserved for her. She'd methodically put her purse on the extra chair and peeled off her white gloves and neatly laid them on the table. Within minutes MJ brought her a perfect Rob Roy that she would linger over, sipping it slowly as she gazed at the people in the restaurant. She never had to look at a menu, of course, as MJ always knew she had the pan-browned lamb hash with wax beans, and would time it so that it would be served to her along with a second Rob Roy just as she finished her first drink. For the past six years, Vi's Monday night routine never varied until that Monday in early October when George Roman walked into her life carrying a Rob Roy.

"Do you mind if I join you?" he asked, startling her, as she hadn't seen him approach. "I see you're alone and my dinner companion seems to have stood me up. I really don't feel like dining alone tonight."

Vi recognized him as someone she'd recently noticed having dinner at Schrafft's with a man who appeared to be a business colleague. He was handsome, in his late forties, early fifties with a widow's peak of salt and pepper hair and warm brown eyes, but Vi did not want company. As she was trying to come up with a way to shoo him off, he continued. "I promise, I'm not Jack the Ripper, and I'm a decent conversationalist."

Vi laughed. He seemed pleasant, maybe even charming. She nodded and removed her purse from the second chair and put it on the floor beside her.

He sat down and placed his drink on the table.

"I see you're drinking a Rob Roy," she said.

He smiled. "As are you."

"It's always been my cocktail of choice. The bartender here makes a perfect, perfect Rob Roy." She said and held out her hand across the table, "I'm Vi Wilding."

He shook it. "And, I'm George Roman."

MJ appeared and asked Vi if she should hold her dinner until the gentleman left.

"No please don't do that on my account," George said. "What are you having?"

"What she always has on Monday night, the lamb," MJ said a bit annoyed that this man seemed to be intruding on Vi's space.

"Sounds perfect. To go with our perfect Rob Roys. I'll have the same," he said to MJ, then turned to Vi and lifted his glass. "Shall we have a second?"

She smiled, "Of course."

During dinner, George told her he was widowed and had recently moved to New York from Chicago where he was a banker in the loan department till the crash. He was living in the Waldorf-Astoria temporarily. When Vi told him that she, too, had been in banking, they swapped banking war stories, laughing at the peccadilloes of some of their co-workers. Vi was actually having fun. He was charming and entertaining, but then the conversation turned serious. Like Vi, it seemed he hadn't been hurt too badly financially when the market collapsed but, after refusing to shut the doors on companies which couldn't make the payments on their loans or foreclosing on people's homes, he was fired. He decided to travel and see how the rest of the country had fared. He wanted to meet and talk to the people most affected, so he sometimes rode in box cars and stayed in hobo camps. He described the devastation made by the dust bowl that, coupled with the collapse of the economy, made life almost unbearable for so many Americans. He saw them on the roads traveling west to California and Oregon looking for food and work and decided to come to New York and find a way to help. He had to do something so he started a non-profit to keep small businesses from going under and keep people in those businesses employed.

Vi was impressed with his passion and enjoyed his company, so when he asked her out to dinner on Saturday at the Waldorf-Astoria, she accepted. She went home that night realizing that, for the first time since Tony died, she had a reason to smile. She wanted to know more about George and about his charitable foundation. She wanted to help.

"That was my first mistake," Vi told the women sitting around her.

"My story is almost identical," Fritzie chimed in. "Ransom certainly knew how to get to me with that whole charitable foundation thing. But in my case, it was health clinics for migrant workers and their children. No matter what name he was using, he seemed to have done his research on the two of us."

"So it seems," Vi continued. "George and I met often that first week to discuss his foundation. Always dinner at the Waldorf. But as our dinners became more personal, they turned into dates. We went to the movies. We picnicked in Central Park. And, after a while, I practically moved into his hotel suite. Yes, he became my lover. One evening he ordered dinner in the room and over vichyssoise, he went down on his knee and proposed. He opened up a little velvet ring box where, perched inside, was an antique diamond ring in rose gold that he said had been his mother's. I dropped my vichyssoise spoon as he put the ring on my finger and told me that I didn't have to give him an answer right away, but he wanted me to wear the ring while I thought it over. It was a little too large, so he asked for it back so he could get it sized for my finger."

"Oh, my God, I feel we were actors in the same play," Fritzie exclaimed.

"It was at lunch in my home, two days later that I gave George a check for one hundred thousand dollars for his foundation and said yes to his marriage proposal," Vi went on. "He seemed overjoyed. Little did I realize what his joy was really about. We made plans for dinner later that evening and he left around one-thirty to deposit the check in the bank and do some foundation business. I never saw him again."

MJ whistled. "Wow. That's a lot of money. What did you think happened?"

"I didn't know. I waited hours for him to pick me up for dinner. Then I began to panic, thinking he was hurt or dead somewhere. I tried his room at the hotel a few times, but no answer. When I hadn't heard from him by noon the next day, I didn't know what else to do so I started calling hospitals, but no one by his name or description had been admitted. Then I began calling police stations. I got copies of every newspaper, looking for reports of accidents or murders of an unidentified male that might be George. Nothing. Finally, after a few days, I had sense enough to go over to the Waldorf. The desk clerk recognized me and after a little persuasion, he told me George had checked out on the same day he disappeared."

"Did you stop payment on the check?" Dot asked.

"It was far too late. My account showed it had been cashed the day I gave it to him."

"Did you go to the police?" MJ asked.

"Yes. But they were very patronizing. Implying that I was the one at fault. That I had been a silly woman who fell prey to a larcenous man."

"That's about what they said to me, too," Fritzie said. "They took my statement and told me that unless I could find the man, there wasn't anything they could do."

Lynne, who had been fidgeting with her hands the whole time Vi was telling her tale, stopped and looked directly at Fritzie. "And what happened to you?" she asked.

"It's almost identical to what happened to Vi," Fritzie said, "though the reason MJ never saw me with him was because we met in Schrafft's front entrance. Probably didn't want any of the staff seeing him with me after joining Vi at her table when he set his sights on her. From what I can figure out, he wooed all of us in the same year."

"It seems so," Dot injected.

"I remember I had three old-fashioneds with dinner that night," Fritzie said. "Something I never did, but I was feeling sorry for myself and was trying to prolong my meal so I wouldn't have to go home to that enormous empty house on Beekman Place."

"I also remember that night because you seemed a little wobbly and I had never seen you like that before," MJ said. "I was going to walk you outside and get you a cab when a customer needed my attention."

"Yes, I was a little shakey, but I didn't think I needed any help. When I got to the front entrance a man bumped into me, or I him, and I almost fell to the ground. He caught me and introduced himself as Ransom Fiske and offered to drive me home because his car and driver were just outside."

"You went with him?" Lynne asked, who was still fidgeting with her hands.

"I hesitated, of course, but I wasn't thinking clearly and I thought what could go wrong since he had a driver who would witness everything."

"Unless he was an accomplice. You're a wealthy woman. They could have kidnapped you for a healthy ransom," Lynne injected.

Dot, Fritzie, Vi and MJ laughed.

"What?" Lynne wanted to know.

Still laughing, Vi chimed in. "Ah, irony. I think Ransom had another plan to get that ransom, Lynne."

Lynne blushed, something she never did, then laughed, too. "Of course."

"So, you got into the car," Dot pressed on.

"Yes. Ransom guided me into the back seat then climbed in after me. He asked for my address and told the driver to take us there. As he drove me home, he told me that he was widowed and had moved to New York from Boston to raise money for health clinics for poor families he wanted to open in cities around the country. But, unlike George, Ransom was living at the Hotel Astor until he could find a more permanent home."

"And, you told him about your history of fundraising for New York hospitals?" MJ asked.

"I might have mentioned it," Fritzie said with a wry smile. "By this time, we were in front of my townhouse and as I was about to get out, Ransom asked if he could take me to dinner at the Astor. He wanted to ask me questions about my New York fundraising experience. I accepted, and the following night I found myself being wined and dined at The Hunt Room in the hotel. He was charming and a great listener. We talked about my husband. He said he knew Ben's work and claimed he actually owned one of his paintings. He couldn't wait to show me which one after he found a place to call home and his belongings arrived from Boston. He didn't say much about himself, not his background, not even if he had children. Nothing. Just that he was a widow. He seemed totally focused on wanting to give good healthcare to the poor and I found that endearing. He made me feel special and important as he eased the conversation to the clinics. He asked intelligent questions about how I dealt with the hospitals when I gave them the money I raised, who my lawyers and accountants were and, after a couple of dinners, he asked me if I would help him organize his first New York fundraiser."

"Ah, yes, the irresistible question," Vi said.

"Yes. I, of course, couldn't say no. We met often, either at my home or at his hotel and one thing led to another and we, too, became lovers. I was happy for the first time in years. I was working on a project I believed in and I had fallen in love. Like you, Vi, he proposed and gave me a beautiful solitaire diamond ring that he had to take back because it was slightly too big and needed sizing. I couldn't say yes fast enough. We talked about having a small wedding right after the fundraiser as a sort of celebration. We were having a light lunch at my home when I wrote him a check for one hundred thousand dollars to be used as start-up money and legal fees to set up the clinic's non-profit foundation and open offices. I even scheduled a meeting for us with my business advisors the next morning, but he never showed. I was stunned. I rushed home thinking Ransom misunderstood and thought the meeting was at my place and was patiently waiting for me outside my front door, but he wasn't there. Like Vi, I thought he was dead or hurt somewhere. The first thing I did when I got inside my house was call the Astor. When I gave them his room number, a woman answered the phone. I asked to speak to Ransom, but she had no idea who I was talking about. In shock, I hung up the phone. A few minutes later I called the hotel again but this time I just asked to speak to Ransom Fiske. It was then I learned that he had checked out of the Astor the morning before…before I even gave him the check, and left no forwarding address. How cocky was that, I ask you?"

The women knew that was a rhetorical question and didn't answer.

"When I realized what a fool I'd been, I called my banker to stop payment, but like Vi, I was too late.

"He certainly knew how to get to us," Dot said bitterly. "He was clever in how he met us and ingratiated himself into our hearts. I first met him on the street right outside Schrafft's. I remember I was all dressed up in a beige summer linen suit. It was a warm night, so I didn't put on a hat, and I had shoved my white gloves into my clutch. I saw him step out of a chauffeur driven car as I walked up the street to the entrance. He was standing there seemingly perplexed."

"How so?" Vi asked.

"Like he didn't know if this was where he was supposed to be. He smiled and tipped his hat, then excused himself for bothering me, but he wanted to know if this was the only Schrafft's in the city. I didn't recognize him and had no idea he was a regular diner at MJ's station, so I smiled and explained to him that it wasn't and asked if I could be of help. He told me he had been sitting in his car waiting for an old college friend to meet him for dinner, but since he hadn't shown up yet, he thought maybe he got the wrong restaurant. We chatted a moment and I told him the locations of other Schrafft's I knew. He thanked me, got into his car and left."

"He just left?" Fritzie asked.

"Yes. Here's the clever part. The next day, as I was overseeing work on a display at Macy's, whom do I bump into but this same man! He went on about what a coincidence it was to run into someone twice in two days. He introduced himself as Sy Levy and told me he just moved to New York from Miami, didn't really know anybody yet, other than former business colleagues and would I have coffee with him."

"And, of course, you said yes," Vi said.

"Of course. He was well dressed, handsome and seemed very nice."

"The worst sons of bitches always start out the nicest," Vi chimed in.

"It had been a very long time since anyone invited me for coffee," Dot continued. "Not that I would have welcomed it. I had become pretty much a recluse outside of Macy's, but here I was, ready to go off with a complete stranger."

"Maybe that's why you said yes. He wasn't part of your life and didn't remind you of anything sad. He was new, so you were new," Fritzie stated.

"You might be right."

"So, what happened after you had coffee? What bullshit story did he invent for you to gain your trust?" Lynne asked, still fidgeting with her hands.

"Over coffee he told me he had been in retailing in Miami…"

"How coincidental!" Lynne interrupted. "He seemed to know everything about all of you before he even met you."

"He certainly did," Vi said. "He studied us before picking us."

"Yes," Dot continued. "He certainly knew me. He told me he had two department stores, though he never mentioned their names and I never asked. He said he sold them after his wife died since he had no children to leave them to and took himself off to visit family in Germany. But the climate there was very hostile to Jews and he tried to convince them to leave and come to America. But they just didn't see it and refused. When he landed in New York, he decided he didn't want to go back to Miami. He wanted a fresh start and since he was familiar with New York and had some acquaintances here from his retailing days, he decided to stay. But those acquaintances were still working so he filled his days going to museums and checking out the stores. Before I left him to go back to work, he invited me to dinner at the Plaza where he was staying till he found a new home. Things progressed from there and we started meeting for dinner almost every night. Eventually, he became my lover."

"No story about starting a charity or a foundation?" Vi asked.

"No, not at first. But as we got closer, he talked more about what was going on in Germany. He became alarmed by cables and letters he received from friends in Europe and wanted to set up a Jewish refugee foundation if things got worse."

"Did you see any of these cable and letters?" Lynne asked.

"Of course not," Dot answered.

"I can't believe he used what's going on in Germany to bilk you out of money. I read about Kristallnacht. How does he live with himself?" Lynne angrily exclaimed.

"Good question. It was after we were deep into our relationship, or so I thought, that Sy told me how he was trying to get his family out of Berlin, but the State Department wasn't being helpful. That's when he asked me to donate. He wanted to raise money and put it safely into a foundation to be used when Jews would finally leave Germany. I have family in Germany and, after talking it over with a few friends, I decided to help. He said he had already raised half a million dollars, but needed at least a quarter million more before he left for Washington to argue his case with the State Department and, perhaps, grease some palms."

"And you wrote him a check," Fritzie said.

"Yes, for one hundred thousand dollars."

"And you never saw him again?" Vi asked.

"No, he disappeared right after he cashed my check. And I didn't even get an engagement ring," Dot said wryly.

"Neither did I," Lynne whispered. "And we never became lovers."

"Well, you didn't miss a thing," Dot said emphatically.

The other women's eyes widened, then they burst out laughing.

"You were lucky," Fritzie said after they finally calmed down. "Your heart wasn't broken."

"No, my heart wasn't. But it was shame and fear I had to face so I don't know how lucky I was."

"What scam charity did he use to get your money?" Vi asked.

"None. He successfully blackmailed me."

"Blackmailed!" Dot exclaimed.

"Yes. My karma."

"Karma? What's karma?" MJ asked.

"When life comes back and bites you in your bottom for past sins. I learned about karma some years ago after a visit to Ojai, California where I met Krishnamurti. I had no religious or philosophical beliefs, but I became fascinated with him after attending one of his lectures. When I got back to New York, I read everything he wrote."

"Did you read other theosophists like Annie Besant, Charles Leadbeater?" Vi asked. "I discovered them some years ago."

"Yes, and immersed myself in various Indian philosophies. I enjoy learning about other people's cultures and beliefs."

"What sin could you have possibly committed that makes you think you deserved to be blackmailed?" MJ asked.

"I hurt my family very deeply as well as the boy I was engaged to."

Fritzie could see that Lynne was struggling to hold back her emotions. "I think it's time for a little break before Lynne tells us her story," she said.

The room fell into an awkward silence which was broken when Fritzie rang a little bell and a maid came out carrying a silver tray with a pot of tea, a silver sugar and creamer set and a beautiful floral porcelain plate of scones. She placed it on a nearby dark walnut console.

"Ladies, please help yourselves."

They each rose and poured themselves tea in china cups nestled in saucers that were laid out on the console next to the tray, selected a scone and a pink linen napkin and returned to their seats.

"I think you need to tell us what happened, Lynne," Vi said encouragingly.

"I've never told anyone this. Not even my benefactor, Alice Holmes. And certainly not my daughter, Spring."

"It's time," Vi continued.

"My name isn't really Lynne Davis," Lynne began. "I was born Pauline Lynne Demarist on a struggling potato farm way out on the North Fork of Long Island. When I was seventeen, soon after I graduated high school, I purposely wooed Silas Vanetsky, the son of the owner of the local general store. We became engaged and I used his love, raging hormones, and male vanity to run away to Manhattan. I had it all planned. To finance my getaway, I stole money from my parents that they had kept for emergencies in a coffee tin in the pantry, and the day I left the farm for the last time I jumped into my fiancé's car and didn't even bother to look back. Silas thought we were eloping to Huntington and he finally was going to get me in bed."

"You married him?" Dot asked.

"Yes, I did. And, I was on a deadline. To kill time after our civil ceremony, I begged Silas to give me a tour of all the mansions in the town before going to the hotel. I had my escape planned to the minute. When the time was right, I teased him in the car by placing my hand seductively on his thigh which I knew would arouse him. When he parked the car, I kissed him passionately. By now he was so excited, he never questioned me when I shyly suggested he check out our room first to make sure it would be a nice setting for our 'first time.'"

"Did you at least sleep with the poor guy?" Dot laughed.

"No!" Lynne snapped, then sipped her tea as they slipped into another awkward silence. Lynne continued to sip her tea.

"I'm sorry," Dot finally said to Lynne. "I didn't mean to make you feel uncomfortable."

"We're not going to judge you, Lynne," Fritzie assured her. "You can confide in us."

Lynne hesitated for a moment, but looking closely at the faces of these women, all betrayed by the man they thought loved them, she somehow felt safe that they would keep her secrets.

"As soon as Silas went off to make sure I'd feel comfortable in the room, I sneaked away and hopped a train to the city," she continued. "I met Alice on the train and introduced myself as Lynne Davis. I made up a sad tale of being a homeless new widow on the way to New York to look for work. Alice was a wealthy socialite living alone, and took pity on me. She took me in, became my mentor, benefactor, second mother and grandmother to my daughter, yet I never told her the truth. My daughter still doesn't know the truth."

"That was a long, long time ago, Lynne. You were young and suffocating," Dot chimed in. "You must have missed your family."

"No, not even a little. Though we all lived and worked on the farm together, we weren't a warm, loving family. My mother was born in Sweden and as cold as the country she came from. Everything about my parents was dark and drab. There was never any joy in our house and I wanted to be part of the world I read about in the books. I wanted to travel. When my parents refused to let me take a scholarship to college, I began to hate them. And, I was selfish. I didn't care what happened to them. They had my dreary brothers to look after them, so I stole their money and ran away."

"You became a wealthy woman. Did you ever give the money back?" MJ asked.

"Yes, I am wealthy, thanks to Alice who left me her estate, but before and after, I always worked. After a couple of years in New York and I could afford it on my own, I secretly retained a lawyer who had legal contacts in Philadelphia. He set up an account in a Philadelphia bank where a check could be drawn and sent to my parents. I made sure they knew the checks were from me, but according to the bank, they never made an effort to find me. Which was fine with me. That's why I chose a Philadelphia bank and not one in New York. I wanted them to think that's where I'd run off to."

"And you wanted them to know you were alive and doing well," MJ injected.

"Maybe so. I know I wanted them to know it was me paying back what I stole. After I did that, I sent them fifty dollars a month until the bank was informed they were both dead. Since my brothers still worked the farm, I started sending the money to them."

"Not even your brothers tried to find you?" Vi asked.

"No. They just cashed the checks."

"Are you still sending them money?" Vi continued.

"Yes, but one passed away, so it's just to my surviving brother, now."

"Well, it seems you've made amends," Dot said. "I still don't get why you allowed yourself to be blackmailed."

"Shame. I never want my daughter to know how selfish and cruel I was."

"She won't hear it from us," Fritzie said adamantly. "We've all done things we're ashamed of. Tell us how you met our mutual con man and how he blackmailed you."

"It's more like he met me. He saw me in Schrafft's while he was staking out the restaurant for lonely women and recognized me."

"From where?" Vi asked.

"From the North Fork. As he told it, he 'cleverly' followed me home, then waited outside for two mornings till I came out, then he followed me to Childs where I still worked part time. When he sat down at my station to order lunch he introduced himself as Hayes Walker. I knew he wasn't Hayes anybody, but didn't let on. After he finished his meal, he paid his bill and left. He came into Childs a few more times when he finally asked me out for dinner."

"And you went," Dot said.

"Yes. I was curious and wanted to know what he was up to and why he was lying about who he was. He said he was staying at the St. Regis and picked a small little French restaurant near the hotel but, when he offered to pick me up after work, I told him I would meet him there. I didn't want my co-workers to think I was going out with a customer. He started his con much the way he did with all of you. He spun a tale of how he had just moved to the city, this time from Los Angeles, and was living in the hotel until he found an apartment. He said he was widowed with no children and went on about his wife who had died of ovarian cancer."

"Oh, dear Lord," Dot whispered.

"Exactly. I didn't say much, wondering to myself where this was all leading. Did he not recognize me? What was he doing? Did he really have a dead wife?"

"But you knew who he was right off the bat," Vi said.

"Yes. It was his hair. It had receded into a widow's peak, just like his father's."

"Who was he?" MJ asked.

"Silas Vanetsky, the boy I humiliated when I ran away."

"Oh, dear Lord!" Dot exclaimed, no longer in a whisper.

"What did you do?" Fritzie asked.

"Nothing. I became even more curious about where this was going, so I led him on. Asked questions about his life in Los Angeles claiming I'd never been there, but, of course, I had. It soon became obvious that he was the one who actually had never been to Los Angeles. I acted like a school girl wanting to know about her favorite movie stars and Hollywood, so I breathlessly asked him to tell me everything…if he ever saw or met any movie stars like Bogie or Bette Davis…and if he'd ever gone to the newly famous Chasen's which had just opened a few months before he supposedly moved to New York. I'd been in L.A. that January right after the restaurant's opening and had dinner there with friends. Everyone was talking about it and it was being glamorized in all the society pages and movie magazines. I went on and on about how people like Kate Hepburn and Cary Grant were eating there and, instead of couching his Los Angeles lies with a truth by saying he hadn't been able to get there before moving to New York, his ego tripped him up. It was just like when we were kids and he wanted to show me all the rich estates and homes in Huntington. As if knowing where they were and who lived in them rubbed off on him somehow. So there he was describing a restaurant he'd never been in, a meal he'd never eaten and movie star diners he never saw."

"When did he finally catch on that you knew who he was?" Vi asked.

"Not for two more dinner dates. I admit I let him think he was seducing me just like I had all those years ago. But, I needed to follow through and find out what his game was. Did he really not know who I was or was this a twisted game to get even with me?"

"You sat through two more dinners?" Vi continued.

"I did. One at that same little French restaurant. The last in his hotel suite where I knew he was going in for the coup de grace, as it were. That last dinner was when I finally couldn't take it anymore."

Lynne got up and poured herself another cup of tea. No one said a word until she sat down again. She took a bite of her scone and sipped her tea.

"OK, now's not the time for tea and crumpets. What happened?" Fritzie asked.

"Yes, don't keep us hanging," Dot said.

"He slid into his real purpose as easily as shifting gears in a car. I actually was giving him the benefit of the doubt thinking that he was living this fantasy existence to start his life over and that he had no idea who I was. Hell, I did the same thing. But then his con started. He caressed my hand as he started his pitch. I can't remember if he was talking about needing investors for a hospital or disease research or a museum, I just knew it was a con and he was trying to seduce me so he could bilk me out of money. I actually started to laugh and almost spit red wine in his face."

"That must have gone over well," MJ laughed.

"Oh, yeh," Lynne answered wryly. "That's the thing with narcissists, they think they're smarter and cleverer than everyone else and they get really, really angry when they feel they've been taken for a fool. And he certainly wasn't going to let me do that twice to him. If I hadn't known who he was, he most likely would have won me over, too. He was a practiced liar and he was charming, if you didn't know he was a liar. He made you feel that he really listened to you. He was attentive and good looking, but when he realized I wasn't falling for him or his story, he turned on a dime."

"What did he do? You were trapped in his room," Vi said.

"At first he didn't know if I knew who he was and I still wasn't sure if he knew who I was, but I found out soon enough. He glared at me as I laughed, then smiled. I could see on his face the recognition that he knew I was on to him and it all became clear.

"'You've always known it was me, haven't you?' he demanded. I nodded and he told me he knew who I was the minute he saw me in Schrafft's…and when he found out I was wealthy, he planned to humiliate me and steal my money. But, now that he couldn't do that, he was just going to ask for my money outright. He wanted me to write him a check for one hundred grand."

"Did you laugh?" MJ asked.

"Not this time. I could tell by his face that he would hurt me if I laughed at him again, so I played along to see what he was planning to do. In the longest hour of my life, I listened to him whine about how I had made him the laughing stock of Long Island forcing him to move away, leaving his father's store and any opportunity he had of inheriting it."

"That's ridiculous," Fritzie stated. "People in your little town might have talked about what you did to him for a week, but the whole of Long Island? Rather self-aggrandizing."

"Very. But Silas' image of himself as a 'ladies' man,' a man no woman could resist, was shattered. He now hated me, but he also hated living in that town and he used his perceived humiliation as his excuse to leave. He wanted the finer things in life just as I did, but really wasn't willing to work for it. His father's store wasn't grand enough for him. I gathered he bummed around a bit in Manhattan before meeting and wooing a wealthy, much older widow from Massachusetts who took him under her wing. He moved to Boston and became her gigolo. He was nineteen and loved it. Not her, but the lifestyle she gave him, and all he had to do was listen to her, flatter her and make love to her. That became his vocation. She took him to the finest stores and bought him a new wardrobe. She taught him about food and wine and what fork to use. She paid for a home for him on Beacon Hill and I gather he lived off her till she died and left him a good deal of her money."

"Did she have children?" Vi asked.

"She did. He either conned or coerced her to put him in her will. Her grown children had put up with Silas for years and they were not going to stand by quietly and let him inherit money they thought he didn't deserve. They sued and eventually settled a tidy sum on him. Here's the ironic part. I really did the same thing to Alice."

"No, Lynne, it wasn't the same thing," Vi said.

"On paper it is."

"So why romance and con women if he got a nice settlement?" Dot asked.

"Because he spent wildly, indulging himself with expensive cars, watches and clothes, extended first class trips to Europe, India and China. He lived like a sultan, so the money was soon gone and he had only one skill to acquire more and that was by charming lonely, older women."

"He admitted that?" Dot asked.

"Not in so many words, but it was the way he bragged about his lifestyle. The people he claimed to know, I read between the lines. As he talked, his contempt for women became more and more apparent. He had no qualms about using them or hurting them. He was proud of how he could just charm them and make love to them and they'd provide for him. He didn't steal from them at first. But as he got older his boyish good looks began to fade and he started conning lonely women his own age or slightly older in a less obvious, sexual way. He studied them and learned all about them then planned how he would meet them and, when he did, he was charming, very attentive and kind."

"Yes, he was," Vi interrupted.

"Then he would find a way into their hearts and pocketbooks. He started in Boston, then lived in Chicago and Detroit for a few years. Also St. Louis, I think, before ending up in New York two years ago."

"Good heavens, how many women did he prey on?" Vi asked.

"Many. He'd con four or five women around the same time in a city, then when he felt he had enough money, he'd go back to Europe or move to a new city and live off what he'd stolen. But eventually the money would be spent because he had no self-control and he'd have to start all over again."

"And he told you all this," Vi continued.

"Yes. You could see it brought him great pleasure to hurt women and he wanted me to know how smart he was. How clever. If a man could preen like a peacock, Silas was preening. He felt no remorse. He knew he should have left me alone. That I was a risk. But he wanted to get even. He learned all he could about Lynne Davis, but he never intended for me to know who he was until after he stole my money and abandoned me. He thought he had physically changed enough. It never occurred to him how much he now looked like his father, a man he never really respected. His plan was to make me fall in love with him and steal my money, as he did with all of you. But since that wasn't going to work out now, he threatened to tell the press how I stole my poor parents' last dollar leaving them penniless and that I bilked society matron, Alice Holmes, out of all her money."

"All that's a lie. Why would the press listen to him?" MJ wanted to know.

"They might not have if it was just about me and what I did to my parents. But Alice, well—she was an important figure in

New York society and reporters would have started to dig into his story. I loved Alice. She was the mother I never had and I never did anything to hurt her, but the world might not have seen it that way when they learned about my real past. If it was just me, I wouldn't have cared, but I had to think of Spring and her future. The next day I wrote him a check for the hundred thousand."

"That's four hundred thousand dollars in total he got from us," Fritzie calculated.

"Maybe more since we don't know how much he stole from Fanny after he killed her," Dot said bitterly.

"Do you think he followed his pattern and left New York to live the high life in another city?" Vi asked Lynne.

"I don't know. He may not be finished here yet. From what he told me, he never conned a sum of money anywhere near a hundred thousand before. If he got that amount from me and from the rest of you, I get the feeling that in his mind New York was to be his last hurrah and that he's building a huge nest egg so that he can retire and continue his high lifestyle for the rest of his life without ever having to worry about money again. Even he understands that he can't count on his looks and charm for much longer."

"You really think that?" MJ asked.

"It's a real possibility," Lynne answered. "I think he's arrogant enough to think he won't be caught and greedy enough to try for a least a million dollars. I don't think he's smart enough to take the money he's already stolen and leave town while he can."

"How are we going to find out?" Vi asked.

"He found you in Schrafft's, approached me in Childs. Maybe he's still in the middle of conning other wealthy women he met in restaurants before leaving town."

"Well, how do we find him, Lynne?" Dot demanded. "I don't care about me, but he has to pay for what he did to Fanny."

"And pay he will," Lynne said, her face set in stone. "And I have an idea how to start."

# CHAPTER 11

ASHLEY — 1968

My reporter's notebook was filled and I was about to drag another one out of my purse, when Vi called a halt to the evening.

"On that note, I think we'll call it a night. The rain has stopped and there's a cab waiting outside to take you all home," Vi said.

"But, Lynne, what was your idea? How were you going to make him pay? You can't leave me hanging!!!" I almost cried.

"You've learned a lot about us tonight, Ashley. Be patient," Lynne said as she and MJ walked to the foyer where Vi's butler awaited to help them with their coats. I slipped on my still damp shoes I'd left by the fireplace and followed. When he finished helping Lynne and MJ, he held up my London Fog and I shivered as I slid my arms into my cold and soggy raincoat.

As the taxi drove us to our homes, I tried getting Lynne to continue her story, but no luck. She was exhausted and didn't want to talk about it anymore. Instead, she talked about Vi's Thanksgiving party and how much she was looking forward to it and that she hoped I would be there.

The cab dropped me off at my apartment building and when I entered the lobby, I saw Marty sitting on the couch. He smiled when he saw me.

"Hi. How long have you been here?" I asked as I gave him a kiss.

"Not long. I got off duty early and thought we could walk over to Clarke's and get a late supper. I have some news."

"Thanks, Sweetie, but I've already eaten, but what news?"

"You're soaked," he said as he noticed my drenched coat.

"Nothing gets by you, detective." I smiled.

"It hasn't rained in a couple of hours. Where were you?"

"Why the third degree?"

"No third degree," he laughed. "Just making conversation with my girlfriend and curious as to how she spent her night."

We headed toward the elevator.

"I'm sorry, doll. I got caught in the downpour on the way to Vi's. She says 'hi,' by the way."

"You had dinner at Vi's?"

"Yes. Lynne and MJ came, too. It was fun."

The elevator came, we got in and it began its slow climb to the eighth floor.

"And, we've been invited to her Thanksgiving soiree."

"A soiree?" Marty asked with a smile. "I've never been to a soiree."

"Well, that's what I called it. Not Vi."

I was about to fill him in on all the details when the elevator bounced a couple of times and stopped between floors.

"Oh, great. Not again. I'm too cranky and clammy for this right now."

I impatiently pushed the screeching alarm button three or four times waking the dead along with everyone in my building. Though what I hoped to accomplish by doing that, I had no idea. Patrick, the doorman on duty, was a hair's breath away from his one hundredth birthday. John, the handyman, had gone home hours ago, and I had no faith that Ralph, our live-in super, could fix the elevator. I was hoping that at least he had the number of a twenty-four hour repair service.

"Are you all right?" I heard echoing up from below. It was Patrick's voice.

"No! I'm stuck in…"

"We're fine, Patrick," Marty said, cutting me off. "How long till someone can get this thing running?"

"I have no idea. I'll get Ralph to call the maintenance people."

"Great, great, great," I sighed. "We're going to be stuck here for hours and I have to pee."

"Hold that thought—and that urge," Marty said laughing.

"It's not funny!"

"Yes, it is."

Then he jumped up onto the brass handrail on the back wall of the elevator.

"Help me balance, Ashley."

I hadn't a clue what he was doing, but I braced my hands against his back as he reached up to the elevator ceiling and pushed open a panel.

"We're only about a foot from the seventh floor," he announced as he pulled himself out of the elevator car.

"Oh, my God, Marty!! What are you doing?"

He sat on the car's roof, his legs dangling down right above my head.

"When you gotta go, you gotta go."

"What?! I'm so not going into the elevator shaft. I'll pee right here, first."

"Don't worry, you'll be fine. I'll try and pry open the doors to the seventh floor, then I can lift you up and out of the elevator."

"No way!"

"Do not argue with a man in his 'rescue the damsel in distress' mode."

I held my breath as he pulled his legs out of the elevator car and kneeled on its roof. I watched through the roof opening as he banged and pulled at the seventh floor doors above and was terrified he would lose his balance and fall to his death. After what seemed like hours, Marty finally pried the doors open then sat back down on the elevator roof and dangled his legs into the car again. He leaned into the car and reached his arm down to me.

"Come on, honey. Grab my hand."

"No!"

"Yes! I promise, I won't let you fall."

"What if the elevator jerks or starts or something?"

"It won't."

"How do you know it won't?"

"Because I said it won't. I'm not going to sleep in the elevator tonight and neither are you."

"Yes, I am."

"Ashley, stop it. I know you're afraid, but you have to trust me."

"No, I don't."

"Yes, you do, sweetheart. You'll be fine, I promise."

I really did have to pee, so I put my arm through my shoulder bag and slung it across my back and grabbed Marty's hand. My heart was beating a mile a minute as he began to pull me up. I can't ever remember being that terrified.

"As soon as you can, grab onto the roof and push yourself up as I pull."

I did as I was told and within seconds I was sitting beside him on the roof of the elevator car.

"Don't look down," Marty ordered. "Just look to your left at the open doors and crawl out."

I looked to my left. The opening was right there. Less than a foot away. I placed my palms flatly on the floor outside the opening and slowly got on my knees then wiggled my way out of the elevator shaft. I did not look down. Not once. As soon as I was out and lying on the seventh hallway floor, Marty followed and took me into his arms. I couldn't stop shaking.

"From now on, let's take the stairs," he whispered in my ear.

I punched him in the arm.

He ignored my feeble punch, helped me up and led me to the stairwell so we could walk up the remaining flight to eighth floor. My floor. Home.

"The elevator guy will be here around two," Ralph yelled up. I looked at my watch as I walked up the stairs. It was ten thirty.

"Thanks, Ralph, we're out of the elevator, so put an *out of order* sign on the elevator door till he arrives," Marty yelled down before entering the stairwell. "And come up to the seventh floor and rope off the elevator shaft, too. The doors are open you don't want anyone falling in."

Marty was right behind me when I reached my apartment door.

"If Henry Kissinger still lived in the building, we'd have new elevators," I said petulantly. My hands were still shaking as I tried to get the key into the lock. He took the keys from me and opened the door.

"Kissinger lived here? When?" Marty asked.

"I don't know. When he had an apartment in New York while teaching at Harvard, I was told. I don't think he ever actually lived, lived here."

Inside my apartment, I ran into the bathroom, quickly shed my damp raincoat and peed. When I came out, relieved in more ways than one, I poured myself a shot of vodka.

"Want one?" I said to Marty.

"No thanks."

I tossed the shot back and poured another one.

"I don't do well in life-threatening situations, it seems, especially if it's *my* life," I said, trying to make light of my fear and threw back the second shot of vodka. Then put the vodka back in the freezer. "Didn't you mention that you had some news to tell me before we almost plunged to our deaths?"

Marty guided me over to the couch and pushed me into it, then sat next to me.

"There's been a development in your robbery."

"Wow, really? What?"

"Your charm bracelet got pawned down in the Village."

"Am I getting it back?"

"It's in evidence right now. But you will at some point."

"How did you find out?"

"Luck. The pawnbroker thought the seller was way too skittish and called the police to see if there was a record of it."

"I'm so glad." I said and reached over and hugged him. "You gave me some of those charms."

"I know," Marty said. "But, there's more."

"They found my pearls?"

"No. But, we know who the thief is."

"Why do you look so serious?" I asked. "That's a good thing, right?"

"Yes, but it's a little complicated."

"OK, you're making me nervous. What's wrong?"

"It was your ex-roommate Eileen."

"No way. She'd never do that to me."

"She did, sweetheart. She did. It seems she did more than just steal from you."

"What are you talking about?"

"Before she broke in and stole your jewelry, she stole your birth certificate."

"That's ridiculous!" I jumped up and went over to my dresser and opened the top drawer, nearly knocking over my bottle of Shalimar. I ran my hand under the lining paper where I kept my birth certificate and social security card. The card was still there way in the back of my drawer, but the certificate was gone.

"Why would she want my birth certificate?"

"To take out a loan in your name."

"What? How do you know that?"

"It seems she defaulted on her monthly payments and an arrest warrant was issued in your name. The police went to the paper this morning looking to arrest you, but Dwyre covered for you. He told them you were out of town on assignment and wouldn't be back in the office for a couple of days. He remembered I was a cop and called me."

Stunned, I plopped back down on the couch.

"It was right after his call I got a call from Vince Fariello. You remember, the cop handling your break in?"

"Yes, of course," I said still stunned there was a warrant out for my arrest.

"Well, I met him down at the pawnshop to interview the pawnbroker. When we gave him Eileen's description, he said it matched the woman who pawned your bracelet yesterday morning."

"I can't believe this! How could she get a loan in my name?"

"By using your birth certificate as an ID."

"That's crazy. It wasn't even my real birth certificate. It was a photocopy I got when I registered to vote a couple of years ago. It doesn't have my signature!"

"That's a whole other issue that Vince is going to deal with. The loan company accepted it and gave her a thousand dollar loan back in May and she's never made a single payment.

"They got a warrant for my arrest for missing payments on a thousand dollars?!"

"Yup. After the pawnshop, I asked Vince to come with me to S & R Loans, and did he make a stink! He told them they were guilty of libel by accusing you of defaulting on a loan you never made. He said he was reporting them to the Better Business Bureau for unsavory business tactics by handing out money to people without proper, verifiable identification and was going to encourage you to sue for defamation of character. By the time he was finished with them, they had called the precinct where the warrant was issued and told them it was all a terrible mistake. I think they called their lawyers as soon as we left."

"Now what?"

"Vince got a warrant issued for Eileen's arrest and has most likely taken her into custody already. You're going to have to press charges."

"But there's no proof she stole my birth certificate."

"Not yet, but Vince is also searching her apartment. Even if he doesn't find any more of your jewelry or your birth certificate, I think the pawnbroker and loan officer will identify her."

"How could she do this to me? She's my friend."

"She's not your friend, Ashley. If your boss didn't know I was dating you, you might be in jail right now."

I crawled onto Marty's lap and put my arms around him.

"Thank you."

"You're welcome. Now, is there anything in your fridge to eat? I'm starving."

As soon as I got into the office the next morning, I went to see Dwyre.

"Thanks, boss."

"How the hell did you get into that mess?" he asked.

After I told him, his eyes lit up. "That's crazy. I want you to do a first person story about friendship, betrayal and S & R for your column."

"I don't want to name her."

"You don't have to. Do an investigative piece and find out how the loan company could get away with giving money to just anyone without proper ID. They have branches all over the city. Find out if it's just this branch or a company policy."

"First, I need to find out why she felt she had to steal from me. She was my roommate. I trusted her."

"Fine. If it enhances the piece, include it. Otherwise leave it out."

"OK." I said, then headed toward the door wondering how I was going to bring myself to talk to Eileen.

"By the way, Wilkes," Dwyre said just before I left his office, "forget your column. I want this to be your first assignment for the City section."

Surprised, I didn't know what to say or where I would start, so I just nodded.

"You'll do fine," he said, sensing my insecurity. "Close the door behind you, the noise is getting to me."

I nodded again and left. I think I closed the door, but I was so shocked, I wasn't sure.

Back at my desk, I just stared at my typewriter, still numb from last night's events and now being given my first real reporting assignment. I was filled with doubt. This wasn't a story about what happened to some stranger. It was about me. *I* was the story. That went against everything I'd ever learned in journalism courses. The reporter is never the story. It's fine for a column, but not straight news.

I needed to talk to Vince Fariello. I called his precinct. He was out on patrol so I left a message. I found the city's yellow pages and looked up S & R Loans. There were five branches in Manhattan alone and a whole bunch in the other boroughs. I decided to start with a branch on Madison and 42nd Street, which was not the one that gave the loan to Eileen.

The S & R office was on the twelfth floor of a pre-war office building with gargoyles at the roofline of the building's facade. When I got off the elevator, the reception area was filled with a few people reading out-of-date magazines sitting on worn, mid-century naugahyde and chrome chairs that surrounded a cheap teak coffee table. In front of a glass wall, a young receptionist with too much make-up and an overly teased and hair-sprayed flip was typing at a large matching teak desk. Behind the wall I could see a middle-aged female operator plugging in calls and pulling out plugs on her switchboard. I strode confidently to the receptionist and waited for her to acknowledge me.

"Can I help you?" she asked, as she glanced up at me while her fingers continued to pound away at the keys.

"Yes, please. I'm here to get a loan."

"Your name?"

"Monique Wilkes," I said automatically, though why my cousin's name popped into my head I have no idea.

"Fine, take a seat. Someone will be out to get you in a while," she said as she yawned and added my name to what appeared to be a list of names on a yellow legal pad. The top names were crossed off, but four names were above mine, presumably matching the four people sitting in the reception area.

I took a seat on one of the naugahyde chairs and started leafing through a three-month-old *Glamour* magazine from the coffee table. It was forty-five minutes before an elderly woman dressed in a drab, inexpensive charcoal gray suit called my name and ushered me into a small cubicle where a middle-aged man in a brown suit, white drip dry shirt and paisley tie sat behind a metal desk. The nameplate on his desk read Bob Bennett. He stood and reached out his hand.

"Hi, Monique, I'm Bob Bennett." He indicated that I should sit on the straight back chair facing his desk.

"Nice to meet you," I said as I shook his hand and sat down.

"Well, it's nice to meet you, too, Monique. Now what can I do you for?"

His phony conviviality instantly annoyed me. I tried to summon up whatever acting skills I had and come up with a plausible story if he asked me why I needed money.

"I need to borrow some money," I blurted out with no such plausible back story in mind.

180

"You know a bank charges less interest than we do. Have you tried to get a loan from one of them?"

"Yes. I don't have any…what do they call it?" trying to sound completely clueless.

"Collateral?"

"Yes, collateral. That's it," I answered. "I don't own anything, so I have none. Collateral, I mean."

"And how much do you need to borrow?"

"Twelve hundred dollars."

"That's a lot of money, Monique. May I ask why you need so much?"

Keep to the truth as much as possible became my mantra.

"Uh, hospital bills. I, um, had a case of vertigo last year and between the ER costs, the doctors' bills and all the tests I had to have to find out what was wrong with me, the bills just piled up. I have no medical insurance and can't possibly pay all this on my salary," I told him. This really happened to me last year, but thankfully, I did have medical insurance through the paper.

"I tried sending them twenty-five dollars a month," I continued. "But I've been getting all sorts of dunning notices threatening me. It's just overwhelming."

"I understand," he said as he put on a sympathetic face. He lowered his voice. "Monique, I hope they found nothing serious."

"No, thank goodness, but I really want to pay the hospital back. They were so thorough and treated me so well and went out of their way to make sure I would be all right," I added, like spooning sugar into coffee.

"That's very commendable, Monique. Let's see what we can do. We'll start with your filling out one of these loan applications, okay?" He pushed the application across the desk and handed me a pen.

This was where it was going to get tricky. For occupation, I was going to write down that I was a legal secretary and make up the name of some law firm, but thought better of it. Law firms and lawyers may make him cautious if he wanted to do anything unethical. The *Glamour* magazine I was just reading popped into my head, so I wrote down that I was a receptionist at Glamour and made up a phone number and an address on Lexington. I made up a social security number hoping that no real person had it and a phony home address. Signed it and pushed it back over to him.

"Great. Now all I need now Monique is a driver's license or some sort of identification."

"I don't drive."

"A credit card or voter's registration is fine."

"I don't have any of those, either. I have my birth certificate at home. Will that do? I can bring that in."

"No, Monique, I'm afraid not. I need something with your signature or picture on it, so I can verify you are who you say you are."

"But I don't have anything like that. I've never needed it before."

"Then, I'm sorry, Monique. We can't give you a loan without it," he said as he looked me straight in the eye.

"Please, Bob. I don't know what I'm going to do. Those dunning letters are scaring me."

"I'm sorry," he said as he handed me my application. "If you get some kind of identification that has your signature or picture, please come back and bring this with you. But right now there's nothing we can do." He stood up, indicating it was time for me to leave.

As I rode down the elevator, I was relieved that Bob wouldn't give me a loan, but even more relieved he gave me back my application. If he was at all suspicious, I didn't want him checking up on me as I planned to hit a few more loan offices to make sure the one that loaned Eileen the money was the only one that wasn't on the up and up.

When I got back to the paper there was a message for me from Vince Fariello. I called him back and he told me that they found my birth certificate in Eileen's apartment but no more of my jewelry and no pawn tickets. The pearls were probably lost to me forever since they looked like millions of similar necklaces. Same was true for my other stolen gold jewelry except my charm bracelet.

"Is she in jail?" I asked him.

"No. The judge released her on her own recognizance and set a trial date."

"So, she's home?"

"Unless she fled the country, I would imagine so."

"Does her office know she was arrested?" I asked, feeling guilty about all this, though I know this wasn't my fault.

"I don't know."

"If she was so desperate for money, how is she going to afford a lawyer?"

"Don't worry about that. The court appointed a public defender. He's the one who got her out of jail. The theft is a minor offense compared to stealing your identity and using it to perpetrate a fraud by taking out that loan."

We talked a bit more and I thanked him for all the help he gave me regarding the robbery and the mess with S & R. When I hung up, I called Eileen at home. No answer. I tried her office, but was told she wasn't in. I suspected she was avoiding my call.

It was close to 5:00, so I decided to go over to Eileen's apartment, since it was just a few blocks away, and wait till she got home. It was cold, but as I stood vigil across the street, I didn't feel anything. I was that upset and angry. A half hour later, Eileen walked up to her building with her long, straight blonde Mia Farrow hair pushed back off her face by a wide head band. I ran across the street, darting through the traffic.

"Eileen!" I yelled.

Her building didn't have a doorman. When she saw me she quickly turned away and started rummaging through her purse looking for her keys. I reached her before she could find them.

"We have to talk," I said, stating the obvious.

"Why?"

"Why? Because I think I deserve an explanation. Don't you?"

"Hey, you're the one who had me arrested," she spat out defiantly, as she glared at me with her big blue eyes.

"Whoa! Are you fucking kidding me? I had no idea the petty thief who ransacked my apartment, stole my jewelry violating my home and scared me to death was a friend. I won't even go into the birth certificate fiasco. The police actually showed up at the paper to arrest me! To arrest *me*!" I yelled. "What the hell's wrong with you?"

As she continued to glare in defiance, her eyes began to fill with tears.

"Eileen, talk to me!"

She pulled her keys from her purse, unlocked the door and held it open for me to enter. I followed her up the stairs to her fifth floor walk-up. Inside, it looked like a hurricane had blasted through, no doubt the result of the police search. She began to straighten up a bit, making a place for us to sit. She grabbed a bottle of white wine from the fridge and poured two glasses, offering one to me.

"It's a good thing I live in a studio. Not that much to clean up," she said as she sat down on the over-stuffed easy chair we had found together on the street when she moved here. She'd had the chair reupholstered in a pretty pale pink velvet. I hadn't been to her apartment in a long time and, as I sipped my wine and looked around, I saw a lot of new and expensive furniture. I was sitting on a new, rich rose-colored brocade couch I'd seen in W. & J. Sloane, the up-scale furniture store on Fifth Avenue but my eyes nearly popped out of my head when I saw a full-length raccoon fur coat and a fitch fur coat lying rumpled on her bed. There's no way she could afford any of her new furniture, never mind two fur coats.

"I never meant to steal from you, Ashley," she said, the words catching in her throat. "I just got in a bit of a bind at Bonwit's for clothes I charged and needed some money to make a payment."

"Eileen, you work in PR and make, what, a hundred and twenty-five dollars a week? How can you afford a fur coat, much less two!!! And half this furniture in your apartment belongs on Beekman Place!"

"I know. I just can't stop buying what I want."

"But why would any store let you buy any of this? This couch alone costs as much as that fitch!"

"They thought I made a lot more money than sixty five hundred a year."

"Why?"

I sat in awe as I listened to her explain how she did it. As she was learning the PR business and writing press releases for Atkins & Beldock, the small firm she worked for, she also answered the phones. She was the office assistant/apprentice. So when she applied for credit cards at all the expensive department stores in the city, she used different names for each application and always stated her place of employment as Atkins & Beldock with a yearly salary of eighteen thousand dollars or more. A lot for a woman in business, especially someone in her twenties, but when the stores called to verify the employment of each alias, it was Eileen who answered the phone and she'd pretend to transfer the call to a non-existent "personnel" director. She'd get back on the line, disguise her voice, give yet another false name as she introduced herself as the personnel director, then did the verification. It gave me a headache just thinking about all the hoops she jumped through to keep it all straight.

"Okay, you used the thousand dollars from the loan for Bonwit's, why did you steal all my jewelry? My grandmother gave me those pearls when I was confirmed. You knew what that necklace meant to me. And my charm bracelet!"

"I needed more money. Collection agency goons began harassing me at the office. I'd tell them that so and so didn't work there anymore, but they knew I did and debts in my own name were also high. I couldn't let my bosses find out." She pulled out a desk drawer and showed me about fifty letters addressed to her and to her aliases at her office. "These are just some of the dunning letters I've gotten at the office when the stores realized the home addresses I put down were fake. Then the harassing phone calls started."

I was shocked at the sheer number of them. "How much do you owe?"

"Thirty-two thousand dollars."

"Thirty-two thousand dollars?! My jewelry's only worth pennies compared to that. What good was it to steal it?"

"The little I got from your stuff, I used as a small payment to Saks."

"Eileen, you have to stop spending money you don't have!"

"Don't you think I know that?!" she said. "I can't."

"What do you mean you can't?"

"I just can't. I've tried, but when I see something I like or just want, I just charge it. I don't see it as spending money when I'm doing it. It's like a drug addiction." She started to cry.

I just sat there. I didn't know what to do or what I was feeling. I didn't understand why she couldn't just stop, but I could see she was struggling and in a lot of pain.

"How are you ever going to pay back all that money? Can you return anything?"

"I tried returning the coats and got as far as my little lobby, then I just turned around and walked back upstairs. I couldn't do it. It's like I'm possessed."

"Can your parents help?"

"I can't ask them."

"Why?"

"They already paid off ten thousand two years ago."

"What are you going to do?"

"I don't know. Die?"

"Don't be ridiculous. Maybe your public defender can help you out. And maybe you need to see a shrink. You need help, Eileen. Even if you declare bankruptcy or something, you'll end up right back here if you can't stop buying stuff and the next time you might do something more foolish or dangerous than steal from a friend."

"I know."

"Have you been able to make any other payments?"

"Yes."

"How?"

"Don't ask."

I looked into her eyes and knew how. She was beautiful and smart. Men loved her. Our friendship was over, but my heart was broken for her.

She took a key out of her purse and gave it to me. It was the one I had given her to my apartment.

Walking home, I had no idea there was even a thing called "compulsive buying disorder" or that it would take decades before it was recognized as a real mental illness. Right then, all I knew was that I needed to get my locks changed, but that would need to wait till morning. I had my key back. Even if Eileen had made a duplicate, I doubt she would be using it tonight. Besides, Marty was picking me up in an hour. We were going to see *Hair* which had moved to Broadway a few months ago after its run at Joe Papp's Public Theater. Afterward, we were off to Joe Allen for a late supper. Young naked actors should help me forget this whole sordid business.

Though I was able to forget Eileen that evening, the whole encounter was still eating me up two days later. I managed to finish my column on pawn shops, but for the last day and a half, I just sat at my desk staring at my typewriter, wondering how I was going to approach the story about S & R Loans. Was writing about Eileen's compulsion going to add anything to the investigation? One article I researched written by a male psychiatrist claimed that this recent "phenomenon" (his word, not mine) was strictly a female one as a result of allowing women into the work force, giving them financial independence from men and letting them have their own credit cards. I was stunned, then angry that any trained psychiatrist would think that, never mind write it. On the surface this appeared to be pure misogyny! Or was this the consensus of the mental health community? I'd have to research that further. Meanwhile, I needed to find out if S & R was preying on desperate people or just providing a legal service and Eileen's loan was an anomaly? I decided to start by going to a few more of their loan offices and see if any of them would give me a loan without proper I.D. Maybe an angle would come to me as I distanced myself from my conversation with Eileen. I still couldn't wrap my head around what Eileen had done. I started feeling depressed about the fact that she had nowhere to turn to get herself out of her situation and resorted to stealing from friends and sleeping with men for money. I was just about to leave the office when Vi called to invite me to join her and Lynne for an early dinner at Schrafft's.

"It's not Monday, Vi," I laughed.

"You're so right, but it's Friday and Lynne loves the fish," she said, laughing. "It's time I try something new there. Expand my horizons. Though I won't veer from my perfect Rob Roys."

"Okay, I'm in. See you at six."

I came out of the second of two S & R offices in lower Manhattan with no loan from either of them. I wasn't going to be
uncovering any major loan scandal if this kept up, but there
were still a zillion more branches to hit. If it turned out that
Eileen's loan was an isolated incident, her part in it might have
to become the story. Though Dwyre might just choose to cancel
it all together. I looked at my watch. It was five fifteen and I had
to get to mid-town to meet my Schrafft's ladies. Of course, not a
cab was in sight. It was rush hour. The subway was probably the
fastest way to get up town. It was dark and there was a real November chill in the air as I walked the few blocks to the subway
station. At the turnstile, I saw a long line of commuters queued
up in front of the token booth. I fished in my bag and found a
token in my wallet. Thank you, Jesus. As I reached the platform
my train pulled in. And, it was an express! I jumped on and
wormed my way through the crowded car till I found a position
next to a pole. I grabbed hold. Yes, God was on my side. Or so
I thought as we raced along, but halfway to my destination, the
train stopped dead on the tracks. The lights flickered on and
off in the tunnel and in the subway car. I looked at my watch.
Five-thirty five. We sat there for fifteen minutes and my fellow
passengers, packed in like sardines, were getting restless. I was
getting pissed. At least the car was warm and because we were
approaching winter, it didn't smell of body odor. After more
starts and stops, we finally pulled into my station at five after six
and I still had a few crosstown streets to navigate in my three
inch Italian leather boots before reaching Schrafft's.

I was fifteen minutes late when I rushed into the restaurant.
Vi and Lynne were already there. Vi with her perfect Rob Roy
and Lynne with her gimlet. Shortly after I sat down, MJ brought
me a very chilled martini, three olives. I took a sip. The ice crys-

tals lingering in the drink added to the enjoyment as I savored that first sip moment.

"Cheers," I said after the fact.

Vi and Lynne lifted their drinks and I took another sip.

"Dear, are you all right?" Vi asked. "You seem tense."

"I am tense, but hopefully this martini and you ladies will change all that."

"Well, let's look at the menu then you tell us what's bothering you," Vi said, solicitously.

We picked up the menus and studied them for a minute before MJ appeared to take our order.

"OK, Lynne's in for the filet sole and mashed potatoes, but what about you two?" she asked, indicating Vi and me. "Ashley, honey, you're looking a tad on edge…as if you'd strangle a steer with your bare hands and eat it."

"Yup," I laughed. "It's red meat for me, MJ. The sirloin steak, *bloody*, French fries and salad."

"And you, Vi?"

"I think I'll try the creamed chicken with biscuits. I'll have a salad, too."

"Creamed chicken it is."

MJ left to put in the order and I popped an olive into my mouth.

"Okay, now that the ordering is out of the way, what's making you so tense, dear?" Vi asked.

"Well, my apartment was robbed of my limited amount of jewelry by my ex-roommate. She stole my birth certificate and took a loan out in my name that she never repaid, so there was a warrant out for my arrest. Other than that, things are swell."

"Is Marty handling it?" Lynne asked.

I finished my martini as I filled them in on all the details and, I confess, I did feel better unloading on them.

"You think she's become a prostitute because of all this?" Lynne asked.

"I don't think she's working Lexington Avenue or the Lincoln Tunnel, but I do think she's getting paid for sex from some of the men she's dating."

"I think 'call girl' is what she'd be called now," Vi said.

"Yes, probably, and I don't know what I should do to help her. Maybe give her some money, but I don't have that much saved."

"Honey, I don't think there's anything you can do," Vi continued. "She's caught in a vicious cycle and can't seem to climb out. Giving her money won't help, as you learned when she told you her parents helped her previously."

"I know. I'm just so sad and angry at the same time. How could she get herself into this situation?"

"Sounds like she needs professional help," Lynne said.

"I told her she needed to see someone, but I don't know if she will. I certainly know she doesn't have the money."

"I'm sorry, dear," Lynne said and reached over and patted my hand.

"Okay, enough about me," I said then took my reporter's notebook out of my purse and prepared myself for the next installment of their story.

"First things first," Vi said. "Let's talk about something pleasant. Is Marty joining us on Thanksgiving?"

"Yes. And he's looking forward to it."

"I knew he would."

"What time?"

"I'm sending out the formal invitations tomorrow," Vi continued. "Thought we'd start with cocktails and hors d'oeuvres at three o'clock with the sit down dinner promptly at five."

"Sounds great," I volunteered.

"It's definitely black-tie. People rarely dress anymore, not even for the opera. What do you think, Ashley?"

"Well, I don't know. I don't have a gown or anything, but I do have a couple of really pretty cocktail dresses. Would that work?"

"Yes. That would be perfect. I really just want to see the men in tuxedos. Even the homeliest man looks handsome in one," Vi stated.

"I agree," Lynne added.

"Well, Marty can always rent a tux," I said. "Though I have a sneaking suspicion he might actually own one. He's become a man of many surprises."

MJ brought a second round of cocktails and some of Schrafft's delicious cheese bread and whipped butter. I love cheese bread and took a slice and put it on my butter plate. Vi and Lynne followed suit. I buttered my slice and took a bite.

"Okay," I said with my mouth full. I swallowed. "When last we talked, Lynne had an idea how to find Silas. I'm all ears."

CHAPTER 12

1938

Vi, Fritzie and Dot looked at Lynne skeptically. If they weren't going to go to the police with their suspicions regarding Fanny's death, what could they do to find out what happened?

"What's your idea, Lynne?" Fritzie asked.

"Well, we know he likes to stay in expensive hotels and was at a different one with each of us. I suspect he's invested a lot of money up front for hotels, clothes, and wining and dining all of us to get these big pay offs and, like I said, I don't think he's finished with New York."

"What makes you think he's still here?" Dot asked.

"He was able to get four hundred thousand dollars from the four of us…"

"And we don't know how much he stole from Fanny," Dot interrupted.

"No, we don't. Let's assume it's at least another hundred thousand making the total we know about half a million. However, because he wiped out her savings accounts, I'm assuming he might have gotten double that. If my guess is right and this *is* his last hurrah, the money he stole from us and Fanny isn't going to be enough for him to live the high-life for the rest of his life. Only when he has the million I think he's going for will he stop and maybe flee to some European playground.

"Maybe he's fled already now that his picture's been in the paper," Vi said.

"Maybe he has. But I don't think so. He's arrogant and probably thinks that we couldn't find him even if we did recognize him in the paper. And if we went to the police, he doesn't believe they're smart enough to find him, either, assuming the police believed us."

"What if we were the last of the women he conned and he's already got his million?" Fritzie asked pessimistically.

"Then we're sunk. I'm willing to gamble that we were his first victims in New York. It makes me livid that he's possibly gotten away with murder..."

"Not possibly!" Dot interrupted.

"I believe you're right, Dot, which is why I think he feels safe to continue. He's emboldened by what he's done. I know Silas and his ego, and I think right now he believes he's invincible, that he's smarter than everyone else," Lynne continued. "The winter is the perfect time to wrap it all up. People are less observant walking the streets as they go from place to place in the cold. It gets dark early, which helps to keep a low profile on the street. And he seems to entertain mostly at his hotels or in his room after the initial meeting at Schrafft's, Childs or other restaurants where he finds his victims."

"So what are you suggesting, Lynne?" Vi asked.

"I'm suggesting we each stake out the other quality hotels in town and see if we can find out where he's staying."

"Stake out how?" Dot wanted to know.

"Go to a hotel and sit in the lobby. Pretend to read a newspaper so you can cover your face if you see him. Watch the elevators and staircases."

"What if the hotel manager gets suspicious or thinks we're ladies of the evening and throws us out?" Vi asked.

"Ladies of the evening? At our ages? Now that could be fun," Vi piped in.

The women laughed at the thought.

"Well, hopefully, we won't be noticed if we don't stand or sit in one spot all day," Lynne said when she stopped laughing. "But, on the off-chance that that happens, politely leave and we'll alternate. In fact we probably should do that anyway. Change hotels. There are four of us, so by end of the week we will each have checked out four hotels. We might miss him, of course, but it's worth a try."

"Okay. I'm in. What hotels? He was at the Waldorf for Vi, the Plaza for Dot, the St. Regis for Lynne and the Hotel Astor for me," Fritzie stated. "What's left?"

"Do you have a phone book, Fritzie?" Lynne asked.

"Somewhere. I'll be right back." As Fritzie left the room, Vi poured herself another cup of tea. Dot joined her and took another scone.

"What do you think of this plan?" Dot asked Vi in a whisper.

"I'm not sure yet," Vi replied.

Dot was about to say something when Fritzie came back into the library.

"Found it," she said and handed it to Lynne. "Here Lynne, I'll let you look it up, I can't find my reading glasses."

Lynne found her bifocals in her purse, perched them on her nose and leafed through the phone book.

"Oh, dear, you, too! I don't really mind getting older, except the vision thing. I probably should pin my reading glasses to my blouse every morning because I can never find them when I need them," Fritzie exclaimed with a chuckle.

"Knock wood. So far, I don't need them," Dot added.

"Any luck, Lynne?" Vi asked.

"Yes. Here we go. We still have the Hotel Paramount, the Gotham, the Pierre, the Essex House, the Algonquin and the Sherry-Netherland."

"We're only four women. We can't cover six hotels," Dot exclaimed.

"Well, I think we should start with the Essex House, the Pierre, and the Sherry-Netherland because of their locations. We need one more."

"How about the Gotham?" Vi asked.

"Isn't that the hotel where a man leapt off a ledge and plunged to his death not too long ago?" Dot asked.

"Oh my, God, yes that's the hotel," Vi answered. "What was his name, again?"

"John William Warde," Lynne said. "He was from Southampton, I think."

"Right. And only twenty-six years old," Vi continued. "What could be so horrible to make someone commit suicide at that young age? Your life is just beginning."

"I remember reading over ten thousand people gathered on the ground as his sister and hundreds of police tried to convince him not to jump," Lynne said.

"Tragic," Vi added. "Maybe we should stay away from that hotel for now. Probably riddled with tourists who love the macabre."

"Okay, scratch that one off the list for now. I can see the Algonquin as a hotel Silas might fancy," Lynne said. "It's a bit apart from the others, but that might work in our favor. He might want to stay at one place in a different section of the city."

"That's settled then. Now let's divvy up our assignments," Vi said. "We can begin on Monday. I'll start with the Essex House if no one objects."

Fritzie grabbed a piece of paper and pencil off the desk in the library. "I'll make an assignment list."

"Before we begin, I need to ask," Lynne said. "It's not a perfect plan and there are so many variables on why we will fail, so, are we sure we want to go through with this?"

"Yes!" Dot stated vehemently. "I owe it to Fanny to try and find out what happened."

"I'm in," Fritzie chimed in.

"So am I," Vi said.

"Okay. Vi'll take the Essex House. Why don't I take the Algonquin," Lynne said. "Fritzie do you want to start with the Pierre? And, Dot, is the Sherry okay for you?"

Fritzie and Dot nodded in agreement.

"Here's what I'm thinking," Lynne continued. "We'll start on Monday camping out in the lobby trying to be as unobtrusive as possible. Dark solid colors are probably best to wear. Less likely to be noticed. Maybe bring a change of wrap to switch into at midday to alter your appearance. Bring a book, magazine or newspaper to read, or pretend to read, as we watch the front entrance, elevator doors and front desk. Then on Tuesday we'll rotate hotels counter-clockwise. Then the same on Wednesday, Thursday, Friday and through the weekend. No one will be in the same lobby two days in a row, so hopefully bellboys and desk clerks won't notice us. One thing about aging women, we become invisible. If he's at one of those hotels, hopefully one of us will spot him."

"Then what?" Fritzie asked.

"We kill him?" Dot answered with her own question.

"Oh, Dot, don't even joke about a thing like that," said Vi.

Lynne sat in the lobby of the Algonquin admiring the décor. She'd been an on again, off again guest of the Algonquin Round Table before it faded away after the stock market crash, but never really noticed the lobby with its elaborate dentil moldings and dark, polished wood columns. She loved the deco influenced chairs and settees arranged in various conversational groupings and the dark wood tables and modern lighting accessories. She sat in a chair that faced the hotel entrance, partially hidden by one of the lobby's potted palms, a copy of Agatha Christie's, *Murder on the Orient Express*, in her lap. It had been sitting on her shelf since it came out four years ago, but she never found the time to read it. She brought it as her "prop," and was about to open to the first page when her mind wandered back to the Round Table days. Of course, they didn't call themselves the Round Table, but rather the "vicious circle" after flirting with a few other "group" names.

She had met critic Alexander Woollcott right after her foray on the Ziegfeld stage and her brief marriage to choreographer Oscar London. His acerbic wit delighted her, so when he invited her to tag along one day to one of the vicious circle's lunches, she jumped at the chance. Frank Chase, the owner of the hotel, had recently moved the group from its original berth in the Pergola Room to the round table in the Rose Room after the group grew too large to accommodate them. "If they stopped inviting new people there wouldn't have been a problem," he once complained good naturedly.

Lynne was a hit as a luncheon guest and was often asked back. She got to hobnob with New York's literati such as writers Robert Benchley, Charles McArthur, George S. Kaufman, Heywood Broun, and his wife Ruth Hale, Broadway producer Brock Pemberton and the glorious actress Tallulah Bankhead. She even traded barbs, but was always outmatched, with Dorothy Parker who became a friend for a while. If it wasn't for her chance meeting of Alice Holmes, she would never have known such arty and clever people.

She felt something furry rub against her leg and realized Frank's cat, Hamlet, had come to pay her a visit. As legend had it, Frank adopted the cat when he discovered him sniffing around for food in a garbage can outside the hotel restaurant's kitchen. He named him Rusty because of his color, but John Barrymore was appalled. That was no name for a proud cat who survived the alleyways of a cruel world to become the prince of the hotel, so he renamed him "Hamlet."

Hamlet jumped into Lynne's lap and she absentmindedly stroked Hamlet's belly while keeping her eye on the hotel's elevators and front entrance. As Hamlet began to purr, she wondered what her life would have been like if she had married Silas. It became apparent as she dated the adult Silas in the guise of Hayes Walker, that he would not have been happy being a merchant in a farming town and would probably have left her for the high life he seemed to crave. She couldn't fault him for that. It's what I did, she thought to herself.

Lynne opened her book and started reading, looking up every time someone new entered the hotel or stepped out of the elevator.

The ladies regrouped at Fritzie's that next morning and compared notes. They realized that they had to come up with a better plan. Other than Vi, who thought to bring a sandwich in her purse, the ladies were starving by the end of the evening, not to mention the various times they had to leave the lobbies on bathroom breaks. Silas could have left or come into the hotel during any of those times. They decided they couldn't keep watch at all the four likely hotels. The new plan was that they would pair up and do two hotels at a time. Lynne and Dot would take the Pierre while Vi and Fritzie would move to the Algonquin. The day after, Lynne and Dot would stake out the Essex House and Vi and Fritzie the Sherry. They would keep alternating so that all four hotels would be covered a few times a week. Being in pairs made sure that there was always one woman at an observation post while her partner went to the bathroom or to get something to eat. It also gave each of them a chance to run home and change clothes to keep from being spotted.

After the first week, the women became discouraged. They had been sitting in various hotel lobbies from nine in the morning till around ten at night and no one had spotted Silas. Dot refused to give up. Her guilt over Fanny's death was strong, even though she knew she had nothing to feel guilty about. She kept going over and over in her mind how she should have tried to repair their friendship because, if she had, they could have enjoyed eating dinner together at Schrafft's when they became older and alone and not been easy prey for Silas.

Lynne still believed that Silas was in New York and she was determined to continue the search. If the others wanted to bow out, she would understand. When Vi and Fritzie saw how adamant the other two women were, they agreed to keep up the surveillance.

"If, after a couple of weeks none of us has seen Silas, we can try a few different hotels," Lynne said.

"Fine with me. Let's give it a month," Vi said. "If we don't find him, we'll have to rethink this plan."

At the end of the third week, Lynne was again sitting on the same chair in the Algonquin lobby, partially hidden by that potted palm, when she saw Silas strut like the cock of the walk into the hotel. Her heart began to race as she saw Dot enter the lobby from her bathroom break and was only about ten feet away from Silas. Dot saw him and immediately turned her back toward him as she made her way to Lynne. She quickly sat down across from Lynne and picked up her newspaper and held it up in front of her face. The two women watched Silas as he went to the front desk, got his key and sashayed over to the elevator.

"He's been here all the time," Dot said.

"Seems so. Let's get out of here and go over to the Essex House and tell Vi and Fritzie we found him."

Dot kept the newspaper in front of her face, as Lynne continued to spy on Silas from behind the potted palm. As soon as he got in and the elevator doors closed, the two women rushed out of the Algonquin. It was time to come up with a plan B.

CHAPTER 13

ASHLEY — 1968

"Oh my, God!" I practically yelled. "You found him!"

"Yes, we did," Lynne stated proudly.

"Plan B! What was Plan B?" I asked excitedly. "I've got to hear about your Plan B."

"It's going to have to wait, dear," Vi said, then laughed. "We've closed the joint."

I looked at the women around the table and noticed for the first time that MJ was dressed in street clothes and had joined them. I had been so enthralled with the ladies search for Silas I never saw MJ sit down. I then noticed that there wasn't a single person left in the restaurant except for us, a couple of busboys and a janitor cleaning up the place.

"Don't worry, Ashley, you'll hear all about Plan B in good time. Everything comes to those who wait," Lynne said, then gave me a wink.

"Waiting has never been my strong suit. When can we get together again?"

"Soon. I'll call you," Vi said.

"What about our bill..." I asked as I rummaged in my purse for my wallet.

"It's been taken care of," Vi offered.

"No, I can't always have you feeding me."

"Why not?" Lynne asked. "Think of it as our way of thanking you for indulging two old ladies by listening to their story."

"I…I don't know what to say," I sputtered.

"Thank you will suffice," Lynne smiled.

The women gathered their purses, gloves and coats and we all left Schrafft's together. As Lynne hailed a cab to share, I declined. I decided to walk home. The air was chilly, but I needed to calm down. I was so excited that the ladies found Silas! I wanted to know what they would do next, but now I had to wait…again. I needed to "walk off" some of my pent up energy. The cool fresh air would do the trick.

By the time I made my way east to Park and 53rd, my "high" was gone and I was cold, cranky and there were no on-duty cabs anywhere. As I crossed the traffic lane going south on Park, the light changed and I was stuck on the landscaped divide between Park Avenue's north and southbound lanes with a teenaged boy about eighteen who seemed to be stoned or drunk. He had long, dirty, matted blond hair and was bundled up in an army jacket covered with rock band patches. He mumbled something to me then pursed his lips and made kissing sounds. Okay, kid, I'm in no mood for this I thought as I firmly planted my feet, readied my purse to use like a club and looked him straight in the eyes.

"If you don't disappear," I hissed, "you'll be splattered all over Park Avenue after I push you into the oncoming traffic."

The kid freaked. He saw no fear in my eyes. Just resolve, and maybe a hint of madness as I stood ready to push him. He rushed across 53rd Street to that side of the divide. When the light turned green, he ran across the northbound lane, then scurried down Park Avenue. I was now shivering more from my anger-fueled adrenalin rush than from the cold, so I hurried east on 53rd till I reached First Avenue, then turned left and walked the two more blocks to my building. Patrick was on duty and held the glass front door open for me as I rushed into the warm lobby of my building.

"Thank you, Patrick," I said, rubbing my cold hands together.

"You're welcome, Miss Ashley. Have a nice night."

"You, too," I answered as I got into the elevator. I was looking forward to putting on my flannel PJs, crawling under the covers and watching some TV. I said a silent prayer that the elevator would make it all the way to the eighth floor.

The next morning I was back at work, continuing my undercover work going from one S&R office to another around the city. Not a single employee of that loan company would give me a loan without proper identification. I finally gave up the ghost and went to Dwyre to let him know that there was no story on S&R after all, but he didn't want to let it go.

"It's possible all the offices were notified about your friend's incident and have become more vigilant in giving loans. Maybe the story should center on the guy who gave your friend the loan. Find out who he is, what happened to him and if he gave out more loans like Eileen's."

"I don't see how one bad employee in a company makes a story."

"Listen to your gut, Wilkes, I am. If nothing comes of it, no harm no foul. But something tells me there's more to this than some guy giving a girl an iffy loan. Take your time. In the meantime, I want a lifestyle piece on the young women my wife tells me are now flooding army/navy stores and thrift shops for clothes and accessories."

"Okay, boss, no problem, since I'm one of them." I smiled.

"Then do the piece in the first person."

"Got it!"

Back at my desk, I was psyched. I loved the idea about a tongue-in-cheek piece about why so many young women, not just hippies, are shopping in army/navy stores. I could almost write this article without a bit a research or interviews. But I had no idea how to write an in-depth article on the individual lender who gave Eileen her loan. Maybe he just thought she was pretty and decided to do her a favor. Right now, however, I was going shopping.

My favorite army/navy store was Kaufman's on W. 42nd Street so I decided to make that my first stop. It was lunch time when I arrived and the store was crowded with women my age. I took out my trusty reporter's notebook and chose a pretty brunette with straight hair just past her shoulders. She was dressed in a navy blue wool A-line mini dress, with brown alligator low heeled pumps and white textured panty hose. Very career girl. Draped on her arm was a camelhair polo coat. I walked up and introduced myself.

"Hi, sorry to bother you. My name is Ashley Wilkes and I'm the style reporter for the *Daily News*. I would love to interview you, if you have a minute."

"Interview me about what?"

"About why you're shopping at an army/navy store. From the clothes you have on, you seem to be more of a Bonwit Teller, Lord & Taylor girl."

She laughed. "I am."

"Then why here?"

"I love the jeans. I have no problem spending a hundred dollars or more on a dress, but on a pair of jeans from France when Levi's makes them so much better? No way."

"So can I ask you a few more questions?"

"Sure, why not," she said as she put out her hand to shake. "By the way, I'm Lauren Bade."

I shook her hand and invited her for a cup of coffee at the coffee shop nearby. Inside, we found a booth. She ordered a Tab then pulled out a sandwich from her canvas "Hunting

World-style" shoulder bag. The waitress didn't care. I ordered tuna on rye.

"Hope you don't mind, but I'm starving and was going to eat this at my desk when I got back."

"No, not at all," I said. "I love your bag. Did you get it at Hunting World? I've been drooling over one for ages."

She laughed. "I wish. This is a copy. Actually, I shouldn't say that. Hunting World probably copied this one. It's an army/navy store original. Duck and deer hunters and fishermen buy these bags all the time and they've probably never heard of Hunting World. They use all the pockets for bullets, duck whistles and fishing flies, I guess, but for me they're great for all the stuff I want to carry and find easily. I heard photographers love these bags, too."

Lauren lifted her bag off her seat and plopped it on the table then flipped open the pocket flaps. "See, one pocket for make-up, one for pens and note pads, another for spare pantyhose, one had my sandwich. The interior is my book bag."

"Book bag?"

"I'm in law school."

"Well, it's very cool. I'm always fishing for my pen and note-book, not to mention my lip gloss and keys," I said. "Do you work as well as go to school? You're certainly dressed for it."

Lauren laughed. "I just came from a torts class and needed to dress the part to be taken seriously. I'm the only female in my class. My part time job is at night. I'm a Playboy bunny."

"You're kidding?!"

"Nope. Half the bunnies I work with are in college or grad school. The job pays great, the tips are great, you can pretty much make your own schedule and the club has strict rules, bunnies are off limits to key holders. I'd have to work a sixty hour week to make what I earn in a night or two and that wouldn't give me the money or the time to go to law school."

"This may be a silly question but things have loosened up a bit for women, did you try to take out a loan?"

"I did and was told what everyone I know was told. Sure you can have a loan if you bring your father or husband in to co-sign. Well, I don't have a husband, nor do I want one and my dad doesn't think women should be lawyers, or even go to grad school, so he refused. And I graduated from Sarah Lawrence Phi Beta Kappa for god's sake!"

"I'm sorry."

"Oh, don't be. Playboy was the answer to my prayers. I don't have to put up with anything from the key holders. Just smile and serve them their drinks and dinner. No touching. No dating. And I'm not beholden to any man for anything. Or bank for that matter."

"Can I quote you on that?"

"Absolutely."

"Which brings me back to what you're wearing now and what you buy at the army/navy store."

"I buy all sorts of things. It's not only political radicals or hippies who love fatigues. I do, too, and I love the army tee shirts and the flannel shirts. Instead of carrying bottled water when I go jogging around Central Park which can be cumbersome, I fill up the canteen I got at Kaufman's and sling it across my back. Look ma, no hands."

She lifted her arms in the air and laughed. "I also have a fabulous yellow, mid-calf slicker that I wear all the time when it really pours. I grabbed it up as soon as Kaufman's started carrying them. I even bought this cool over-sized army watch." She pushed back her sleeve so I could get a better look at it.

"Beats the Mickey Mouse watch I have," I laughed. "And, I'm with you. I love the jeans and tees. And my London Fog that I love to death is useless in the rain. I'll have to check out one of those slickers. I've only seen them in the movies on fishermen who seem to fish only in hurricanes."

"I promise, you'll love it. You can get the green army version or the yellow fisherman version. They're really cool."

When we finished lunch, I had filled a few pages of notes and we exchanged telephone numbers. I liked her and thought it a hoot that Playboy was paying for her tuition and law books. I paid the check and as we walked out, promised to give her a call when my article was published, then went back inside the store to interview a few more female shoppers and the manager to see if the store was stocking anything different since women invaded the stores.

I ended up going to a couple more of my favorite army/navy store haunts and found that they were now carrying more workmen apparel. Flannel shirts. Jean jackets. Denim work shirts. Bandanas. All popular with today's Manhattan young working women. I had found a fabulous tweed hacking jacket with suede patches last year at one of them. All I needed was a deerstalker hat and a pipe. The only real problem with shopping at these stores was the sizing. Most of these apparel companies only made men's sizes, but it didn't stop any of us from shopping there. The look was great and the merchandise was cheap. But according to the owners and managers of the stores, that was changing and prices would probably go up. Ah, capitalism! Supply and demand.

When I finally got back to the paper, I decided to give Vince Fariello a call to see if he could fill me in on the man who gave Eileen the loan. I wanted to get his name and find out if he'd been arrested or at least fired from S&R. But before I could make the call, Dwyre called me into his office. Inside, Marty was leaning against a wall. My heart sunk. At least it felt like it did. I knew something terrible had happened.

"What?"

Dwyre left his office and closed the door as Marty led me to a chair.

"Sit."

I sat. I prayed that whatever this was, it had nothing to do with my parents.

My hands were shaking. "Please. Tell me."

"It's Eileen."

"What about her?"

"She's dead."

"Dead! What do you mean dead? She can't be dead, I just saw her a couple of days ago."

Marty dragged another office chair in front of me and sat down. He took my hands in his.

"I'm so sorry, sweetheart. She killed herself around two this morning."

I started to jump up, but he gently pushed me back down into the chair. I was now shaking all over.

"I don't believe you. She wouldn't do that!" But, even as the words came out of my mouth, I remembered what she had said when I asked her what she was going to do about the mess she was in and she answered, "I don't know. Die."

"She couldn't really do that?" I whispered as I shook my head as if to shake out all thoughts of Eileen being dead.

"She left a note. Actually, it was quite a long letter."

"I want to see it!"

"You can't, Ashley," he said softly as he wiped away the tears I was too numb to feel as they fell down my cheeks. "The police have it."

"Tell me what happened."

"Evidently, she'd been thinking about killing herself for quite a long time. Years, maybe. According to her letter, she bought an entire wardrobe of expensive nightgowns, still with their tags on them, and kept them in a dresser drawer so that when she was ready, she could choose the one she thought would look best on her when she was found."

"That's crazy! How did I not know she was suicidal if it's been years?"

"I don't know. She seemed to live a dual life. The life you knew was the woman who was outgoing and funny, good at her job… the other, was a woman living a life of profound desperation."

"But if I'd known, I could have helped her."

"Eileen had demons, sweetheart. They led her into an abyss of debt that just kept growing. She saw no way out except prostitution and she just couldn't live like that any longer."

"But what if S&R had never given her that loan and I never found out she was the one who stole from me? She wouldn't have been humiliated and arrested."

"Stop it. This is not on you!" Marty stated firmly. "The excessive shopping and her collection of nightgowns prove that she's been in emotional trouble for a long, long time."

My shaking had stopped, but I couldn't stop my tears. Marty, still holding my hands, sat quietly as I cried and tried to come to terms with all he told me. Finally, I stopped crying and pulled one of my hands free to wipe my face.

"If it just happened not that many hours ago, how did you find out so soon?"

"Vince called me. He was called to the scene because he had been her arresting officer in your theft."

"Scene!?" I asked. "What kind of scene?"

He ignored my question and took out his handkerchief and finished wiping my face.

I knew he was stalling. But I had to know.

"How, Marty? How did she do it? Drugs?"

"She jumped," he said so quietly I could barely hear him.

"Jumped?! What do you mean she jumped?"

"She jumped out of her fifth floor window."

My mind was racing. Why would she jump? Hadn't he just told me that she bought all those nightgowns so she could control how she looked when they found her dead? It made no sense.

"What was she wearing?"

"Some kind of pink peignoir."

"It just doesn't make sense. I'm not denying she was suicidal since all the evidence you mentioned points to her killing herself. But why would she jump out of a window? She bought those nightgowns to look beautiful in death and being splattered on a sidewalk is not beautiful."

"Vince thinks she was tripping. He's asked the lead detective to request an autopsy."

"What do you think?"

"I don't know, Ashley. Vince is a smart cop and is on his way to being a good detective. He thinks she was hallucinating because the last few pages of that long epistle she wrote became illegible with words that were all over the page, some written with large letters, others tiny, none making a sentence or any sense at all. There were even weird scribbles on the last two pages."

"And tripping can make you jump out a window?" I asked.

"If it's a bad trip, I think so. Who knows what she could have been seeing or was thinking. With her suicidal tendencies, the hallucinations might have literally pushed her over the edge. Vince just wants to make sure she was on acid before the police make any final verdict."

Dwyre came back into the office and looked at me.

"How are you?" he asked.

"Awful."

"Do you think you can work?"

I thought a second, then told him yes.

"Then I want you to finish up the army/navy store piece then follow up on that guy from S & R and your friend's death. See where it leads."

"Why?"

"Because my gut tells me there's an important story here."

"I don't know if I can."

"Give your friend a voice, Ashley. There may be more Eileens out there that you can help."

Marty escorted me out of Dwyre's office and walked me over to my desk.

"Let me take you to Danny's tonight for supper. I'll see if Vince can join us."

"I don't think Vince can afford Danny's, Marty."

"I'm paying. I think it might do you some good to talk with him."

"OK."

East 45th Street was known as steak row because it had one great steak house after another, including Joe & Rose's, The Press box, and Danny's Hideaway, one of Marty's favorite watering holes. Owned by Danny Stradella, the restaurant was famous for its steaks and lobsters and its celebrity clientele such as Johnny Carson, George Plimpton and Mickey Mantle. Being young and living off a starting reporter's salary, this was not my crowd, so I had never eaten there until I started dating Marty. The first time he took me to Danny's we were the guests of John Lindsay, the city's mayor, and Marty's boss. We ate in the dark, paneled room filled with pictures of movie stars, comics, TV and radio personalities, as well as politicians and athletes hanging on the walls above the upholstered black leather banquettes. The tables were covered with white linen, and blond wood chairs were perched on the other side of the tables facing the banquette. I loved the room—masculine, but not unfriendly to women, like a good date. Across from us that night, Sammy Davis, Jr. was sharing a table with Liberace. They appeared to be friends. Since the Mayor was picking up the tab, I hadn't thought much of it until Marty and I started going by ourselves. I was concerned at first by his desire to eat there on a detective's salary, but I didn't say anything till that night at Arthur's, so I just relaxed and enjoyed star gazing.

We were early, so we went into the bar to wait for Vince. There was one unoccupied stool so Marty pulled it out for me and once I was perched on it, he pushed it close to the glass-topped, mahogany bar. I thought this was the coolest bar in town not because the drinks were good, though they were, but because well-known reporters, cartoonists, and magazine editors had written Danny's praises all over the walls. I dreamed one day of being a famous enough reporter that I could write something for the wall.

Marty ordered a dry martini for me and a scotch on the rocks with a splash of soda for himself. Our drinks came and as I lifted my glass to take a sip a very soused man sitting on the stool to my right suddenly leaned his body against me, causing me to spill half my drink. The bartender quickly wiped up the bar.

"It's on the house," he said as he leaned forward and tried to move the man upright as he had now put his head on my shoulder. I looked at the guy and recognized him. He was Steve Carson, a well-known comic whom I'd seen often as a kid on the Ed Sullivan show. Marty, who was standing behind me, put his right arm between me and Steve and grabbed hold of the edge of the bar as he gently, but firmly, elbowed Steve's head off my shoulder allowing Steve to just lean on his arm and not on me. Within a second Steve snapped out of his stupor and jumped off the stool.

"What the fuck, get off me," he said as he took a swing at Marty. Marty caught his arm before Steve could land his punch and held it in a vice grip while Steve tried to punch Marty with his other fist. No one in the bar seemed to notice.

"Danny, get the fuck in here," Steve yelled, "and throw this asshole out. Danny!"

Danny, a small man with dark hair, was an ex-boxer and a WWII vet and could handle most men twice his size. He quickly came into the bar, assessed the scene and looked at Marty, who was now holding both of Steve's arms as he struggled and tried to kick Marty. He knew Marty was a cop and knew that this wouldn't go well for Steve.

"I'll take care of him, Marty," he said as he engulfed Steve in his arms. "Calm down, Steve, I'm not throwing anyone out. Not even you," he continued as he forcibly led the man out of the bar. The other bar patrons briefly applauded, then went back to their drinks and conversations.

Marty sat down on the now empty bar stool as I gulped down what was left of my martini. Before I put the glass down, another appeared in front of me.

"Again, on the house," the bartender said.

"Thanks, Nat," Marty said.

Marty was still nursing his scotch when Vince finally arrived and we headed for our table.

"I'll have the drinks sent over," Nat said as Marty left him a twenty on the bar.

Once seated, our drinks arrived and Vince ordered an old-fashioned. I was anxious and really didn't want to have this conversation, but I wanted to know what Vince knew about Eileen and the man who gave her the S & R loan. It was also now my job since Dwyre insisted I investigate who, what, where and when, and maybe find out why this all happened.

Our waiter came over and both Marty and Vince ordered steaks, but I was still upset about Eileen. Plus, the embarrassing altercation at the bar didn't help. Food was the last thing I wanted, but I knew I had to have something if I was going to drink.

"Can the chef make me a plain chicken breast?" I asked.

"Of course," he said.

"Great. I'll have that and maybe some mashed potatoes." Mashed potatoes had always been my go-to comfort food.

The waiter left to put in our order and I sipped my martini. I tried to think of a way to start this conversation when Marty started it for me.

"Ashley needs your help, Vince. She wants to find out more about Eileen's suicide and the man who gave her that loan."

"Please, anything you can tell me will help," I said and reluctantly took my reporter's notebook out of my shoulder bag hanging off the back of my chair. "All of this is overwhelming me. I still don't understand why she left my apartment such a mess when she went to steal my jewelry. I know you wouldn't know this, but why? Why would she trash my place like that? She knew where I kept everything. She lived with me for god's sake."

"I think she wanted you to find out, Ashley. She wanted you to stop her," Vince said. "Maybe she thought you could save her."

"Well, I certainly didn't do that. I only made things worse."

"Not true," Vince said pointedly. "Nothing you did caused any of it."

Throughout the rest of our dinner Vince told us that Doug Posner was the name of the S & R guy. He had been arrested and, after speaking to his attorney, admitted that he did give Eileen the loan without a proper I.D. He bragged about how clever he was, letting her think she was seducing and sleeping with him to make him bend the rules. He went on to say how women were weak and stupid and that he often slept with those who came to him for a loan. His own quid pro quo. Vince said he even winked when he said that. Since these women were desperate for the money, they did what he asked of them. "Nothing illegal about that," he stated. "They were willing."

Since technically no one was raped, at least not physically in the eyes of the law, the police released him, but informed S & R what he was doing. He was fired that day and from what Vince had heard, he left New York for parts unknown.

Tears welled up in my eyes.

"I'm sorry," I said. "My emotions are right on the surface and I'm so angry that a person like Posner can get away with what he did to Eileen and those other women. How can anyone prey on vulnerable people like that?" I was a master of rhetorical questions.

Vince then told me more about Eileen's death and her long suicide letter. It seemed, to him, that she just couldn't go on. She couldn't stop buying before or even after her arrest. She'd been borrowing money from shylocks to pay off her credit cards and, as I already knew, had started sleeping with men for money. What I didn't know was that that money went to pay off the vig to the shys. It was a vicious circle and she saw no way out.

I was so stunned, I couldn't stop thinking, my god, I'm listening to someone who says "vig to the shys" and I know what he's talking about. I laughed to myself. Living in New York was quite an education.

"I think it was a sickness, Ashley," he said. "She needed to be in someone's care who understood addictions. I've seen this kind of thing with gamblers, but never heard of a shopping junkie before."

As we left Danny's, I thanked Vince for all he told me and he gave me his home number if I needed to ask him anything else. I impulsively threw my arms around him and hugged him.

When Marty took me back in my apartment, I realized I didn't want to be alone and asked him to stay. He had left some clothes and a toothbrush at my place a while ago. As we got ready for bed, Marty tried to lighten the mood and take my mind off Eileen's death.

"So, what time do you want me to pick you up on Thursday?" he asked as we brushed our teeth.

"Thursday?" I answered his question with a question, trying not to swallow any toothpaste.

"Vi's Thanksgiving bash!"

I spit out the toothpaste and rinsed my mouth. "That's this Thursday?"

"Yup."

We walked into my one room and climbed into bed.

"I don't even remember what time it's supposed to start," I told him.

"Three o'clock for cocktails and appetizers. Dinner at five."

"Did you get a tux?"

"I have a tux."

"Thought you might."

"I actually bought one a couple of years ago 'cause I needed to go to so many black-tie functions as part of the mayor's police detail. It was a write-off," he explained, with a big grin on his face.

"Well, my dress isn't, that's for sure," I laughed.

"Let's see it."

"Nope, not till you pick me up."

"Is that like the groom not seeing the bride in her dress till she walks down the aisle?"

I laughed again.

"So, what time?" he asked again.

"I don't know, three. I don't want us to be the first ones to arrive."

Marty was at my apartment exactly at three and whistled admiringly when I opened the door. My cocktail mid-thigh, long-sleeved mini-dress was black velvet with a white lace collar and cuffs that I bought at Bergdorf's for almost a week's salary. I had on black lace panty hose and black velvet pumps. I felt good. And Marty looked gorgeous. The black tux jacket contrasted with his blue eyes and made them seem even bluer. I grabbed my little black beaded evening purse, and slipped my arm into his as we headed out.

We arrived in minutes and when we stepped out of the taxi and went through the gate into Sniffen Court, I actually gasped. Though it was still daylight it was night inside the courtyard which was totally covered by a tarp forming a roof over the entire space. Shimmering white twinkle lights were strung across the courtyard just under the tarp. And, though I had on a mid-calf, black wool crepe cape I had borrowed from Kate, I realized I didn't need it. The enclosure was warm as toast and the lifestyle reporter in me couldn't resist noticing every décor detail. Trashcans filled with coal were burning at every coach house doorway giving off heat. In the middle of the courtyard was a long banquet table covered with a gold linen tablecloth that displayed what appeared to be place settings for more than fifty guests. Place cards were at every seat. The napkins pulled through silver rings matched the tablecloth. The china was white with gold rims and the silver was sterling. A half dozen silver candelabras were on the table, though not yet lit. Each chair surrounding the table was covered in a gold damask slip-cover. Decorating the table were fall leaves and tiny pumpkins. A large buffet table, also covered in a gold tablecloth was set up outside Vi's open front door. Inside, she had set up the bar. The buffet table was filled with cheese and pate platters and other appetizers. As more guests arrived and her Sniffen Court neighbors came out of their coach houses to join the party, waiters in white dinner jackets began to mingle through the crowd serving hot hors d'oeuvres off silver trays. Others balanced silver trays filled with flutes of champagne.

"Wow, Vi certainly has a lot to be thankful for," Marty said with a smile.

"You think?!" I'd never seen anything like it, not even the black-tie charity galas I'd had to cover for the paper. The fall-like gold linen elegance playing off a cobblestoned courtyard, heated with trashcans like a depression era hobo camp was design genius.

"And raising money for a women's shelter at the same time," Marty added.

"What? Vi never told me that."

"The Mayor told me when he heard I'd been invited. Vi's starting a women-only shelter in the East Village to get them off skid row and cared for. This dinner is costing a small fortune for most attending."

Vi entered the courtyard and headed toward us.

"You're here," she said, stating the obvious as she kissed each of my cheeks, then Marty's. "Don't you look scrumptious, Mr. Lambert. You wear a tux well." She took his hand and led him into the house. "Follow us, Ashley, there's a couple of people I want you to meet."

As we walked to her front door, Vi grabbed a glass of champagne off a waiter's tray and handed it to me.

"There's a bartender inside, Marty, if you want something a little stiffer," she said with a twinkle in her eyes.

Entering her home, I noticed only a few table lamps and sconces were glowing, but lighted candles were everywhere. The rooms looked ethereal. As we walked down the hall, I saw a full bar set up in the living room, and another in the dining room, but Vi veered us into the library where two gentlemen in tuxedos were sipping highballs. I recognized Bob Klein, the fortyish, tall, slender man with graying hair as the CFO of Saks Fifth Avenue. I had written a life-style piece on him and his wife last year, but I hadn't a clue who the other man was.

"Nice to see you again, Ashley," he said as he shook my hand.

Vi introduce Marty to Bob, then both of us to Dr. Joel Weiss, the head of the psychiatric department at Mount Sinai Hospital. We shook hands.

"I wanted you to meet both Bob and Joel, Ashley, because I think they can help you with the story you're working on about

Eileen. Joel's department has been working with women who seem to have the same problem."

"As more and more women have entered the work place and have become independent financially your friend's story has become more commonplace," he said as he moved to sit down on one of the brown leather club chairs, then indicated that I should sit on the yellow brocade settee.

"I'll leave you to explain what we're going to be doing with the shelter, as I need to get back to my guests," Vi said. "Marty, why don't you follow me to the bar and get yourself a drink."

After Vi and Marty left the library, Bob and Joel told me that they had been recruited by Vi to be on the board of her new non-profit women's shelter which she hoped to turn into a full women's center to include education and medical facilities, alongside the bedrooms and living quarters. Saks would be underwriting the day-to-day clothes for the women, as well as professional outfits to help give women the confidence they needed when they tried to enter the workplace.

Joel asked me about Eileen and after I told her story, he explained that her shopping addiction wasn't a new affliction and wasn't strictly a female problem. I was glad to hear that and told him about the psychiatrist's article I had read that blamed it all on women working and allowed to have credit cards.

"Sadly, even my profession has its sexists and fools," he said, then went on to say that this addiction also manifested itself in men who buy fancy cars and other high-ticket items they can't afford, or entrepreneurs who over-expand their businesses and end up filing one bankruptcy after another. He further told me that therapy had helped many women with this shopping phenomenon and more therapists were learning how to deal with it. Initially, however, the shelter would serve as a safe haven for homeless women and a place for those women from the streets who needed to detox and get other medical attention. Joel would help provide pro bono doctors who could mend the body and therapists who would try to mend the mind, but he would continue to research and treat men and women with shopping addictions privately.

When Joel and Bob were finished telling all that Vi hoped to accomplish, it was time for dinner. As we left the library, Joel added, "Feel free to use my name in your article, Ashley, and let people know that there is help for compulsive shopping." I now knew that the psychological angle to Eileen's story was what my article would emphasize. By the time we reached the banquet table, I had set up an appointment to meet Joel at the hospital to interview him in depth.

Outside, people were gathering at the long table, looking for their names on the place cards and taking their assigned seats. Marty had found his in the middle of the table. Mine was right across from him. Sitting to my right was Vi's Sniffen Court neighbor, Randolph Chapman, the renowned opera singer, and to my left sat Frank Giadelli, a judge on the New York Court of Appeals. It was going to be an interesting dinner. I spotted MJ seated near Vi who was at the head of the table. I looked for Lynne and finally saw her at the other end, seated next to the Deputy Mayor. While sequestered in the library with Joel Weiss and Bob Klein, I never got a chance to talk to either of them.

As my dinner partners and I began small talk, servers walked up and down the length of the table pouring our choice of white or red wine into gold-rimmed crystal wine glasses, followed by more servers who placed a salad in front of each of us atop the white china plate that served as a charger. The red and green salad was made up of fresh greens with a bit of radicchio and cranberries and a delicious mustard vinaigrette with a hint of sugar. I'm not a salad lover, but I liked this one.

By the time the entrée was served, Randolph was regaling our section of the table with stories of singing with Maria Callas in Europe and gossip about Ari Onassis. Just as he finished, dinner was put in front of me on yet another white and gold china plate. As the servers delivered the entrée to the other guests, I marveled at how beautifully the food was arranged on the plate. There were slices of moist turkey breast meat, green beans with sliced almonds, and a mustard yellow casserole I recognized as lanttulaatikko, made from lanttu, the Finnish word for turnip. I was touched that Vi had included this dish in the Thanksgiving meal, knowing I was half Finnish.

"Does anyone know what this is," the Judge asked pointing his fork to the lanttulaatikko. "It has quite an unusual taste, bitter, yet sweet. I like it."

"It's a Finnish casserole called lanttulaatikko," I chimed in, using my limited Finnish accent. "It's mashed turnips with a bunch of other ingredients that I can't spell."

"Lanttulaatikko?" Randolph asked, pronouncing it perfectly.

"Yes," I answered, "and only the Finns would have a casserole spelled with double t's, double a's, and double k's."

When the Judge asked me how I know all that, I explained that my grandparents were Finnish and that my mom and grandmother always made this dish during the holidays.

The conversation turned to Finland and I was surprised to learn that both the Chapmans and Giadellis had been there. Randolph to perform in Helsinki, accompanied by his wife who always wanted to see the city and buy some Arabia pottery, and the Judge to Lapland.

"I always wanted to experience aurora borealis and mush with the huskies," the Judge said.

"So he says now. What he really wanted was to find Santa Claus," his wife, who was sitting next to Marty, said with a laugh.

The conversation turned to a high profile case Marty had worked on and the Judge presided over a year earlier. The Judge knew Marty from the Mayor's detail and as they talked, I kind of tuned out catching a comment here and there as Randolph and others jumped into the conversation, since most had read about it in the papers. By the time the servers delivered dessert, an assortment of thinly sliced pieces of pie to each of us and placed platters of cookies along the middle of the table, I started thinking again of Eileen. What if she had had the kind of money that most people at this banquet had? Would she have been able to indulge in her addiction without fear or would her purchases become more and more expensive, putting her in the same predicament she found herself in the end?

When dinner was over and people started to leave, Vi came to me and took my hands.

"Dear, are you free tomorrow night?" she asked. "MJ and Lynne are coming. My cook's making leftovers."

Oh, my God, I thought. I knew that she wanted to tell me more of the story. I looked at Marty. He saw that I was conflicted.

"Honey, have dinner, I know you want to," he said. "I can pick you up after dinner and we can head for the Hamptons then."

"Are you sure?" asked Vi. "I wouldn't want to spoil your trip."

"Not a problem. Be less traffic this way," said Marty.

Vi smiled. "I'll pack a coffee thermos for you."

"Okay, then. What time?" Ashley asked Vi.

"Come at five. I'll send my car for you at 4:45. Bring your weekend bag and Marty can pick you up here," Vi said. She turned to Marty: "Say around 9:30? We have a lot to talk about." She winked at him.

"Nine-thirty it is," Marty agreed.

I hugged Vi goodbye and thanked her for a truly amazing Thanksgiving and looked around for Lynne and MJ, but they were either inside the house or on their way home.

Marty gave Vi a kiss on the cheek and thanked her, too. "It's always a pleasure to see how the other half lives," he joked.

Marty draped Kate's cape over my shoulders as we walked out. "What was that all about?" he asked.

"All about what?"

"What do Vi, Lynne and MJ need to talk to you about?"

"About my story and Vi's new women's shelter," I lied.

Marty dropped it, but I knew he didn't believe me. As we left Sniffen Court and I looked back…it truly was like a fairytale palace. But it wasn't real and I instinctively knew that what they were going to tell me would be very real and far from a fairytale.

The smell of brewing coffee woke me up. Marty, in a tee shirt and boxers was in my galley kitchen. He poured two cups. Still groggy, I sat up and realized I was naked and pulled the sheet up to my chin. I never sleep naked! My little black velvet dress, lace panty hose and bra were in a heap on the floor. I smiled as I remembered Marty slowly undressing me when we got home, whispering how he'd been waiting all evening to make love to me. As he kissed and teased my body, my arousal grew and all thoughts of Eileen and my Schrafft ladies disappeared. All I could think about or want was Marty.

"What are you smiling about?" Marty asked as he handed me a cup of coffee.

"Last night," I said indicating my clothes on the floor.

"We can repeat that if you like."

"I like."

We stayed in bed most of the day. We made love, drank cold coffee, made love again, had tuna sandwiches as we read the New York Times and did the crossword puzzle together in bed. When he left to go home and pack for our weekend, I did the same, then got ready to go to Vi's. At 4:45, my doorman buzzed to tell me that Vi's car and driver were waiting. I grabbed my overnight bag and headed downstairs.

The streets on Friday after Thanksgiving were pretty deserted. Well, deserted for the city. So many Manhattanites leave town for Thanksgiving weekend. We zipped our way to Sniffen Court, making all the lights on the way. I arrived at Vi's promptly at 4:55. You would never have known that the day before she had given a dinner party for more than fifty people.

"I thought we'd forego appetizers and just sit down to an early dinner so we'll be finished by the time Marty comes to pick you up," she said as she led me into the dining room. "My cook made turkey tetrazzini from the leftover turkey and baked some country bread." MJ and Lynne were already sitting at the dining room table which was simply set with white ironstone plates and white linen napkins. Candles in sterling silver candlesticks were lighted, however. On the buffet table was a tossed green salad in a wooden bowl from Africa that Vi had found when she was on safari years earlier, some sliced homemade bread on a large wooden cutting board, again from Africa, and a warmed, silver chafing dish with the tetrazzini. This was the most elegant leftover dinner party I ever attended.

"Please, help yourselves, ladies, we have a lot to talk about tonight," Vi said as she uncorked a chilled bottle of white Bordeaux.

We filled our plates and sat down.

"It's time to tell Ashley about Plan B."

I took my napkin out of its ring and placed it on my lap, then reached into my bag, pulled out a fresh reporter's notebook and pencil and placed them on the side of my dinner plate ready to be filled with...what? Anticipation and trepidation washed over me. I had become very fond of "my" Schrafft ladies and wondered, did I really want to know what happened all those years ago?

CHAPTER 14

1938

Dot and Lynne rushed into The Essex House and found Fritzie and Vi sitting separately in the lobby doing their surveillance much like they had been doing at the Algonquin. They signaled Vi to join them where Fritzie was sitting as they sat down beside her on one of the sofas.

"What are you doing here?" Fritzie whispered.

"Is something wrong?" Vi piped in as she joined them.

"We found him!" Lynne and Dot announced simultaneously.

"Lynne was right," Dot continued. "He wasn't finished with New York. He's at the Algonquin."

"Now what?" Fritzie asked. "We never did discuss what we would do if we found him!"

"We make him confess to murdering Fanny!" Dot declared full vibrato.

"Shhh. I don't think the lobby of The Essex is the place to discuss this. Let's go to my apartment," Vi said. "It's the closest."

When they arrived at Vi's apartment, Vi played hostess and showed them around, then ushered them into the cozy, oak-paneled library while she went into the kitchen to brew some tea. After sitting on the matching dark plaid upholstered sofa and chairs, the three women remained silent until Vi came in, pushing a tea cart laden with matching cups, saucers, cream and sugar and teapot, over the antique Turkish area rugs. Vi poured each woman a cup. Still, no one said a word.

"Help yourselves to milk and sugar," Vi said, breaking the silence.

The only sound was the muted noise of the traffic down below and silver spoons stirring the tea. Now that they were there, no one knew what to say. They sipped tea in awkward silence.

"I like the plaid upholstery," Fritzie finally chimed in. "Looks stunning against the light paneling."

This was the first time any of the women had been in Vi's home. In fact, they'd only been in Fritzie's townhouse on Beekman Place. As close as they had grown and as much as they had learned about one another since meeting in January, they still didn't know one another's day-to-day lives. Their shared experience with Silas is what bound them.

"Thank you. I wanted something a bit masculine in this room."

They fell back into silence.

"Okay. We seem to be at a crossroads," Vi continued after a few minutes more of silence except for the sound of sipping tea. "What are our goals now that we found him? Do we want him to give us our money back, assuming he still has it?"

"Yes," Lynne answered. Dot and Fritzie agreed.

"Getting back the money is all well and good, but I want to know what really happened to Fanny. I feel I owe it to her," Dot said. "Why didn't I go to her when I found out her husband died? If I had, we could have had each other, eaten in Schrafft's together and not be prey for Sy. I mean Silas."

"I agree we should try and find out what Silas' relationship was with Fanny and if he really was the one who was responsible for her money disappearing," Lynne said.

"I know she didn't just flit it away," Dot chimed in. "She was a practical woman and, even though I never met her children or knew their relationship, I doubt she would have given it all away without consulting them."

"It does seem suspect," Fritzie said. "I remember when she took over for her husband in the assembly. She was a strong, accomplished woman. I, too, doubt she would just give her money away without at least her banker or lawyer knowing about it."

"And where was her will?" Dot asked, beginning to get upset. "Impossible that she didn't have a will."

"Didn't the paper say that her safe was open when they found her?" Vi asked. "Lynne, do you still have the article MJ saved?"

"Yes," Lynne answered as she picked up her purse and pulled it out. She scanned the article. "'The police have determined the death of Mrs. Friedman as suspicious due to an empty, open safe in the apartment and that no suicide note or Last Will & Testament was found.' At least that's what they thought at first."

"Didn't some lawyer come forward saying he wrote a will for Fanny?" Lynne asked.

"Yes, but he claimed that Fanny had the signed original," Dot answered.

"Did her family know what was in the will?" Fritzie asked.

"If they did, it was never revealed to the press," Dot again answered.

"Her attorney knows," Vi said.

"So, we don't know if the police ever investigated the lawyer's claim or who her heirs were?" Fritzie continued.

"It seems so. All we know is the police eventually ruled it a suicide," Vi said. "To me it sounds like they couldn't figure out what happened, so suicide was the simplest answer."

"But she was an assemblywoman, her husband had been an assemblyman, her children are successful people in the community!" Dot stated. "Why would the police not pursue this further? I don't understand."

"Maybe they did, Dot, but didn't come up with anything. Hopefully when we get to talk to Silas, he'll know the answers to some of our questions," Fritzie said.

"I know she was murdered. The thing is, do you think Silas could have murdered her?" Dot asked, directing her question to Lynne.

"Not the boy I grew up with, but the man he became? Maybe," Lynne answered. "I saw a different adult Silas than you ladies did. He had no love for women. He was cold, calculating and certainly not above blackmailing, not to mention stealing."

"Well, how are we going to get him to talk to us?" Fritzie asked.

"Exactly. It's not like we can invite him for tea," Dot said as she held up her tea cup to emphasize her point.

"No. We need to ambush him and force him to come with us." Vi said.

"Ambush him? Are you serious? And, take him where?" Fritzie asked, surprised at Vi's suggestion.

Vi was about to answer when Lynne jumped in. "Some place private. Secluded. Where we can question him without interruption."

"Okay, I'm in. Where and how do we do that?" Dot asked.

"We kidnap him!" Lynne stated emphatically.

"Kidnap him! Are you joking? How do you kidnap a grown man?" Fritzie wanted to know.

"We lure him into my car and drive him to my country home upstate in Rhinebeck."

"Just like that," Fritzie said.

"Well, no, not exactly. It will take a little planning, but I think we can do it."

"How?" Vi asked Lynne.

"I've been thinking about this for a while. First, we need to follow him and find out if he's wooing a new victim," Lynne continued. The ladies seemed skeptical. "Then we find out her name and leave a message at the Algonquin that she needs to see him right away. In the message she'll tell him that a car will be outside the hotel waiting for him to take him to the rendezvous and when he gets in, it will be we who are waiting for him and we'll whisk him away to my house in Rhinebeck."

"You know, you're diabolical, right?" Vi laughed.

"Of course. How do you think 'Pauline' stayed undiscovered all these years," Lynne answered with a smile.

"Diabolical or not, that all just sounds too easy. We need a real plan," Fritzie said. "I like the idea of luring him into the car and taking him to Rhinebeck, but that's a long drive and he's not going to go without a fight."

"We could chloroform him," Dot chimed in.

"And how do we get chloroform, just walk into a drugstore and buy some?" Fritzie asked.

"I don't know, but I think that wouldn't be the most discreet thing to do even if we could," Dot answered.

"We're getting ahead of ourselves," Vi said. "The first thing we need to do to see if Lynne's plan is even feasible is to find out if Silas is working another con and who his victim is. Once we do that, we can figure out the rest. If we still want to chloroform him, I think I can get some without anyone knowing about it."

"You're right. We need to find out who *she* is and how he might be preying on her," Lynne added. "Once we learn who she is, we can plan the kidnapping in more detail."

"That sounds reasonable. And when we get him to Rhinebeck we can tie him up and interrogate him," Dot said.

"But first we need to follow him and see what he's up to," Lynne continued. "We can do shifts, again. But we have to be very careful. He cannot ever see us. He must not know that we have found him. Agreed?"

Vi, Fritzie and Dot nodded in agreement, although the expressions on their faces showed they weren't quite so sure about all this.

Silas made no appearance in the Algonquin lobby the first day of the surveillance. The women alternated an hour each so as not to draw attention to themselves. They felt they had pushed their luck the first time they waited in hotel lobbies. But at 9:30 a.m. on day two, Dorothy was about to end her first shift when Silas strolled in from the street, checked with the desk clerk then headed to his room. She watched as the elevator climbed to the third floor and stopped. She waited to see if it continued. When it didn't, she made the logical assumption that Silas' room or suite was on the third floor. She assumed that he had spent the night elsewhere and would probably be in his room for a while and decided to gamble on his not returning to the lobby right away and spotting her. She approached the desk clerk who seemed to be shuffling papers from one end of the desk to the other, pretending to be busy.

"Hello. I know you're busy, but can I ask you a question?"

"Of course, madam. What can I do for you?"

"I think I just saw my friend Robert Johnson go into the elevator. I've been waiting for him, but he didn't see me and I didn't have a chance to catch him before he left the lobby. I thought I might ring him up and tell him I'm here. He's staying on the third floor but I forgot the room number."

"Are you referring to the gentlemen who was just here?" the clerk asked.

"Yes, that gentlemen. I caught a glimpse of him at the desk as I was coming into the hotel and tried to get his attention."

"Oh, I'm sorry madam. That was Marshall Woods, not your Mr. Johnson."

"Really? Then I'm the one who's sorry," Dot said contritely.

"Let me look up Mr. Johnson's room number for you. You can give him a call and see if he's in his room," the desk clerk said as he leafed through the register.

"No, you don't need…" she started to say, but the clerk finished running his fingers down the list of guests.

"I'm so sorry ma'am, there doesn't seem to be a Mr. Robert Johnson staying with us at the moment," he interrupted. "Are you sure he said he'd be at the Algonquin?"

"Well, um, I don't know now," Dot answered feigning confusion. "I was, ah, so sure he was here. I just don't know what to say. I'm so sorry."

"Please, no apologies necessary. The Algonquin is always ready to help."

Dot headed for the hotel's front entrance as Fritzie entered the lobby. Flushed with excitement, she walked right past Fritzie, whispering, "Follow me out of the hotel." Fritzie stopped, a perplexed look on her face, then turned around and did what she was told. As she got outside, she watched Dot hurry down the street then disappear around the corner. She scurried after her and when she turned the corner, Dot was waiting for her.

"What's going on?" Fritzie demanded, out of breath.

"Oh, my god…Oh, my god, Fritzie, he's here."

"Yes. We know he's here, Dot."

Dot practically squealed as she tried to contain herself. "I just saw him!"

"You actually saw him?"

"Yes, in the flesh. He's staying on the third floor."

"How do you know that?"

"I watched as the elevator went up and stopped on the third floor. No one else was in the elevator with him and it didn't continue up or down."

Excited, Dot grabbed Fritzie's arms. "That's not all," she continued excitedly. "He's using the name Marshall Woods."

"You're sure?"

"Positive! The desk clerk told me. I feel like Nancy Drew!"

Fritzie laughed. "You're a regular sleuth. You'll have to tell us how you got his latest name after we find the others and tell them the good news."

They found Lynne at home, then the three of them went to Vi's who had just grabbed her purse and was about to go out when they arrived.

"I was just leaving for my shift," she said, surprised to see them as they pushed past her and entered her apartment. "Is something wrong?" Dot took the purse out of Vi's hand and placed it on the entryway's console.

"You're not going anywhere," she told Vi as she physically ushered her down a hall and into her own library. The others followed. Before anyone sat down, Dot, still bursting at the seams, blurted out "We got him!"

"Silas?" Vi asked.

"Yes, Silas! We got him!"

Vi plopped down on the sofa. Lynne and Fritzie sat down as well, as Dot paced back and forth.

"Now what?" Vi asked.

"We go kidnap him!" Dot answered without hesitation.

"Sit down, Dot," Lynne commanded. The ladies tensed as Dot sat down next to Vi. "How are we going to do that?" Lynne continued. "Four more than middle-aged ladies go blazing into the Algonquin and physically wrestle the guy into my car? We need to carefully figure out our next move."

"You don't think I know that?" Dot snapped. "It took everything in me not to run up to him in the lobby and demand he tell me about Fanny."

"First tell us what you found out, if anything, other than he's at the Algonquin which we already knew," Vi said to Dot, trying to calm her down.

Dot filled them in on how she found out what floor he was staying on and what name he registered with.

"Marshall Woods?" Fritzie exclaimed. "Where on earth does he come up with these names? All so…Episcopalian."

Dot laughed. "You're forgetting my Sy Levy. He went Jewish for me."

They all laughed with her. The tension was broken.

"Nothing like playing to your audience," Lynne chuckled. "If he had been this clever when we were kids, maybe I would have married him."

"Well, you did marry him," Fritzie said with a smile.

"Ah, but you forget, that was Pauline," Lynne returned the smile.

Fritzie, Dot and Vi stared at Lynne for a minute then began to laugh again, not just at what Lynne had said, but the absurdity of it all.

"OK, ladies, back to our kidnapping business," Vi said, through more fits of laughter. "Now that we know who he is this time, we need to find out if he has a new victim as we discussed and the only way I can see us doing that is to continue our shifts at the Algonquin. Eventually, as he did with all of us, he's going to bring her back to his suite or room, depending how much of an impression he wants to make."

"And when he does, we'll follow her if necessary to find out who she is, then take it from there," Fritzie said.

"That could take too long," Lynne said ruefully, more than a little frustrated at their dilemma. "I say we follow Silas as soon as one of us sees him. I think we might find 'her' more quickly that way."

"If there is a new 'her,'" Vi piped in.

"Yes," Lynne continued. "If she comes to the hotel with him first, all the better. Otherwise we can't just wait around the lobby in the hopes she'll show up with him. I have an uneasy feeling that he's ready to bolt."

"Why?" Vi asked.

"I don't know. Fanny's death. All of his marks, we four and who knows who else, living in Manhattan where he could bump into any one of us. I think it's getting too risky for him to stay in town."

"You're probably right. So, we go back to the Algonquin and when he leaves the hotel we follow him!" Dot said emphatically.

"Yes. But, we'll have to be vigilant, so he doesn't see us. Dress plainly. Wear comfortable shoes," Lynne said. "Maybe team up in pairs. One of us outside the hotel. One of us in the lobby. This way, if he jumps into a cab or is picked up by someone the person outside can see which direction he's going. Get a license plate and describe the car, if necessary. Maybe even grab a cab to follow him because whichever one of us is inside won't be able to run out after him. She might not see where he went by the time she follows him out of the hotel. What do you think?"

"I can't think of any other way to find out what we need to know," Fritzie remarked. "But if we don't know how long Silas plans to stay in New York or if he is even running another con, and if we don't see him with a woman in a week, I say we come up with another plan to kidnap him."

The ladies agreed.

"Should we fill MJ in?" Fritzie asked.

"I think we should leave her out of it in case something goes wrong," Vi answered.

"What could go wrong?" Dot wanted to know.

"Well, we could get arrested for kidnapping for starters," Vi said. "MJ should not be part of our revenge. If all goes as planned, we can always tell her about it later."

The temperature was in the forties and Vi, bundled up in a dark wool coat with a shawl over her head, was standing across the street from the Algonquin when she spotted Silas leaving the hotel. This was the third day of watching for him and though they saw him numerous times coming and going, he never had a companion and trying to follow him was a complete failure. Each time he either got into a cab and took off before they could find another and follow him, or they were too far back tracking him on foot trying not to be spotted and lost him. This time, however, Vi got lucky.

When Silas left the hotel, Lynne, who was inside, waited a few moments, then followed him out. Just as she came onto the sidewalk, she saw Silas still standing in front of the building. She was about to duck back inside when a taxi pulled up to the hotel and an attractive older woman in her mid-sixties, her silver hair pulled off her face in a bun and wearing a full-length mink coat climbed out. Lynne immediately recognized her and quickly went back inside as Silas gave the woman a kiss on the cheek. Just what she needed, she thought, someone from her "crowd" calling attention to her being there. Silas would not think it a coincidence.

Vi watched Lynne disappear back into the hotel as Silas leaned in and paid the cabbie. He then took the woman's hand and steered her toward the hotel entrance, but she pulled her hand away and stopped. The cab drove off as they appeared to argue. Finally, Silas seemed to acquiesce and the woman took his arm and they began to walk toward Fifth Avenue. Vi followed from her side of the street at a discreet distance.

When the couple reached Fifth Avenue, they turned right and headed south. It was noon and the street was packed with people on their lunch break hustling to and fro, but Vi was determined not to lose them. The couple stopped in front of the New York Public Library on 42nd Street. Vi stopped, too, and though she was half a block behind them, turned her back to them in case Silas looked in her direction. She watched their reflection in a glass window of the building she was standing in front of and saw the couple climb the stairs, past "Patience" and "Fortitude" the two stone lions standing guard, so named by Mayor La Guardia at the start of the Depression.

Now what, she asked herself? Then decided to chance it and follow them. Once inside the library, however, they were nowhere to be found. Not in any of the reading rooms that she surreptitiously checked out or any of the other rooms. She had lost them. Again she thought, now what? She decided to walk back to the hotel and see if Lynne was still in the lobby. By the time she reached the hotel, she saw Lynne about to get into a cab.

"Lynne!" she yelled out.

Lynne heard her and held the door open, holding the cab till Vi reached her. "What happened?" she asked Vi.

"Let's get out of here," Vi said, and jumped into the cab. Lynne followed.

Vi gave the driver Fritzie's address.

"I think she's home. We can find Dot later."

"Did you follow them?" Lynne asked.

"Yes, all the way inside the library. But I lost them."

"I know who she is," Lynne said bluntly.

"What? You do? Tell me."

"Let's wait until we're at Fritzie's to talk about it," Lynne said, indicating the taxi driver.

Vi agreed, realizing that Lynne didn't want the driver to hear what they were talking about or who they were talking about.

Fritzie's housekeeper let them in and escorted them out to the back terrace with its lush rolling lawn that sloped down towards the East River till it hit a tall, black wrought iron fence covered in morning glory vines. Fritzie had on a full gardening apron over a heavy, wool, oatmeal colored sweater and gray, whip chord flared, pleated trousers. Her white sneakers and garden-

236

ing gloves were covered in dirt from digging dead plants out of the large cement urns at the edges of a huge flagstone terrace.

"Hi," she greeted them. "Frost seems to have killed my beautiful pink geraniums." She took off her gloves and threw them on a potting table and took a seat at a round patio table perched in the sun. Lynne and Vi joined her.

"I hope you don't mind sitting outside. I love the brisk, cold air on a sunny day," Fritzie said lifting her face into the sun. "Tuula, will you bring us some tea, please," she yelled into the house, then focused on her friends. "What happened?"

"I know who Silas' next mark is," Lynne stated. "So do you, I think."

"Who?" Fritzie asked.

"Daisy Hunt."

"Daisy? Oh, my, lord, he has set his sights very high."

"Daisy Hunt?" Vi asked.

"Yes. One of New York's true grand dames. And grand damn rich!" Fritzie said. "I'm surprised you don't know her, Vi. She was married to Freddy Hunt, philanthropist extraordinaire. He basically managed his family's fortune into a bigger fortune, then started giving it away."

"Of course, Freddy Hunt. Forgot all about him, he's been dead for so long. His widow has got to be at least ten years older than Silas," Vi said.

"At least. I'd say she's pushing seventy, don't you think, Lynne?"

"Probably. She's older than us, that's for sure," Lynne answered.

"Do you think he's sleeping with her?" Vi asked.

"Who knows," Fritzie laughed. "He probably is if Daisy wants it. She's been widowed a very long time."

"Didn't she have a lover a few years back?" Vi asked.

"Yes. Some accountant or banker she was grooming to chair her foundations since her son is such a ne'er-do-well, prancing around the great cities of Europe, living off his trust fund and avoiding alimony payments to his three ex-wives," Lynne said. "If Silas did his homework, I'm sure he'll figure out how to please her."

"The library makes sense," Fritzie piped in. "Daisy, and Freddy before he died, have been involved with the library since it opened in 1911. She helped with acquiring its vast Dutch art collection and her voice was prominent in the choosing of the furniture that adorns the various rooms. If I remember correctly, her pet project is creating and subsidizing libraries in parts of the country that have no access to any books. Towns and counties that barely have a one room school house. Last I heard she was raising money to build one somewhere in the Smoky Mountains."

"Yes," Lynne said. "I heard from her a couple of weeks ago about a donation."

"The thing I don't get is this," Vi stated, "when I watched them in front of the hotel arguing, it appeared he wanted to take her inside, but she seemed to insist they leave. She took his arm and led him away from the Algonquin. As they walked toward Fifth Avenue I followed. I have no idea why they were arguing. I couldn't hear a word since I was across the street."

"My guess. He did not want to go to the library," Fritzie said. "If you remember, he never took any of us anywhere too open or public, especially during the day. Always his hotel restaurant and always in a dark corner, or an out-of-the-way restaurant downtown that no one we knew would patronize. Otherwise it was room service or he'd dine at our houses. He never seemed to want to go anywhere he might run into someone he knew."

"Or one of the women he bilked," Vi cut in sarcastically.

"Exactly! The library is a very busy place with tons of people on the streets and inside," Fritzie continued. "Being in the open like that makes him vulnerable."

"Yet, he went," Vi said.

"Probably because he couldn't come up with a believable reason not to go and see whatever it was she wanted to show him or meet whomever she wanted him to meet," Lynne chimed in.

"Well, what do we do now? Do we warn Daisy?" Vi asked.

"No, not unless we have to," Lynne answered. "No one should know our involvement with Silas except us. I think we put our plan into motion. Fritzie, you compose a letter telling him that you, as Daisy, have to see him. You have a surprise for him upstate, so you'll send a car for him at 7:00 a.m. next Friday, but you don't deliver the letter until Thursday evening, after we see him return to the hotel. I'll make a date with Daisy for an early dinner. Maybe take her to see a play afterward so he won't be able to contact her. I'll think up something to keep her with me till way after midnight. Maybe twist my ankle and have her come with me to the emergency room. Vi, you get the ether or chloroform, however you planned to do that. Since Fritzie is the only one who knows how to drive, she'll dress up in my chauffeur's uniform and be the driver."

"I'll put my hair in a bun and stuff it under the chauffeur's cap," Fritzie said, excited by the intrigue.

"Good idea," Lynne answered. "I'll give my chauffeur the day off and you and I will go to my garage and get my car early that morning and drive it to the Algonquin. When Silas comes out to the car, you'll keep your head down and hold open the back passenger door. You know how most people never really look at those who serve us. I'm hoping that Silas is the same and won't even bother looking directly at a chauffeur's face holding the door for him."

Lynne took a breath, as the other ladies listened intently.

"As soon as he climbs in and Fritzie's back in the driver's seat," she continued, "Vi and I will rush into the back from both sides, lock the doors and place a sedative soaked handkerchief over his mouth and nose. Dot, you'll quickly get into the front passenger's seat and lock your door. As soon as we're all in,

Fritzie will take off. I just pray we can contain him while he's struggling to get free."

"And if we can't?" Dot asked.

"Don't even think about it," Lynne answered.

Vi hadn't seen her friend Betsy Howard in months, but she was going to need her help to get the chloroform. After doing some research at the library when they first started talking about kidnapping Silas, she decided against ether. Though it acted more quickly, it was highly flammable. She'd rather risk it taking longer for Silas to succumb than burning them all up. The only thing she was unsure of was how much she'd need without giving the man a heart attack, something that could happen with too much chloroform or if someone had a bad heart. She decided Silas probably didn't have a heart which was another reason to go with the chloroform. She called Betsy and asked her over for lunch.

Before Betsy arrived, Vi arranged the luncheon plates with a bed of butter lettuce and a chicken salad she had made that morning—Betsy's favorite. She sliced some fresh bread she'd bought at the Swedish bakery on First Avenue and chilled a rare bottle of Chablis. Betsy loved white wine. She put everything on a tray and brought it into the library for what she felt would be a more intimate lunch. The doorbell rang. She looked at the clock on the fireplace mantel. Right on time.

As they sat at the game table that Vi had covered up with layers of white linen tea cloths they caught up on each other's comings and goings and how Vi was hoping to put together a new benefit for Bradley's hospital where he was now chief of surgery. She asked many more questions about the hospital, but when she asked if Betsy knew where drugs were kept, Betsy cut her off.

"OK, we've been best friends almost all our lives, what gives? My favorite chicken salad. A bottle of wine. You're buttering me up for something."

"What do you mean?" Vi answered feigning innocence.

"You're a terrible actress, Vi. Why on earth do you need to know where hospital drugs are kept?"

"Because I just can't walk into a pharmacy and buy what I need."

"Why not?"

"Because I don't want anyone remembering me buying it. I could make it, but you remember how bad I was at chemistry."

"Make it? What are you talking about?"

"Chloroform. I need a bottle of chloroform."

"Good Lord, Vi, why the hell would you need chloroform?"

As Betsy had pointed out, they had been best friends for decades. Having blundered in her attempt to get information from her, Vi decided she would confide in her. Betsy knew how Vi had been swindled and was almost as angry with Silas as Vi was, but she hadn't know about the other women. Vi told Betsy everything, praying she wouldn't regret it, but she needed the chloroform or their plan wouldn't work.

"Vi, I don't know if the hospital even uses chloroform any-more," Betsy said when Vi finished. "There were some studies that were done that showed it could be dangerous for some patients."

"I know. I've done all the research. But I don't want to use ether, too volatile to handle."

"I'll ask Bradley…"

"No, please don't involve him," Vi said, cutting her off. "If we can't get it ourselves, I'll have to think of another way to subdue him."

"OK, let's go play cat burglar. Come with me," Betsy said as she walked out of the library.

Puzzled, Vi followed her to the foyer and watched as Betsy grabbed her coat off the coat tree, then picked up her purse from the hall table.

"Come on. Get your coat. We're going to the hospital."

When they arrived at the hospital, they went straight to Bradley's office. Betsy had decided to tell him that they were out having lunch nearby and thought it would be nice to just drop by so Vi could say hello. She pretended that she didn't remember that he had told her over breakfast that he had a big surgery scheduled at two-thirty. Betsy was a much better liar than Vi. So, they weren't there but a minute when Bradley had to leave. He kissed Vi on the cheek and thanked her for stopping in.

"It was good to see you, Vi. We need to all go out for dinner soon," he said as he left his office.

"Yes, soon," Vi said as he disappeared from sight.

Betsy immediately opened a desk drawer and found Bradley's keys. They left his office and went searching for the room where drugs were stored. They were about to give up after a half-hour, when they saw a nurse come out of a supply closet. Before the door shut, they could see that there were boxes and bottles of medication in the room. They waited till she was gone, then Betsy tried key after key to open the door. Finally, she got the right one.

"You stay here and keep watch," Betsy directed. "If someone comes down the hall bang on the door once. When they're gone, bang on the door twice. Let's just hope the hospital still keeps chloroform." Betsy slid halfway into the room. "Oh, and one last thing. I'll knock twice when I'm ready to come out. You knock twice back if it's all clear."

She then quietly closed the door behind her as Vi stood guard, trying to act as if it was totally natural for a non-hospital worker to be loitering in a hospital corridor. She prayed that no one would come who wanted to get into the room. She almost panicked when she saw a young nurse walking toward her pushing a cart. Vi reached behind her back and knocked once on the wall. What if the nurse needed to get into the supply room? Her breath quickened and she struggled to control it. As the nurse drew closer, Vi thought she might just faint. But if she didn't and the nurse really did want access to the room, she would pretend to faint to distract her. All this was racing in her mind as the nurse approached her, then just continued down the hall past her without even acknowledging Vi's presence. Vi let out a sigh of relief as she knocked twice. One more worker in a hospital coat and one male "civilian" came down the hall and she did the requisite knocking. Finally, Betsy knocked twice. No one was in sight, so Vi returned her knocks. Betsy slowly opened the door, then slid out, locked the door and headed back to Bradley's office. Vi faltered a moment, then hurried after her.

"Did you get it?" she whispered.

Betsy didn't answer as she walked into the office and put the keys back in the drawer, just as a middle-aged nurse came in with a folder. She looked at the two women quizzically. Then recognized Betsy.

"Oh, hi, Mrs. Howard," she said. Betsy knew the woman and hoped that she had moved away from Bradley's desk before she and Vi were even noticed.

"Hi, Iris. We were just leaving. If you're looking for my husband, he just went into surgery."

"Oh, OK. Thanks. I just wanted to drop off these charts he asked for. I'll leave them on his desk."

Iris left and Vi felt faint again and flopped into a chair. Her heart had been racing a mile a minute ever since they entered the hospital. "I'm not cut out to be a criminal," she whimpered, as she tried to calm down.

"Come on, Vi. We should get out of here," Betsy said as she rushed out of the office and down the hall.

Vi reluctantly stood up and followed.

Outside the hospital Vi suddenly stopped. "The suspense is killing me, Betsy," she said between breaths.

"I got it!" Betsy announced proudly.

CHAPTER 15

ASHLEY — 1968

Vi looked at the grandfather clock in the dining room corner and saw that it was almost 9:30. "I think we should end tonight's tale. Marty's going to be here in a few minutes to whisk you off to your Hampton's getaway."

"You've left me hanging, again," Ashley said and put down her pencil and closed her reporter's notebook. "Did your plan work? Did you kidnap him? I'm not going to be able to think about anything else all weekend."

"Probably not *all* weekend," Lynne smiled.

Ashley blushed and Vi let out a laugh. "Don't be embarrassed dear. We've had our share of romantic weekends."

"When can we meet again?" Ashley asked, wanting to change the subject.

"As always," Vi said. "I'll call you."

"You're going to love the house, Ashley, so your style. It's off Old Town Road, so walking distance to all the shops and restaurants," Marty said as we drove toward the Hamptons. "I think the house was built in the 1700's, but the bathrooms and kitchen have been totally renovated."

"Whose house is this, again?" Ashley asked.

"Mark Slovik. Remember? He and I played basketball together. We reconnected a couple of years ago when he did some legal work for the Mayor. I told you. He married Judy Blakely who was on cheerleading with you."

"Oh, right," I said, as I tried to act excited about our getaway, but I couldn't stop thinking of my ladies and the fact that they were planning to actually kidnap Silas. I was nervous for them which was ridiculous since they obviously aren't the worse for wear. But maybe they got caught and had to go to jail or something and the trauma of it all has faded after so many years. I wanted to tell Marty everything, but what they had told me and were still telling me was "off the record" to a journalist, and I promised I would never tell anyone while they were still alive. What happened back then? I didn't even know if I still wanted to find out but, of course, I needed to hear it all, and no matter how bad, I was keeping it to myself. Marty was a cop and if they did kidnap Silas, he'd be obligated to report them, assuming there are no statute of limitations on kidnapping. I'd grown way too fond of these ladies to let that happen. I thought about Dot's death and how deeply it had affected me and wished I had gotten to know Fritzie. How these women navigated a system that was so female-phobic, for the lack of a better word, was beyond me. Yes, they were privileged because of their wealth, but money did not give women much freedom. Yet these women managed to have rich, fulfilling, independent lives, despite a society controlled by men, often doing things that were frowned upon, especially for women in their economic bracket. And I thought I had it bad trying to break through gender barriers.

"It's the ladies, isn't it?" Marty suddenly asked.

"I'm sorry, sweetheart, I'm just imagining the house and our weekend," I lied and put my hand on his leg. "It's going to be wonderful."

"You're never going to tell me, are you?"

"What? Tell you what?"

"Their secrets."

"What secrets?"

"Ashley, I know you. I've come to know Lynne, Vi and MJ and I care about them, but I know they're hiding something and it's bothering you. Are you in trouble?"

"No. No, of course not."

"Then what?"

"It's nothing, honest. I just love hearing all their stories about how hard it was for smart women back then and how they persevered."

"As I said, you're never going to tell me, are you?" he asked again not believing my explanation.

"Maybe someday."

"Someday?"

"Maybe not."

Marty knew me well enough to know that he wasn't going to get anything out of me till I was willing to share, so he changed the subject and began describing Mark and Judy's house and telling me about the weekend he spent there with them and a few friends a couple of years ago. I loved him for that.

It was almost midnight when we pulled into the driveway. Marty hadn't lied, it was perfect and looked like the house my family had rented on the Vineyard when I was growing up. I immediately fell in love with this two story, cedar shingle house with its wrap-around porch that had dark green wicker chairs on it and a faded floral couch swing hanging on chains from the wainscoted porch ceiling. I was charmed and, for the moment, totally forgot my ladies. I grabbed my weekend case and followed Marty inside.

The large living room was perfect. White-washed shiplap, over-stuffed sofas and easy chairs in floral and striped fabric slipcovers made up two cozy seating areas. Worn oriental carpets were layered on top of the pine wood floors. In the corner was a square wooden game table with an inlaid chess board surrounded by four upholstered, green slipper chairs. An amber glass-shaded desk lamp sitting on an oak mission-style desk near the front door was on, but the inviting glow in the room came from the lighted fire in an imposing river rock fireplace. For whimsy, large colorful "souvenir" satin throw pillows, edged with gold fringe were displayed on a dark green corduroy sofa. One was from Coney Island and showed off the Cyclone rollercoaster and Steeplechase building. Another, from Atlantic City, featuring the boardwalk. And, yet another from Montauk Point, highlighting the lighthouse. Weird, all places I'd been to with Marty when we were dating in high school. The walls were covered with vintage black and white photographs of Long Island and Hudson River school paintings. The real deal paintings. I loved every inch of the room.

Marty poured two snifters of brandy from a bar cart and handed me one. "Welcome to my Southampton home." He clicked my glass and took a sip.

It took me a minute to realize what he had just said. "Your home?"

"Yes."

"But you told me it was Mark and Judy's."

He smiled. "And 'was' is the operative word. It was theirs 'til last month. Mark opened a second law office in L.A. last year, took the California bar, and when he passed, they decided to live the Southern California dream. He knew how much I loved the Hamptons, how much I loved this house so he made me an offer I couldn't refuse."

Stunned, I plopped down on a sofa, almost spilling my cognac. I took a big sip. "Marty, this must have cost a fortune! How can you afford this?"

"Ashley, we've been over this. I can afford it. Besides, I knew you would love it."

"Me? Please tell me you didn't buy this house for me."

He smiled. "Well, you did cross my mind."

"What if we break up?"

"Then I will still have a house that I love and want to spend time in." He took the snifter out of my hand and sat down next to me.

"You know I've loved you all my life, right?" he said.

I didn't know what to say. He took a ring box out of his corduroy jacket and opened it. Inside was what looked like a three carat, emerald cut diamond ring. It was huge. Yet the setting was simple.

"I had the jeweler set it in yellow gold, because I know how much you dislike platinum."

I was still speechless. He took my hand.

"Ashley Wilkes, I can't see my life without you. Will you marry me?"

My heart was pounding so hard, I thought it could be heard in Manhattan. To say I was shocked would be an understatement.

"You do love me, right?" he asked.

I managed to nod, then finally said, "Yes."

"Yes, you love me or yes, you'll marry me?"

"Yes, I love you," I said somewhat in shock.

"I don't care if you don't become 'Mrs. Lambert' as long as we're together. I don't care if you want to go cover a war, though I would be terrified for you. I don't care if you never want to stop working. I will always support whatever you want to do. Just say you'll marry me."

I stared into his blue eyes. My mind was racing. This was crazy. It hadn't even been a year since we started dating again. But, at the same time, I did love him and couldn't imagine my life now without him.

"Yes."

"Yes?"

"Yes. But can we just move in together first?"

"Yes," he said. "Your place or mine?"

"I don't know, let's see. A studio the size of a closet or a basically unfurnished, except for a bed, two bedroom penthouse with a terrace on Central Park West. I think door number two."

"Deal. You can pick out furniture," he smiled, then put the ring on my finger, took me in his arms and kissed me. I put my arms around him as he grew more passionate and leaned me back onto the sofa and began to hurriedly undress me and himself. The fire's glow made his lean, muscular body glisten and feeling him deep inside me as he caressed me with so much tenderness, I knew I had made the right decision.

We never made it to the bedroom and when I woke up at eight the next morning the fire had died and I was still on the sofa, naked under a down quilt. A plush, white terry cloth robe was draped on a nearby chair. I put it on and followed the scent of bacon into the kitchen. Marty, showered and dressed in faded jeans and an NYPD gray tee shirt, was hovered over a vintage Chambers stove frying bacon.

"Scrambled or fried?" he asked as I sat on a tall, wicker stool at the kitchen island.

"Coffee. Black," I said almost pleading.

He poured a mug for me and placed it in front of me.

"Now, scrambled or fried?"

"Fried, over easy, please," I answered and swallowed some hot, strong caffeine. "Can I ask you a question?"

"Just one?" he asked as he took the bacon out of the cast iron frying pan and broke four eggs into the sizzling bacon grease.

"Well, no. I have a hundred. But one immediate one."

"Shoot?"

"Who set the fire in the fireplace last night just in time for our arrival? Elves?"

Marty laughed. "My houseman."

"You're kidding, right? You have a houseman?"

"I do. Well, he's more like a caretaker. He came with the house."

"And everything else?"

"Most of the furniture I bought from Mark and Judy. The artwork is mine." He flipped the eggs.

"And those wonderfully tacky tourist pillows?"

"I bought them for you," he said. "Do you remember?"

"Of course."

"I was hoping you would." He slid the eggs out onto two white ironstone plates. Added the bacon, then placed a plate in front of me. He grabbed napkins, knives and forks from a drawer and put a basket of croissants and butter on the island, then sat on a stool across from me.

"*Bon appetit,*" he said as he bit into a slice of bacon.

I broke my yolks with the tip of my croissant. Still runny, with hard whites. Perfect.

"I'm beginning to think you're too good to be true," I smiled.

"I'm in love. What can I say?"

When we finished breakfast, I quickly crammed the dishes into the dishwasher, then Marty gave me a tour of the house. Besides the kitchen and large living room, the downstairs sported a sunroom that had been converted into a dining room off the kitchen with a slate floor, braided rugs and a long pine farm table that could comfortably seat eight for dinner. Also on the main floor was a large three-quarter bath, a dark wood paneled library/office and a screened-in porch. Upstairs was a roomy master bedroom, vintage quilts atop a four-poster bed, a master bath with a claw foot tub and separate shower, a full bath in the hall, and two guest rooms. Like my eggs, the house was perfect.

Marty had brought my weekend case upstairs to the master bedroom and laid out thick white towels. I gave him a kiss and went into the shower. My hair was full of shampoo when the shower door opened and he joined me. He buried his head in my neck and kissed me. The hot sudsy water from my hair ran over us as we made love. It wasn't until one in the afternoon that we finally left the house.

Marty had thrown on a worn fisherman's sweater over his tee shirt and I bundled up in my burgundy college duffel over a thick, wool cable knit sweater. The day was chilly and overcast, but for me, perfect weather for walking the beach. As soon as we hit the white sand, my Converse sneakers came off and I felt the cool sand between my toes. Neither Marty nor I cared if our feet or jeans got wet as we walked the shoreline. We didn't talk much, but walked together for what seemed like hours. I collected shells and sea glass in a basket I had brought with us, but as the sun set the air grew colder and we both realized we were hungry.

Back at the house we made a salad, grilled steaks, played backgammon and made love again by the fire. The weekend went along the same path for the remaining two days, though we did stop for fried clams at a little seafood stand we discovered on the way home from going back to see the lighthouse on Montauk Point. I never wanted the weekend to end. We returned to the city very late Monday night and crawled into bed in my studio exhausted from the sea air and long drive home. I set my alarm for six. I needed to be back at the paper bright and early.

"Next weekend we're moving you to the west side," Marty said as he turned out the light. I fell asleep smiling.

After checking in at the city room the next morning, I hit the pavement and two more S&R loan offices. Neither one gave me a loan, solidifying what I already knew, the piece I needed to write was not an exposé of S&R, but on shopping addiction and people who prey on those addicted, specifically women, now that more and more of them were in the work force and were finally allowed to get their own credit cards. Eileen's tragic story would highlight the piece. I did a follow-up interview with

Dr. Joel Weiss on the new psychiatric measures that were being used to deal with this phenomenon and wrote the first draft of my article. I submitted it to Dwyre to see what I needed to shore up and where I needed to investigate further if, in fact, he wanted to actually publish it. I said a silent prayer that he'd approve and that I had done Eileen justice by telling her story.

It had been two days since I'd been in my apartment as I had been staying at Marty's, but when I got home around seven-thirty on Friday night, I found that while I was gone, he had arranged to have all my clothes, dishware, linens, *everything* packed up in boxes. My bed was stripped. My pots and pans were in one of the boxes. I thought of going back to Marty's, but I was tired and hungry and the thought of getting into a cab and schlepping to the west side made my brain want to explode, so I threw on my coat, took the elevator back downstairs and went into the drugstore in my building. I almost cheered when I saw that its lunch counter was still open. I ordered a cheeseburger and fries to go and with sustenance in hand, headed back upstairs to my apartment.

At least my TV wasn't packed. I found a half bottle of open white wine in the refrigerator. No glasses, so I just took a swig out of the bottle as I sat on the naked bed and turned on *The Name of the Game*, one of my favorite shows. The show revolved around three actors I liked: Gene Barry played the publisher of Howard Publications, Robert Stack, a crime reporter for Barry's magazine called *Crime*, and, Anthony Franciosa, a reporter for a magazine called *People*. Franciosa's episodes were my favorite as his character was more of an in-depth lifestyle feature reporter. I wanted to do in real life what he did as a fictional writer, so I was happy that it was one of his episodes being aired. I found some packing paper on the floor and made a "placemat" on my bed, pulled my cheeseburger out of its brown paper bag and started eating it while still partially wrapped in waxed paper. The fries I dumped out of their container right into the paper bag, using the bag as a bowl, all the while slugging back white wine between bites. *Tres elegánt!* After I finished eating, I peeled off my panty hose, took off my bra under my top, rolled up my coat into a pillow and leaned against the wall to watch the rest of the show. I finally fell asleep sometime during *The Dick Cavett Show*.

I was still sleeping at eight-thirty the next morning when Marty let himself in and woke me up.

"Hey, why didn't you come home last night?" he asked as he kissed me awake.

"I'm sorry. I didn't know you had my place packed up. I just wanted to sleep in my own bed one last time. By the time I got here, I was too tired and cranky to go out again, so I went downstairs and got myself something to eat."

"Did you tell your landlord you're moving out?"

"Not yet. I only have two months on my lease, so I'm just going to pay next month and let them keep my security as the last month's rent. Though I'm sure my super will tell him. It's not going to be hard to figure out when the doorman holds the door open and watches as my furniture and all these boxes leave the building."

"Did I mention, the movers are here?"

"What?" I jumped out of bed. All my clothes were packed and I didn't even know if my toothbrush was still in the bathroom. I ran in to see. Well, I didn't run actually, my studio was only seven hundred square feet, but I almost cheered when I saw that it was still in its holder. No toothpaste though, but at least I could brush away the film on my teeth. I put my bra and pantyhose back on and was ready to rock 'n' roll. Almost. Marty buzzed downstairs and told the movers to come up.

Two hours later I was in Marty's apartment taking a hot shower while we waited for the movers to deliver my stuff. I threw on my favorite pair of faded Levi's and an oversized cashmere sweatshirt I had brought to his apartment a week ago, and wondered where I would tell the movers to put my loveseat in the large, empty living room. I'd already decided to have them put my desk in the living room by the window overlooking the New York skyline. The desk was the only nice piece of furniture I had. My bed, of course, would go into the second bedroom. It was only a double. Marty had a king.

My stuff finally arrived and Marty watched, amused, as I directed the movers to put my few possessions here and there when his phone rang. He dragged the phone across the living room, untangling the long chord on the way, and handed it to me.

"It's Vi. She tried calling your apartment, but the phone's already been disconnected."

"Hi, Vi," I said, then just listened. "OK. Tuesday night. I'll be there. See you at seven." I hung up.

"You're still never going to tell me, are you?"

"Tell you what?"

Before leaving the paper Monday night, Dwyre called me into his office.

"You did good, Wilkes," he said. "I've made some edits over the weekend, but it's all there. It's going in tomorrow's paper."

"Tomorrow?"

"Yes. Page 3. Your byline."

I just stared at him dumbfounded. I had waited so long to be able to do a real piece of journalism, but had begun to think that my column and lifestyle pieces would be the end of the line for me at the paper.

"You should be proud of yourself. It's a solid, informative piece."

"Thank you."

I rushed home to share the news with Marty. To celebrate he opened up a bottle of Dom Perignon he'd been saving, then made me one of my favorite dinners—broiled lamp chops, mashed potatoes and fresh peas.

Sometimes, for a moment, life can be just grand.

Back in the office the next day, fellow reporters came over to congratulate me on my first real feature. Jimmy Hamill, a major columnist for the paper since papyrus, actually slapped me on the back. I was thrilled. But me being me, I thought—now what?—and spent the rest of the day wondering what I would write about next. Would Dwyre give me another feature to write or send me to cover another charity event? I also had a new column due in two weeks.

I finally left the office, blank paper still in my typewriter, and headed out to Vi's. When I got down to 42nd Street and looked at my watch, I knew I'd be early if I hailed a cab. It was a beautiful, crisp evening, so I decided to walk to Sniffen Court. I loved walking the streets of Manhattan, who knows, maybe I was a "street walker" in another life. I reached Vi's front door exactly at seven o'clock and had barely lifted the antique knocker when it opened. Her butler, whose name I finally learned on my last visit to Vi, was stoically standing there ready to help me off with my coat.

"Hi, Regis," I said as I entered the foyer.

When Vi had finally told me the name of her silent butler (no pun intended—or does anyone remember what a silent butler is anymore?), I had to laugh. How perfect. Regis. She then told me a little about him. He had been a soldier in WWI and barely eighteen when Vi had nursed him back to health after he was badly wounded and mustard-gassed. A few years later she found him begging on the street and took him home and fed him. Though his bullet wound had healed, he was still suffering from shell shock and the residual effects of the gas. He couldn't hold a job and his family couldn't deal with him, so he ended up living in doorways. Vi took him in and nursed him back to health again, then hired him as her butler. She trained him and helped him find an affordable apartment nearby. My heart broke when she told me his story but I now understood why he was devoted to her.

As always, he said nothing as he took my coat and left to hang it up somewhere. I walked into the living room where Vi was waiting. She greeted me and poured me the usual, a pony glass of sherry. The caviar, butter and toast points were on the coffee table as always, so feeling more at home in her home, I sat down on the sofa and helped myself.

"My cook needed the night off and I didn't feel like cooking, so I've ordered pizza from Rocky Lee's." Rocky Lee's Chu Chu Bianca was a popular Italian restaurant not far from my apartment that made the most fabulous thin crust pizza. Thin crust! Something unheard of in the city at that time.

"Perfect. I love Rocky Lee's."

I was on my third toast point loaded with caviar when Lynne arrived at seven-fifteen.

"Vi, so sorry I'm late," she said as she rushed into the room. "Traffic."

She joined me on the sofa as Vi handed her a sherry. She lifted her glass. "To Ashley. We read your article and couldn't be more proud."

"To Ashley," Vi chimed in.

I actually blushed. "Thank you."

"And we both want to say that we think that you did your friend a real service writing about her struggle and what it did to her. I hope the information you imparted in your story will help others," Vi continued.

"I hope so, too. I wish I'd known about Dr. Weiss before Eileen killed herself. Maybe he could have saved her."

Lynne patted my hand. We talked a bit more about Eileen and shopping addiction, then Regis came in with two large pizza boxes. He put them on a console next to the silverware and china plates that had already been set up.

Vi pulled out a stack of white paper napkins from a console drawer. "No linen. We're slumming tonight," she said, then laughed. "I even have cold ale on ice."

I laughed, too. Paper napkins and beer, excuse me, ale…not the Violet Rose Wilding I knew!

"Ah, yes, caviar and sherry. Definitely slumming it," Lynne injected.

I smiled. Right then I had to admit the aroma of the pizza was overtaking my love for caviar. We all helped ourselves right out of the boxes as Regis brought in a chilled mug of ale for each of us. I devoured my first slice and was so happy Vi had ordered two pies. I could probably eat one all by myself. If I'd known what they were about to tell me I might've lost my appetite.

CHAPTER 16

1938

Lynne had purchased a new uniform for her chauffeur and though it was too big for Fritzie, it was passable. She bought it to fit him so no one would question why she'd buy a uniform that didn't fit her employee when she knew what size he wore. She also decided to give the chauffeur the whole week off with pay, explaining that she would be out of town and wouldn't need the car. She invited Daisy for dinner at her home, along with Vi, and the two conspirators managed to keep Daisy engaged until late into the night. Vi had hired a car for the evening and dropped Daisy off at her uptown mansion a little after midnight. If all went according to plan, Daisy would be unable to get in touch with Silas, and vice versa, until long after they had kidnapped him. Lynne had planned it all methodically, preparing for almost any contingency, just as she had prepared her escape from her parents' potato farm on the north fork of Long Island all those years ago.

Fritzie, dressed in the new uniform, met Lynne at her garage early that morning. She started up Lynne's black 1937 Ford Deluxe Sedan and they headed to the Algonquin. When they pulled up in front of the hotel, Lynne immediately got out of the car and moved into the shadows against the hotel wall, but not too far from its entrance. Vi and Dot were already in position. Fritzie checked her watch. It was almost time for Silas to leave the hotel if he believed the note she had sent him in Daisy's name. She left the driver's seat, went around the car, opened the backseat passenger door and waited. Vi took out her chloroform soaked washcloth and held it behind her back. Two minutes later, Silas walked out of the hotel and spotted the car and chauffeur. Fritzie bowed and swept her arm, gesturing for him to get in. Without looking at her or anywhere else, he climbed in. Within seconds Fritzie had returned to the driver's seat, Dot was in the front passenger seat and Lynne and Vi came at him from both sides in the back seat locking the doors behind them. Confused, Silas didn't react when Vi pushed the washcloth onto his face. He looked into her eyes and, at first, didn't recognize her as his mind tried to grasp what was going on. When he did recognize her and then Lynne who was pressing him against the seat, he started to struggle, but the women were able to keep him pinned as Fritzie sped away. Silas' struggle became more violent as he thrashed around. The women were losing control and beginning to panic.

"The chloroform isn't working," Vi said, trying to keep the cloth over his mouth and nose.

Dot turned around in the front seat and faced Silas. She held a pearl handle derringer in her hand and pointed it at him. "Stop struggling," she commanded. "Or I won't hesitate to shoot you."

From the deadly look in her eyes, he believed her and stopped struggling. Five minutes later the chloroform worked and Silas was unconscious.

"A gun, Dot? A gun!?" Vi asked. "What were you thinking?"

"That what just happened would happen. Even if he didn't escape the car, he might have overpowered us in Rhinebeck. I wasn't going to let that happen."

Nobody else said a word for the rest of the long drive. Their adrenalin had normalized and their bodies began to shake. They all took deep breaths to help stay calm until they got him into Lynne's house and could interrogate him. If he stirred, Vi put the cloth back over his face for a bit till she felt it was safe to remove it again. She kept checking his pulse, making sure his heart hadn't stopped. Though if it had, she had no idea what she would do.

It was afternoon when they finally drove down the long dirt driveway and pulled up in front of Lynne's three-story Victorian home. There were no neighbors nearby, so the women were not afraid of being seen carrying Silas' inert body into the house. At six feet, one hundred and eighty pounds, it took all of them to accomplish that goal. Once in the house, Lynne dragged a sturdy, straight-backed wooden chair into the middle of the living room and they propped him on it. She got the clothesline she had brought and they wound it around him and the chair as they tied his hands behind the chair and wove the rope into the slats of the chair's back, then tied his ankles to the chair legs. When they finished restraining him, they sat down and waited for him to regain consciousness.

They didn't have long to wait, though it took a full five minutes before Silas put it all together and realized he was their captive. He looked at each one of them with a mix of anger and hate and as his anger turned to rage, he began to struggle to get loose. He rocked the chair back and forth and wiggled his hands trying to escape the ropes. The chair tipped over. Dot and Lynne got up and righted it again then checked to make sure the knots were still tight.

No one was talking. The women stared at him and he stared at them. He started struggling against the ropes again. Dot took her pistol out of her purse and pointed it at him again.

"I told you before. Stop struggling. You'll be fine once we get what we came for."

"What's that?" he hissed. "Your money? It's gone."

"All of it? I doubt that, George. Or is it Ransom or Sy? No wait, it's Marshall now isn't it, Silas?" Vi stated.

"You know you can't get away with this," Silas yelled.

"Of course we can," Lynne laughed. "Who's going to prosecute four silly old women for wanting to get back the money you stole from them? Besides, you're not going to tell anyone about this because you know you won't be quite so handsome in prison stripes."

Silas started thrashing about again. Dot pulled back the hammer of her little gun. He quieted down.

"I can't give you back your money," he said.

"Oh, I'm pretty sure you can," Fritzie snapped. "But first, I want to make sure that you don't do to my friend Daisy what you did to us."

"OK, I'll leave Daisy. Hell, I'll leave New York if that's all you want."

"Remember when I said that I was sure you could give us back our money?" Fritzie asked.

"And how do you suppose I can do that?" he sneered.

"Fanny Levitt," Dot said matter-of-factly.

"Never heard of Fanny Levitt," he flatly stated.

Dot took out the newspaper picture from her purse.

"Then you must have a doppelganger right here in New York City," she snapped sarcastically.

Silas looked at the picture and said nothing.

"Funny thing is, that when she was found hanging in her home, her safe empty of all its cash and her bank account cleaned out, you didn't realize that you had conned a woman I knew, a fellow 'con-ee' you might say. Someone who, besides her children, would not believe she gave her money away, then killed herself. I want to know exactly what you did to her!"

Silas continued to deny knowing her. "That was just some woman I danced with. I had no idea who she was before or after that picture was taken."

Dot put the gun next to Silas' temple. "Are you sure?" she hissed.

Silas realized that he wasn't going to be able to lie his way out of knowing her and he instinctively knew Dot's threats weren't idle ones. "I did to her exactly what I did to all of you. I admired her. Flattered her. Wined and dined her. Paid attention to her. Made love to her. Then took what I thought those services were worth."

Furious at his arrogance, Dot smashed him in his face with the gun in her hand. She was about to hit him again when Vi pulled her away from him.

"Stop it!" Vi told her. "We'll get to the truth, Dot."

The women questioned Silas for hours, but he continued to deny that he'd had anything to do with Fanny's death. He asked to go to the bathroom, but the women refused to untie him. When he couldn't hold it any longer, he urinated in his pants. He was humiliated and they used that to their advantage as they continued to ask him the same questions over and over again, all while Silas was still trying to wiggle his hands free. The rope around his wrists loosened but not enough. Feeling defeated and exhausted, he finally confessed.

"Look, I never meant for her to die," he said belligerently.

"What?" Dot asked.

"She wasn't supposed to be there. I didn't know her lunch got canceled and that she had just gone out to run a few errands. When she got home she found me at her safe."

"If you were going to clean out her bank account, why did you need to break into her safe?" Fritzie asked. "That makes no sense."

"I was having a hard time convincing Fanny to write an investment check and wasn't sure I was ever going to. I saw her put ten grand in her safe, so I considered that my back-up plan."

"If you hadn't gotten her money yet, why kill her?" Vi asked.

"Wasn't my fault. She flew at me in a rage and started punching my chest.

What was I supposed to do, just let her pummel me?" Silas stated defiantly. "I grabbed her by the throat and squeezed till she stopped."

"So you hung her?" Dot said coldly.

"I didn't want an investigation," he said matter-of-factly. "I wanted the police to think she'd committed suicide. She suffocated…"

"She didn't 'suffocate' you bastard," Dot interrupted. "You strangled her!"

"Be that as it may, the police would think she was murdered…"

"She *was* murdered!" Dot screamed at him.

"Fine. I didn't want an investigation, so I couldn't leave her on the floor like that. The first thing the police would think when they found marks on her neck would be murder, so I staged the suicide, then left. I had just started courting Daisy and needed her money to reach my financial goal to leave the States forever," he explained, "especially if all I got from Fanny was that measly ten grand."

"If Fanny wasn't buying your scheme to give you money, how did you get her to give you power-of-attorney?" Vi asked.

He smiled, thinking how quick-witted he had been. "I didn't. Her signed will was in the safe so I traced her signature onto a power-of-attorney I had in my briefcase for Daisy to sign, then stole the will along with the money. I could always draw up another power-of-attorney for Daisy," he answered boastfully. "However, the bank was closed when I finally left her apartment, so I had to wait until it opened the next day. Have to admit, I was nervous they'd find her before I could get her money."

"Poor Silas. Why continue on with Daisy, then? All of Fanny's money wasn't enough for you?" Lynne asked.

"What can I say, I'm greedy," he snapped. "Look at all of you. So privileged and spoiled. Everything given to you. Well, except you, Pauline. How is she any different than me?" he asked the others.

"If you don't know the answer to that question, you never will," Dot screamed no longer able to control herself. Enraged, Dot fired her gun, hitting Silas in the shoulder. Blood seeped out all over him. Horrified, at what she had just done, she ran out of the room. Shocked, the others rushed after her. Lynne went to find a first aid kit and some towels to stop the bleeding. Vi gently took the gun away from Dot as she hovered over the kitchen sink and vomited.

While they were gone, Silas ignored his pain and furiously worked the ropes around his wrists. He finally loosened them enough to slip his hands free and slide his arms out of the ropes. He had just finished untying his legs when the women came back into the room. He saw that Vi now had Dot's derringer and was holding it in her right hand. Lynne rushed to him, wanting to put a towel on his wound to stop the bleeding, but he grabbed her, knocking her to the floor. Still entangled in the chair, but able to stand, he lunged at Vi, grabbing the gun away before she even knew what was happening. Fritzie grabbed his arm and tried to get the gun back, while Dot began to pummel him. The three women wrestled him and the chair to the floor. With Lynne already down, the four women fought to get the gun from him as they scuffled on the floor. The gun went off and Silas stopped struggling. Blood spurted out of his chest and onto the women's clothes and faces. Vi tried to stop the bleeding. She grabbed a towel and pushed down on the new wound as she had learned to do as a doctor's aide all those years ago. Lynne pushed another towel onto Silas' shoulder wound. Fritzie felt for a pulse in his neck. At first it was faint, but then it was gone. Silas was dead.

Shocked, the women sat on the floor around Silas' body in silence.

"My God, I did this." Dot asked. "We have to call the police."

No one moved. They just sat, staring at the body. Finally, Lynne stood up. "No. We're not calling the police. No one's going to miss him except Daisy. And as far as she's concerned, his death is the best thing that could have ever happened to her."

"But won't she report him missing?" Dot asked.

"I'm sure she will," Lynne continued. "But when the police try to find Marshall Woods, they'll reach a dead end."

"Right," Vi said. "If she didn't introduce him to her friends, the way he conned us in keeping our relationships private, he doesn't exist beyond the Algonquin Hotel personnel. But even if she did, when the police follow all of Daisy's leads, they'll come up empty and Daisy will learn that the past he'd shared with her was a lie."

"There'll be no trace of him anywhere," Fritzie said. "She's going to be heartbroken when she finds out the man she was involved with didn't even exist."

"She'll get over it," Lynne bluntly said.

"I really think I should call the police. It was my fault. I killed him," Dot declared.

"No, we all did. And we need to keep this to ourselves," Lynne argued.

"Fine. Then what do we do now?" Dot asked again.

"We're going to bury him, clean up this mess and burn our clothes. I have enough of a wardrobe here to dress all of us. Even if nothing fits properly, it will be fine until we get home. I'll never get my rug clean, so we'll bury him in it."

"Bury him where, Lynne?" Vi asked.

"Right here in my backyard. It's pitch black out right now, so we'll have to wait till morning."

No one protested.

Lynne found a sheet in her linen closet and covered Silas' body with it. They stared at the misshapen form before Lynne brought them out of their reverie.

"I think we all need a drink," she said. She grabbed a bottle of scotch from her liquor cabinet and poured each of them a large glass full.

"Let's go into the kitchen and away from the body," she continued, as she picked up the bottle of scotch and walked out of the living room. The others followed. By the time they gathered around the kitchen table, they had finished their scotches. Lynne refilled their glasses, then opened the pantry to see if there was any food they could make. She found a can of SPAM and a box of soda crackers.

"We better eat something or the alcohol will make us sick."

"I'm already sick," Fritzie said.

"I know," Lynne added. "We all are. But it happened and we're going to have to live with it."

"It's all my fault," Dot said. "If I hadn't brought my gun, none of…"

"Stop it, Dot," Vi said. "You were right. He would have eventually overpowered us, maybe even killed us if you hadn't had the gun. It's done! Nothing can change that."

"The only thing that's keeping me sane is remembering that he murdered Fanny."

"Are you sure we shouldn't call the police?" Fritzie asked.

"To what end?" Lynne answered her question with a question. "It won't bring him back. We didn't kill him on purpose," she rationalized.

"No we didn't," Vi said. "I agree with Lynne. No one will miss him but Daisy. And believe me, her pain would have been far worse if he was able to betray her and steal her money as he did to us. At least when she finds out that he was not Marshall Woods, she'll have her money and her dignity intact."

Lynne opened the can of SPAM and put it on a plate along with a knife. They drank more scotch and ate cold SPAM on crackers and sat in the kitchen in silence till dawn.

In the distance, they heard a rooster crow as they all went to the gardening shed for shovels and a pick ax. The morning was very cold and gray as they dug the grave by a nearby maple tree about twenty-five yards from the storm cellar entrance. They took turns chopping through the almost frozen ground with the pick ax and shoveling the loose dirt. It was slow and arduous and when they finally finished around noon, they were covered with dirt and Silas' dried blood. They had stopped feeling the cold hours ago. They returned to the house and rolled Silas' body into the rug then dragged him outside to the gravesite where they pushed him into the deep hole they had dug. Lynne threw the sheet into the grave, as well as the bloody towels and they began shoveling the dirt back into the hole. When it was done, they walked back toward the house, totally exhausted. At the kitchen back door, Lynne instructed them to strip off all their clothes and leave them in a pile on the ground. They did and entered the house naked and shivering. Lynne gave them blankets and bath towels to wrap around themselves till it was their turn to bathe. When they were all done, she provided them with underwear, socks, pants and sweaters that would do until they were back home. They gathered outside again and built a small barn fire and burned all their clothes. Lynne added a little gasoline she found in her garage so that the fire would consume every last thread. They took turns watching the fire and when it finally burned out, it was dark. Too tired to make the long drive back to the city, they decided to stay in Rhinebeck one more night. Lynne foraged through her pantry again and this time came up with some canned pork and beans and a box of rice. They hadn't eaten all day and knew that they'd better have something to keep up their strength. They made the whole box of rice, heated up the pork and beans and opened up another bottle of scotch.

EPILOGUE

ASHLEY — 2000

The eulogies for Vi continued as I heard her voice in my head. "We drove home the next morning and went back to our regular nights at Schrafft's. We never looked for our money and we didn't see or contact each other for over two decades, not until 1959 when MJ told us Fritzie had died."

"At her funeral Lynne, Dot and I decided that it had been long enough not to reconnect. We needed to talk to each other. It's a funny thing about the human brain. Our guilt and nightmares over what we had done eventually faded and we realized that if the police had found anything or suspected us they would have done something a long time ago. We found strength and comfort in the fact that Fanny received justice and Daisy would never have to feel the hurt each of us felt."

Marty squeezed my hand gently as a comforting gesture and I thought how he had been through all of this with me without ever knowing what "this" was. He was next to me in the very beginning when I went to Dot's funeral. He was next to me in 1976 when Lynne died at eighty-seven from pulmonary fibrosis. Never demanding to know what it was about these women I loved so dearly and why they meant so much to me.

As I became more successful as a writer, I moved from reporting full time for the *Daily News* to writing in-depth features for the *New Yorker* and *Vanity Fair*, in some ways becoming the reporter that the Anthony Franciosa character was in *The Name of The Game*, the show I'd loved all those years ago. I also published two novels that were moderately successful.

Marty and I got married in 1973 after living together for five years. Our wedding was in St. Peter's Church on Lex and 53rd. Vi hosted a big party for us at Sniffen Court. After I suffered a couple of miscarriages we decided to call it a day on having a family. We had each other and that seemed to work just fine. In 1991, he became the police commissioner for New York City and there are rumblings afoot that a lot of people in City Hall want him to run for Mayor.

The last eulogy was over and people were slowly leaving the funeral home. I gathered up my bag and the white gloves that I had worn as a tribute to my Schrafft's ladies and followed Marty out onto the street.

"You going to tell me now?" he asked.

"Thought you'd never ask."

ACKNOWLEDGMENTS

My heartfelt thanks to Susan Addison, Kyle Crowner, Joan Kemper and Jule Selbo for their proofreading eyes and suggestions, and to all my friends who have listened to me over the years ruminating over the ladies who dined alone at Schrafft's, wondering who they were. I've finally given a few of these ladies a backstory.

A special thanks to my brother, Bob Saari, for his book cover creative vision, and...

... to my husband, Richard Camp, for all his love, support and editing skills. I never could have finished this book without you.

ABOUT THE AUTHOR

Ilona Joy Saari is a freelance writer who's worked in many genres, from television/film to essayist to rock'n'roll press to political campaigns. She was a Deputy Press Secretary for a U.S. President, a press liaison for two Presidential conventions and has written many speeches for celebrities on the stump for presidential candidates and women's issues. Her essays have been published in the *NY Daily News* and other newspapers across the country. Ilona is currently a columnist for the glossy magazine, *Ojai Quarterly*, and a contributor to *Huffington Post*. Her first novel, *Freeze Frame*, was published in 2012.